THREE LITTLE LIES

BOOKS BY DANIELLE STEWART

The Girl at the Party

The Teacher

THREE LITTLE LIES

DANIELLE STEWART

bookouture

Published by Bookouture in 2025

An imprint of Storyfire Ltd.
Carmelite House
50 Victoria Embankment
London EC4Y 0DZ

www.bookouture.com

The authorised representative in the EEA is Hachette Ireland
8 Castlecourt Centre
Dublin 15 D15 XTP3
Ireland
(email: info@hbgi.ie)

ISBN: 978-1-83618-120-0
eBook ISBN: 978-1-83618-119-4

To Amelie, our beloved exchange student and forever family member. Thank you for the laughter, lessons, and memories you've shared with us, for making time to come back to see us, and—thankfully—for not causing us the kind of worry the characters in this book do! Jack is lucky to call you a big sister, and we are all better for having you in our lives.

PROLOGUE

There is no room for vanity at a crime scene. I'd rushed out of the restaurant and run toward the car so wildly that my hair had fallen from the tight bun it was spun into. I'd kicked off my heels and torn the bottom of my tights against the asphalt. My mascara is smeared and the strap of my dress keeps falling from my shoulder.

As we pull up to the house I try to tame my hair, painfully aware that my neighbors might be watching. It shouldn't matter what I look like right now, but it's a voice in my head I never can quiet. They'll glance out the window and think I've gone mad. I can hardly blame anyone who does. If I saw this scene unfolding, I'd certainly be lurking by my door to get a glimpse of the chaos.

"Here!" I shout, waving to the officers as I spill out of the car before Everett can even put it into park. The word bursts from my lips raw and unpolished, shattering the tense silence as blue police lights dance rhythmically against the front of my house, then splash violently across my lawn.

The officers approach, their faces grim. It feels as though they should be moving with some kind of urgency. But instead, they walk with restraint. I want to shake them. Beg them to tell me what to do. Instead, I fold my hands nervously together and squeeze them to keep from fidgeting wildly.

"Josephine Marie Hargrove?" one of them calls out, reading stiffly from a small notepad in his hand. It's the name on my driver's license, a name I never use; it sounds foreign, official—a stark reminder that this surreal scene is very much happening. Normally, I am Jo. Since middle school, always just Jo. Except to telemarketers and apparently now to these policemen.

I nod, stepping into the formality of the name and the inescapable horror that's taking hold of me. How did this happen? There's yellow tape being rolled out like the red carpet for a premiere no one would ever want to attend. A van pulls up, stark and ominous, the word "Forensics" stamped on the side, a gravely macabre scene.

I squint against the harsh lights, trying to read the officer's expression, searching for a clue as to what I should do next. He's a wide man with a substantial beard and strange-colored eyes. For a moment I try to decipher if they are blue or green but realize with a start that it could not matter less. Nothing so trivial will ever matter again.

Somewhere behind me a door slams, a neighbor's curious gaze hidden quickly behind a hastily drawn curtain, and I'm sharply reminded of how public our ordeal has become. We are now *that* house, *that* family, caught in a storm of police lights and whispered suspicions. My bare feet are cold against the wet grass and a chill runs up my spine. I have to get us out of this. I have to get my family back to the normal, mundane life we were living. The life we had before *she* arrived.

The officer finally snaps me back to attention with a stern question he's clearly tried to ask me more than once. "How long has she been missing?"

I open my mouth to answer, but the words clog in my throat.

I have no idea how long she's been gone. I've only just found out myself.

"I don't know. I was at dinner with my husband when my daughter called." The realization slaps me across the face. I catch sight of my children huddled together by the front door, their faces pale and eyes wide with fear. The sight of them sends a fresh wave of panic crashing over me.

I rush over, my breaths coming in short, sharp gasps. "Are you okay?" I manage to choke out, my voice trembling. They nod, but their eyes tell a different story. They're just as scared as I am.

Before I can say anything more, another officer approaches. "Ma'am, we need you to come with us." His tone is firm but not unkind. "We have some additional questions."

"I want to stay with my children." I squeeze them close to me, but feel his hand come down on my shoulder.

"We need to speak with you over here." Though I'm reluctant to let go of Ashton and Megan, I am a lifelong rule follower. I can't imagine challenging this man's authority, even if it means having to step away from my scared children. I follow him back to the driveway, where a third officer is unrolling more yellow tape around the garage. My stomach twists into a tight knot as I watch him.

The officer glances at me, then at his colleague. "We found something," he says slowly, each stretched-out syllable showing his reluctance to break the news to me. "Some blood in the garage."

My legs buckle beneath me, and I nearly collapse. "Oh my God," I whisper, my vision blurring with tears. "No, no, no..."

The officer catches me before I hit the ground, guiding me to sit on the curb. "Take deep breaths," he instructs, but it feels impossible.

I nod numbly, struggling to comply. Karma feels like a shadow looming over me, casting me into darkness. I've been anticipating my perfect life would be upended by some tragedy, and it's happened. It was inevitable. I sold my soul to get all that I have, and the universe has finally come to collect.

Through the haze of panic, I see one of the officers talking to my daughter. She's sobbing and shaking, but pointing toward the house. My husband is cornered by another officer being questioned just as intently. I want to pull my family toward me. To hold them all and never let them go. But I know in an instant we're fractured and no matter what I do, we will stay that way.

ONE

JO

Megan's ponytail is a little crooked. I see it in the rearview mirror and consider letting her know. A year ago, this would have been a passing comment from me and a quick fix from her. But now that she's twelve, everything is serious. Our mother–daughter relationship has taken a turn. A sharp turn, and I'm having whiplash. The teen years are notoriously difficult, but somehow I was naive enough to think I'd be immune. I put in the time. Read the parenting books. Listened intently to all of my daughter's breathless retellings of disjointed little stories at the end of her day. I had been gentle. Patient. Attentive. And, most importantly, involved. I pride myself on being an integral part of my children's lives. And yet all that work and what did it get me? Right now, a lot of eye rolls and heavy sighs.

"Did you want me to straighten your ponytail before you hop out?" I ask, keeping my voice so cheery it sounds more like the start of a song than a criticism.

"No," Megan moans, covering her hair with her hand. "Mom, I can do my own hair. What's wrong with it?"

"Nothing is wrong with it. It's just more to one side. I can straighten it." I pull my SUV to the curb designated for school drop-off and pray one of the teachers doesn't overhear this exchange as they approach the car.

Megan's voice is shrill and frustrated. "Now I'm going to be all worried about my hair. Why did you have to say anything? You always do this. It ruins my whole day."

"I was only trying to help." I hold my hands up disarmingly, but she doesn't let up.

"Control. You're trying to control everything. What I wear. How my hair is. Who I can talk to. I'm the only person in my grade without a phone. Do you know how embarrassing that is?"

"We're not having the phone conversation right now, Megan. You know our rule. You're not old enough for the responsibility of a phone. You've got your smartwatch to contact us if you need to."

"This isn't a smartwatch. It's for babies." She rips the watch off and shoves it into her bag. "I'm the only one who doesn't have social media. That's why I miss half the things everyone is going to. And you don't let me do sleepovers. There is one every weekend now. I'm the only one who doesn't get to go."

These conversations are never productive. There is no level of emotion Megan can bring to me that will outweigh the statistics and data about the risks. When I don't answer, Megan yanks her backpack up from the floor and it smashes into Ashton's leg.

"Ouch," Ashton cries. "Mom, she hit me with her bag."

"I didn't even mean to," Megan huffs, swinging the door open and jumping out without an apology or a goodbye. "It's always my fault."

Ashton's eyes fill with tears, and I snap around quickly to try to stop this before it starts. He's a tender soul. Endlessly sweet and quick to cry. It drives Everett crazy that our son is still frequently weepy even at seven years old. But I refuse to give in to that macho patriarchy crap that says my son can't feel his feelings. That's half of what's wrong in the world today. He's seven. If he needs to cry, then he should. I know fathers want their sons to be strong, but I'd like our son to be mentally healthy too.

But... if he could possibly not do it right now, that would be great.

"Buddy, she didn't mean to hit you. You're okay. Can you grab your bag and give Mommy a kiss?" The SUV door is still open, and I can hear the chatter and laughter of the other kids lining up for the start of the day. I can also feel the judgment of whoever just watched my daughter storm off.

"Bye, Mommy," Ashton says through a sniffle as he kisses my cheek. "She's so mean," he whispers.

"It'll pass." I sigh. "Have a good day at school. I'll be right here to pick you up." I never miss an opportunity to say this. It feels important to remind my children I'll be there. Physically and emotionally, I never want them to wonder if I will show up for them. My childhood had been plagued with gaps in security. Never really knowing which version of my parents I might get. My kids would not endure the same. It was exhausting but important.

As Ashton steps away and closes the door, I give myself a few seconds to catch my breath. We're not supposed to linger here in the drop-off line. Things have to keep moving, but I need to get my blood pressure down with a few deep breaths. It's only another second before I realize my mistake. I pay the price for that selfish little indulgence of breathing deeply.

The knock on my passenger-side window sends a shock of lightning up my spine. There is no one here I'm prepared to talk to this morning. That wasn't the plan.

I look over to see a familiar face and immediately think of how I rushed out the door with less makeup on than usual and my denim jacket pulled over a plain gray T-shirt. The sip of coffee I spilled on it now looks like a bullseye ready for an arrow of judgment. And Eloise at my window will not miss the chance to survey my shortcomings.

My children are blessed to be able to go to a school like Windsor Knoll. But it's a stretch for me. Not financially. Everett's career has afforded us many luxuries, including comfortably paying tuition here. It's more about the people. Their status. Fitting in with the haves when I spent most of my life as a have-not.

Windsor Knoll is prestigious. The kind of place where mothers like Eloise, with their designer clothes and perfectly styled hair, congregate and compete. I can feel the pressure to fit in, to look the part. My hastily applied mascara is likely smudged, my hair thrown up in a messy bun rather than the sleek styles I usually admire on the other moms. Most days I do fit right in. I take the time to get my nails done and make sure my clothes are sharp and dry-cleaned. Lately, however, my mornings with the kids look less like a routine and more like a war zone. Right now, I'm definitely giving off battlefield vibes.

Eloise is the perfect example of the woman I try to model myself after. She's standing at my window, pretending not to peek around looking to see if my car is clean. Quick little glances before she fixes her gaze on me. She's of a certain pedigree and it's maybe what I envy the most. Her parents own the largest, most lucrative ski resort in the area, and it is apparent that money is no object for Eloise.

Pulling my jean jacket closed enough to cover the coffee spill, I smile wide, glad I have my sunglasses on to mask my tired eyes.

"Just who I was looking for," Eloise sings happily as she leans a little further into the window of my SUV. "Do you have a second? I want to run something by you."

I look in my rearview mirror. The staff that try to keep the cars moving don't come our way. They wouldn't dare try to rush

Eloise along. The donation she writes every year affords her this freedom.

I clear my throat and try to sound as chipper as she does. "Absolutely, what do you need?"

"I know mornings are hectic. Especially with tweens." Eloise gestures with a subtle head nod in the direction Megan had stormed off in. "I'll make it quick. Just don't say no right away."

My stomach lurches. Even though Eloise is smiling, the tone feels foreboding. I like to be prepared for conversations with people from school. Swirl them around in my mind like wine in a glass. Let them breathe and open until I know just what to expect. This isn't meant to be an ambush, but it feels like one. I only smile and let her continue.

"You know that Trent and I are always hosting exchange students. We're really dedicated to the idea of opening our home as often as possible. We're so blessed. All of us, really." Eloise pauses with precision, waiting for me to agree this time. Another nod will not do.

"We really are. I think it's wonderful what you do." I croak the words out and feel my cheeks pink a bit.

"I'm glad you think so." Eloise smirks playfully. "The RAS Foundation that we work with has a group of students coming in about ten days. Trent and I are taking a darling boy named Christian. He loves soccer and hiking. Our little Tommy will be just obsessed with him."

"That will be fun," I reply, glancing up at my rearview mirror again, willing someone to please come tell me to move my vehicle.

"Well, there is one student that hasn't been placed yet. It's really down to the wire, and when I read her little profile, I thought of you instantly." She waves her hand animatedly in my direction.

I curse the broken part of myself that is flattered by this. To be thought of by a woman like Eloise in a positive light is a tantalizing drug I can't seem to quit. My shoulders rise a bit at the idea. I wish I could say it was a mystery to me why I loved this attention so much. But I know how I got to this place. You can't forget something like that. "You thought of us to host?"

Eloise launches into her pitch. "It's only six weeks. It flies by. It's a girl. She's seventeen. It's been a long-held dream of hers to come to the United States and specifically a STEM school like Windsor Knoll. Her grades are impeccable, and she has her sights set on a job in tech. Her little town in England is short on opportunities. It's just her and her mother. I get the feeling resources are limited. With your husband working in tech, Windsor Knoll's specialty programs, and the allergies, I think it would be just meant to be."

"Allergies?" The word always makes my palms sweat. My son's life is on the line far too often because of that horrible word. Any free brain power I have normally goes to combatting the risk. Mitigating the threats his little body might encounter every day from simple foods he's surrounded by.

"She has food allergies. I believe it's why she hasn't been matched with a host family yet. In all my years of doing this we've never had to turn a child away. But people are intimidated by hosting a student with that kind of problem. But when I saw her file, I immediately thought of a super mom who would absolutely take on a challenge. You'd knock this out of the park." Eloise makes a flying motion with her hands and beams.

Again, I take the hit of a compliment, and the high is even better than the last. I've given chunks of my soul to make sure Ashton has a safe world to live in without the worry of allergy-induced anaphylaxis that might kill him. I've fought against the image of being "too much" or crazy. Overbearing. Controlling. One of those irrational moms that can't relax. These kind words from Eloise are like a balm to those burns inflicted by other hypercritical mothers.

"What are her allergies?" I lean in again, intrigued.

"I'm not entirely sure. I know they are different than Ashton's. He's tree nuts, right?"

"Yes, among other things. Are hers very serious?"

Eloise furrows her brow, thinking deeply. "I believe so. That was the impression I got from the coordinator who asked if I could help find a host family. Honestly, you were the only one who came to mind. Think of all you've done here at Windsor Knoll for children with allergies. You've fought so hard. Really elevated our school in that way. And you're already set up in the kitchen for cross-contamination, or whatever you call it. I've been to your house; it's whacky how you have to do it, but I think it would be perfect."

This compliment feels laced with a tinge of malice. The one time Eloise did come to my house to pick her oldest daughter up after babysitting my kids, it was clear she was turning her nose up at plenty. And her daughter seemed disinterested in all the rules of the kitchen. It was why she'd only babysat once. I don't have the luxury of putting a lax person in charge of my son's life.

"There is another perk," Eloise continues, her penciled-in brow lifting slightly. "Nothing was better for my relationship with Shelly when she was in her young teen years than hosting a student."

"Really?" I can't help but be drawn in to this possibility. Megan is pulling further away by the second. And with each inch she moves from me, I worry I'll never be able to get her back. The dread that the best years of our relationship are behind us keeps me up at night.

"Oh, yes. These older teen girls come in from other places in the world and offer new perspectives. They align with me far more than a bratty tween, and that would snap Shelly right out of the crap she was doing. She's still in touch with Jana, the student we had stay with us when she was about Megan's age. I think it helped her see me as a person again, rather than just some terrible mom who didn't let her do what she wanted. Jana would often remind Shelly how lucky she was to have me. And for the first time, she started to listen."

All of that sounded like a dream come true. "And you've always had a good experience with the students?"

"The only time we struggle is when the child has a lot of homesickness. But you wouldn't have that problem at all." She waves off the idea but I'm not so convinced.

"Why wouldn't I have that problem?"

Eloise makes a face as though the answer is so obvious. "Jo, you're the mom every mom wants to be and every kid wishes they had. If this child comes into your home and feels an ounce of anxiety or unease, you'll be right there. I know with Megan it probably feels a bit disorienting right now. You're doing everything right but she acts like you're always wrong. Maybe shaking it up a bit is what you need."

"You said the students arrive in ten days?" I scan through the loaded-up mental calendar I keep and try to imagine how I could make this work. If I should at all.

"You've got a spare room, right? It's really all you need. I'll have Barbara from RAS call you in about an hour. She'll be so excited. They were really stressing about this."

"I need to talk to Everett first. He'll be tied up until the end of the day." My words are cut off by a car gently honking their horn behind me.

Eloise waves off the idea of Everett getting a say. "Oh, please, he's always gone. My husband too. We're the ones in the house doing the work and keeping everything moving. How much would he even be home over that six weeks?"

I want to protest, but she's right. It's the end of the quarter for him, and he'll spend the majority of the time traveling. Likely on a different time zone and hardly even able to have a decent conversation that doesn't have one of us up at an ungodly hour just to connect.

"Have her call me," I say as the horn beeps again. "I should pull up. I'm not supposed to stop here."

"Girl, let them hit me with their car if they don't like it. I paid to have this whole parking circle repaved and those flowers planted. They should know beeping that horn makes me stand here even longer." She laughs and taps my SUV as she finally takes a step back. "You're a lifesaver, Jo," she calls as I slowly pull away. "Super mom!"

TWO

The mail carrier is late. They usually come between noon and three. That gives me enough time to get the mail before I leave to pick up the kids from school. But the box was still empty when I left to pick them up, and now as I drive back home it's all I can think about. Megan is trying to ask me a question about going to the movies this weekend. Ashton is trying to tell me about what they played at recess. But I tune them out. All I can think about is the happiness-ending bomb that might be waiting for me with the coupons and utility bills. I pull the car up directly to the mailbox and flip it open, yanking out all the contents.

"Can I get the mail?" Ashton asks, peering out his window at the mailbox.

Megan grumbles. "You know she has a 'system'." She puts the last word in air quotes sarcastically.

"There is a lot of stuff that comes in the mail that requires work." I shrug off her snarky comment. "Bills that need to get paid. Documents to file. Tax papers. I'm in charge of all of that, so I don't like anyone messing with the mail because something gets ripped open or tossed out. I do have a system but there is a reason for it."

I pull the stack of mail from the box and see the letter. The exact reason I don't let anyone else get the mail. It's addressed to me and the handwriting on the front always makes my heart stop. They began arriving two years ago. Sporadically at first. Once every few months. Then like clockwork, once a month. Now sometimes even more often. It's why I have to be so diligent.

Burying it under the coupons and junk mail, I clutch it tightly as I pull into the garage and the kids get out. The sweat is gathering at the base of my back and I can feel my heart thudding against my ribs. I should be used to it by now. I know what the letter says.

Repent. Face the truth. Killer.

It never changes. And how I deal with it doesn't change either. I burn these letters. Every one of them. Every time. That's why I have a system. To make sure no one in my family knows what really happened all those years ago.

"Are you coming in?" Megan asks, eyeing me closely. She senses something is wrong and it only makes my cheeks grow hotter. She's not concerned with my well-being. We don't get along well enough right now for that to be the case. What she's really doing is looking for a weak spot so she can find some way to needle at me.

"Yes, I'm coming. I've got a nice dinner planned. I need to get started." I step out of the car and squeeze the mail tightly. "I just need to run upstairs really quick." The lump in my throat grows larger as I brush past her and run upstairs to dispose of this letter.

Why I still feel the need to read it is beyond me. The letters don't vary much. It's always about the blood on my hands. About coming clean. Paying for what I've done. Thinly veiled threats that make my skin crawl.

Getting rid of the letter should be cathartic but that's not possible when I know another will be coming soon enough. All I can do is beat my family to the mailbox and pray they never find out.

I put it out of my head an hour later and regain my composure as I focus on dinner. It's an important meal with a purpose. I've got a plan and the salmon will help. It's his favorite. It took a little extra time to make the orange glaze Everett loves, but it'll be worth it. Megan doesn't like salmon, so I put on a piece of cod for her. Like always, Ashton's meal is prepared separately and safely to avoid any cross-contamination. I've worked up a sweat in the kitchen and am barely finished loading the dishwasher when Everett walks in.

Luckily, he's on a work call, which buys me extra time. I call the kids down and gesture for them to be quiet while he finishes his call in our home office. Their drinks are filled, and they are sitting at the dining room table quietly when he comes in. It's picture-perfect.

"That smells amazing," he comments as he plants a kiss on my lips. His cologne is my favorite smell on the planet. With his coming and going all the time for work, it's the reminder that he's here. Present. That things are safe and calm and he's all ours for the moment.

Everett is solidly built and handsome, with dark hair that's starting to show a few streaks of gray. I sometimes envy how he makes time for the gym no matter what kind of chaos might be happening in our life. I'm always squeezing in a sporadic yoga class or a long walk in between everyone else's schedule. But he's been able to maintain his fitness routine and it shows. His eyes are a piercing blue, and his smile is as charming as ever. I remember how his broad shoulders drew my eye from across a large auditorium back in college. He was well-dressed and clean-cut. Two of my favorite traits in a man back then. Mostly because it was the opposite of all the men I knew in my life up until that point.

Though he's still handsome, the man I married is not the man I have now. The long hours, the constant travel, it's taken a toll. He looks run-down these days and the sparkle in his eyes has faded a bit.

"Just some salmon. I did the asparagus the way you like it." I take a seat, and a moment later he does too. I notice he's poured himself some whiskey and he places it down on the table. That normally indicates it's been a tough day at work, but I won't let that deter me. I have a plan.

"I don't like asparagus," Megan groans. "Or salmon. It's so gross, and it makes the house smell. Why do you have to make it?"

"That's why you're having cod and mashed potatoes." I lift the covers off the dishes on the table and start serving each of them.

The only thing that cuts deeper than Megan's attitude is Everett's apparent ability to act as though he doesn't notice it. The case he makes when we have this discussion privately is that giving it attention and engaging will only make it worse. To me that feels like a cop-out. He's lucky like that. I've found frequency breeds frustration. I'm here on the front lines with Megan, constantly having to tell her no or insist she does what she's supposed to. It all adds up and feeds the tidal wave that eventually comes crashing down on me. Everett gets to 'not engage' and then hit the road again.

Sometimes he takes it a step further and actually sides with Megan. Always through jokes and quips. But he finds a way to make me the punch line. I'm the crazy, overbearing mother and it's amazing I haven't had a stroke from all the unnecessary stress. Tonight, however, I put aside the annoyance I feel toward solo parenting a tween monster.

"Thanks," Megan says with all the exuberance of a hostage. "Can we eat in the living room?"

"Not tonight," Everett answers, looking at me to make sure he's parented correctly for the evening.

"You can," I reply, with a shrug. "Set up the trays and help your brother. Put something on the television he'll like too."

"She never does." Ashton pouts, but it doesn't stop him from grabbing his plate and heading toward the television.

"I figured you'd want them at the table." Everett looks perplexed. "Usually when I get home from a trip, you make a big deal about us eating all together."

I can hear it even if he thinks he's being slick. The way he says "make a big deal" is far more accusatory than observational. Everett and I grew up in completely different worlds. He was the oldest of four and the only boy. While his sisters were controlled and held to a high standard, he had endless freedom. The expectations I have for my children seem suffocating to him. But tonight, I'm the one bending the rules.

"I wanted to run something by you anyway, and I figured it would be easier without the kids interrupting every five seconds. I spoke to Eloise today in the drop-off line."

"Dear Lord," he says with a huff. "Are we hosting that awful art show again? I don't think I have it in me. The kids smear one smudge of blue paint across a paper, and we have to all parade around the performing arts building like we're viewing Picassos."

"No, it's nothing like that." I watch him sip his whiskey and consider letting him finish the small glass. Maybe he'll be more receptive if he does. But I know he'll rush me along.

Everett is efficient. Tidy. He's in the senior leadership of a major tech company, and those meetings move fast. That urgency and inability to wade through small talk spills over to our conversations, but I give him grace. I can't imagine the stress of his job, and hearing some trivial gossip from school doesn't hit his radar.

"Don't leave me hanging," he says, filling his mouth with salmon and smiling. "This is delicious, by the way."

"I hadn't made the orange glaze in a while." I smile back. "Anyway, Eloise stopped me today because she thought we would be the perfect fit for an exchange student they have who hasn't matched with a host family yet. They are really under the gun and it's causing a lot of stress at the foundation she works with. Eloise was singing our praises and talking about how wonderful we are as parents." I throw the "we" in to be generous.

"Are you serious? No way we can do that. You've got your hands full already, and work is a lot for me right now. Someone else will step up." He takes another bite and shakes his head.

"We were the only people she asked. She really thought we'd be perfect." I expected some pushback. Everett says no before he says yes when I bring anything up. I didn't notice it early in our marriage, but over time I began to see that was his natural setting when it came to my ideas. But men are like that sometimes. Especially powerful men. I'm well practiced at over-coming the objection. This is happening; I just need Everett to back down. I fold my arms and smile as he finishes his drink. I walk to the bottle of whiskey and refill his glass. He doesn't smile back, but I'm not worried. I'll get what I want.

THREE

After twenty more minutes of every reason why we cannot invite an exchange student into our home, he hits me with the one he knows will hurt the most. "Megan seems to be going through a tough phase. You two are butting heads like crazy. I think that's taking up so much of your time and energy these days."

"I did some reading today," I counter coolly, fully ignoring how he categorizes Megan's behavioral problems as "butting heads", implying she and I both share the blame. That won't distract me. "Hosting an exchange student can shift family dynamics in positive ways. Children might be less likely to argue or may see their parents in a new light, leading to improved relationships. The exchange student can serve as a role model, demonstrating different behaviors and attitudes that might positively influence your children's behavior. Eloise mentioned this has been her experience too."

"I'm sure she did," Everett groans and punctuates it with a heavy sigh. "When is this anyway? Over the summer?"

"Ten days from now. Well, it's nine actually. But just for six weeks. That's hardly a blip on our radar, yet would make such a difference in this girl's life. She hasn't been matched with a family all because she has food allergies. Severe ones. Think of Ashton. Wouldn't you want to know he'd be placed with someone safe who knows what they're doing? It would be terrible if she misses out just because no one can do what we can."

"You don't let Ashton go to the bathroom at a restaurant alone; I doubt you'd let him go to another country. Even when he is a teenager." Everett sips his drink again and looks down at his plate. "I'm leaving next week for ten days. I wouldn't even be here when she arrives. Not to mention I don't have time to jump through whatever hoops we'd need to in order to be approved for this program."

"There are no hoops," I answer cheerfully. "It's a background check which we'll both pass with no trouble, and the woman from RAS will come next Tuesday to do a home inspection and interview. I told her you'd be traveling for work, and she said since Eloise vouched for us so vehemently, as long as our application and background check are good, you won't need to be there for the meeting."

"You've scheduled a meeting already?" He leans back in his chair slightly to get a better look at me. He already knows what I'm about to say.

"I filled out the application as well and signed the contract." I don't let my voice crack as I tell him. "You complain that I'm not spontaneous enough. Well, here is a little spontaneity."

"No, this is reckless impulsivity. When I say spontaneity, I'm talking about booking a ticket to come on one of my business trips and trying to turn it into a second honeymoon."

"You know that's not possible. We don't have anyone to watch the kids for something like that." I shouldn't let the conversation stray down this path. It's a long-standing point of contention between us that I won't leave our children with just anyone. Or... if I'm being honest... anyone at all. I try to reframe it quickly. "You're going to be gone. Work is crazy right now. The kids and I need something to break up the tension and the monotony. I think this will help."

"Bringing a stranger from another country into our home on short notice will help? What do you even know about her?"

"There's a little flyer." I grab my phone and show him the attachment that had come to my email. It's vague, only her initials for privacy until we clear the background check, but I take the highlights I think will resonate with him. "She loves science and technology. Her grades are amazing. She's into folk music and has always dreamed of coming to the United States."

He doesn't bother looking at the information I flash in his direction. "I'm just not that comfortable that I know more about the barista who makes my coffee in the morning than a person coming to stay with us."

"A child. She's a child coming to stay with us. We're so fortunate, Everett, and we have the opportunity to make an enormous impact on her life."

Everett pushes the asparagus around on his plate and seems to be contemplating his options. He knows as well as I do he doesn't have any.

"You'll be wonderful at it," he says, flashing that charming smile my way. "I'll be shit at it, but you'll make it great for this girl. She's lucky as hell to come to this house with you."

A lump of emotion forms in my throat, and I swallow hard to make room for the words. "I'm sorry I didn't talk with you first. I know that's not like me at all. I'm just so untethered lately with how things are going with Megan. I need a win."

"I was thinking about it the other day. You're this excep- tional mother who is always there for her children. If I had a client who I'd dedicated all my time and energy to who thought I was the best at what I do then suddenly hated me, I'd be pretty pissed off. Confused. Frustrated. I know this is a phase that kids go through and maybe more for mothers and daughters, but you're going to be okay."

I don't cry. I could, but I don't. Mostly because I'm the type of person who'd rather burst into flames than burst into tears. I understand on a logical level that emotions are healthy. Crying is a normal part of life, but for me, it feels like a rip current, something I have to swim against to survive. I walk over and sit on his lap.

"Spontaneity, huh?" he asks as he wraps his arms around me. "You'll make it work."

That's my reputation. Every vacation, there's a spreadsheet of thoughtful activities with everyone's needs and preferences considered. Weather studied. Parking checked. Every single thing thought through and measured. The goal is to make the plans look effortless and the fun endless. The same for Christmas. Every holiday, really. I am the maker of the magic. The keeper of the calendar. The doer of all things. And Everett was right. This would be a great experience, because I will make sure of it.

As I sit in Everett's lap, I can't help but think back to our wedding day. The peach roses in my hands were as lush and alive as my hopes for our future.

Everett looked so handsome in his tuxedo, his dark hair perfectly styled, his blue eyes sparkling with love and excitement. I wore a white lace dress that had a laughable amount of puffy tulle and a veil that floated in the breeze. Like everything else in my life I'd planned that day in excruciating detail. We said our vows under an archway of ivy, promising to love and cherish each other for the rest of our lives. What I loved most about Everett in that moment was his confidence. There were no cold feet. Not a hint of apprehension.

The reception was held in a grand ballroom of the country club his family belonged to, decorated with twinkling fairy lights and elegant centerpieces. We danced our first dance as husband and wife to our favorite song, and everything felt magical. Our guests laughed and celebrated with us, toasting to our future and the love we shared. It was all exactly how I'd designed it.

If I'd have seen a glimpse of myself here today, would I have been so hopeful? I didn't realize Everett would grow his world so large, while mine would shrink down to the neighborhood we live in and the school our children attend. We love and cherish each other, just like we vowed, but we're drifting apart in the vastness of our separate worlds.

Everett's career has taken him to heights I never imagined, and while I'm proud of all he's accomplished, it's hard not to feel left behind. His days are filled with meetings and travel, while mine revolve around car pool schedules, field trips, and keeping our home running smoothly. We still have moments of connection, like the quiet evenings when the kids are asleep, and we sit on the porch reminiscing about the past and dreaming about the future. But those moments are becoming fewer and further between, swallowed up by the demands of our diverging lives.

I've stopped asking for more connection. More support. When we tried for baby two, Everett promised hand on heart that things would change. That was eight years ago and nothing improved. If anything, I'm more alone in parenting than I've ever been. Yet I don't tell him what I need. I don't beg him to show up. I've come to terms with the deficits in our relationship and remind myself that all marriages have challenges. Rough patches. On the other side of all this parenting and climbing the corporate ladder, we'll have plenty of time to connect.

Or maybe we'll find that when all the noise goes quiet, we don't have all that much to say to each other.

FOUR

Megan was trying not to seem excited. That was her favorite thing these days. Apathy. Actively working to make sure she didn't like anything initiated by me. About a hundred times a day I would remind myself it wasn't personal. This was the pulling away that happened in adolescence. I was the person she knew loved her unconditionally, which makes me the perfect person to test boundaries with. She can't lose my love, so she keeps trying to.

Luckily Ashton's excitement is unmistakable. He wiggles with anticipation as he holds the welcome sign at the airport gate. It's taking far longer than I promised them it would. The customs line is long according to the gate agent, and though Eden's flight landed forty minutes ago, we'll need to be patient.

"And you know nothing about her?" Megan asks for the fifth time today. "What if she hates it here? Or thinks you are cringy and she wants to go home?"

"I read a letter she attached with her application and I have a good feeling she will not hate it. You've lived here your whole life so it might not seem that impressive to have the city fifteen minutes away, the mountains an easy little escape for the weekend. But where she is from it's very different. They don't have any skyscrapers like we do in the city. No mega stores where you can buy tires, fruit, and a computer all in the same place. She lives in a little town by the sea and has never traveled anywhere. Can you imagine getting on a plane and going all this way to meet strangers? She must really want to do this to take that risk."

"You'd never let me do that." Megan huffs as she turns her shoulders slightly away from me. I see a small burn behind her ear and know she's been battling the curling iron all week to try to get her hair to align with the current style. I offer to help in the mornings, but she always declines. Apparently, I'm worse to be around than a second-degree burn.

"Well, she's five years older than you. You're right, I couldn't put you on a plane to strangers right now, but in five years—" I stop because I refuse to make some sort of verbal contract that I have zero intention of keeping. Megan is right. I can't imagine sending my teenager across the world to strangers and she knows that.

"Is that her?" Ashton asks for the hundredth time to any person coming across the security gate. So far, he's asked about an elderly woman using a walker, a man with a baby in a stroller and two flight attendants. I almost don't bother following his eyeline to the gate but I need a distraction from Megan's hunched shoulders and bored stare. And it's a good thing I do, because down the small ramp comes Eden.

She's a beautiful girl with wavy chestnut hair that cascades down her shoulders, framing her angelic features. She's wearing a cute travel sweatsuit, the top hanging casually off one bare shoulder, giving her a relaxed and stylish look. Her bright eyes scan the crowd and she spots us, a warm smile spreading across her face.

I can't believe how put-together she looks, even after an international flight. Girls these days seem so polished and fashionable. I think back to my own teen years in the nineties, when neon colors and big hair were still clinging to the fashion scene. I remember awkwardly trying to emulate those trends, often ending up with frizzy hair and mismatched outfits that seemed cool at the time. Seeing Eden, so effortlessly chic, I marvel at how times have changed. It's all perfect hair, contoured makeup and crop tops. Not to mention they get endless chances at taking the perfect selfie. Our disposable cameras with limited shots that took a few days to get developed didn't offer the same success rate.

"Eden," I say, trying to read her face and decide if she would prefer a hug or, like Megan these days, want as little fuss as possible. I don't even have time to decide before she's letting go of her suitcase and grabbing onto me.

"Mrs. Hargrove," Eden sings cheerfully and pulls me in for a hug. I can feel a bit of desperation in her grip. It's understandable. She's so far from home, and for the first time. If I can be what she tethers herself to for the next six weeks to feel stable, then I'm happy to do so.

"Did you have a good flight?" We let go of each other. "I know it's a long way. Then customs can be a lot." A gaggle of other teens pours down the same ramp and are greeted by other waiting families. "Did you have friends on the flight?"

"No," Eden replies shakily, her accent giving her words a distinctive lilt. "They don't go to my school. I'm the only one who could come from my town. People there don't travel much."

Her cheeks pink a little and I take note. That's what I do. I sop up all the emotions and subtle cues from the people around me and make note of what makes them uncomfortable. Careful going forward not to cause the stress again.

"This is Ashton," I say, shuffling him forward even though he looks a bit sheepish suddenly. He's half hidden behind the sign as he giggles a hello. "And this is Megan." I am endlessly grateful that Megan is not sulking or making a poor impression. She's smiling and blinking fast. Something she does when she's nervous.

"Hello," Eden says to each of them in turn. "I love that coat. Is that a Treble Ink?"

Megan lights with pride. "Yeah. I got it for my birthday. You have these in England?"

"Some people do." Eden shrugs. "I saw it on television. I love the television from here. Reality shows. *Million Dollar Listing. Hollywood Hotties.* You're a season ahead of us, so I'll be able to watch episodes I haven't seen while I'm here." She beams with excitement.

"I love those shows too," Megan agrees, though we both know she's not allowed to watch that kind of television. She gives me a little sideways look and seems relieved that I don't contradict her. What she doesn't know is I'm so thankful to see her smile that I don't care what we're talking about.

"You must be exhausted," I say as I take Eden's suitcase and we begin heading out of the terminal. "The long flight and the time change. We have a room ready for you and you can rest."

"I am a bit knackered." Eden arches her back to stretch it out and I watch Megan eye her and become completely enamored.

"What does that mean?" Ashton asks, dropping the small welcome sign to his side. "Knackered."

"Tired," Eden explains. "Sorry if I say strange things. I'm trying to get it right. Is my accent difficult to understand? I've been working very hard since I knew I was coming."

"I love it," Megan chimes in quickly. "No one I know sounds like you. Everyone here sounds all boring and the same. I like knackered better than tired. Tired is boring."

"Cheers," she says, then shakes her head. "Thanks."

"What other weird words do you say?" Ashton asks as we walk toward the car. It was in the valet station. I'd paid a bit extra for them to leave it accessible. I didn't want to park and have to lug everything all the way to the garage. These are the little perks I try to remember when I'm frustrated over something Everett has done. I'd never even used a valet before I met him.

Eden laughs a bit. "I dunno. They aren't weird where I'm from. But when you hear me say something you don't know, then tell me."

"We're right over here," I say, pointing to the SUV. "You can ride up front. I'll put your bags in the back."

"That's a huge car. I've never been in one that big. But I don't want to take a seat from one of them." Eden gestures to Megan and Ashton. "I can sit anywhere."

"They don't ride up front. They aren't big enough." I click the button to unlock the SUV and hear Megan mumble something. She's small for her age. A late bloomer in many ways, and she doesn't meet the weight requirement to safely sit up front. And the safest recommendation is to wait until she's thirteen anyway. It's just one of the many things we argue over every single morning on the way to school. She insists she's the only kid in her grade to not ride in the front seat. Just like she's the only one who doesn't have a smartphone. She's the only one who doesn't get to go to sleepovers, though I do let her have them at our house. But nothing is good enough these days.

"Oh," Eden says, looking surprised. "We don't have that at home. Or if we do, my mum just didn't listen."

As we get in the car, I feel an ache in my chest. I can recite the next words out of my daughter's mouth before she says them.

"You're lucky. My mom is crazy about that stuff," Megan says right on cue.

"No." Eden shakes her head and turns to look at Megan in the back seat. "Trust me, you are the lucky one. I'd have saved myself a lot of trouble if my mum was like that. See this scar?"

She pulls her brown curls away from her forehead and exposes a small zigzag line just above her eyebrow. "My mother let me sit in the back of our friend's car while he was messing about out by the sea. I smashed my head and needed seventeen stitches."

"Woah," Ashton says, leaning in from his booster seat. Another safety element we're hanging onto longer than most of his peers. "That's so cool."

"Are you hungry?" I pull out of the valet station and turn the music on. I've given lots of consideration to my playlist. Something that won't embarrass Megan but isn't so edgy I'm introducing Ashton to some new words he'll be asking about.

"I couldn't really eat on the plane," Eden replies almost like an apology, keeping the words noticeably small. "But don't change anything for me. I'm used to that. There's lots of places I can't eat, so I'm good."

I feel my chest tighten and then smooth over with warmth. I love when I get ahead of someone's worry or discomfort and disarm it like a ticking bomb before it ever explodes. "I've got the list of your allergies and I've already handled it all. There isn't too much overlap between your allergies and Ashton's, but our safe areas in the kitchen will work for both of you. We have a separate fridge and countertop oven I use. Now I don't know that I'll be any good at cooking food you're used to back home, but I've got plenty of things you can try. Just tell me what you like and we'll get more of it."

"You didn't... Mrs. Hargrove, you didn't need to..." She looks incredibly touched and relieved.

"It's no trouble at all. You and Ashton both have the dairy allergy. The eggs and wheat will be easy to accommodate. I'll make sure what I prepare for you doesn't have any tree nuts so I can make it safe for Ashton too. And please call me Jo. We just want you to be completely at ease here. It's such an amazing opportunity for us all and it'll go by fast. So we're going to make it as easy and fun as possible while you're here."

"That's cracking." Eden claps her hands together excitedly. "It's so nerve-racking not knowing what you would all be like. I heard the rest of the kids in the program got chosen months ago, so they've been chatting with the host families for ages. Talking about what they'll do, and getting to know each other."

"You must have been so worried about not being placed with anyone." I offer a gentle look of empathy but I'm secretly pleased to know we were able to save the day.

"It was stressful, but my mum kept saying it would all work out. I didn't get told I was matched with anyone until five days ago when the paperwork went through. I got the email while I was at school and literally screamed. I was so excited. This is a dream come true."

"Why?" Megan asks, her brows furrowed a bit with skepticism. She has no concept of the rest of the world. Everything she knows about England is posh things she sees on television and in movies. Just like it was here in the United States, there were pockets of places where the experiences of people were vastly different than all Megan had known. I'd researched the town a bit and understood that Eden was going to have a good amount of culture shock considering she'd never left the town she was from.

"Why is it a dream come true?" Eden asks, seeming stunned by the question. "Everything I watch on the telly is from here. I'm obsessed with makeup tutorials. We don't have a mall, not like what you have. The music scene. The mix of cultures. You have access to everything."

"You have Ulta though, right? Or Sephora?" Megan is enthralled with the details in a way I haven't seen in ages.

"No." Eden laughs, turning around halfway in her seat to explain it to a completely gobsmacked Megan. "We don't have anything like that. And it's not just the shopping. My town is so small I've never been into one of the big cities. I know that sounds mad but we haven't been able to travel with my mother working as much as she does. Plus I'm so focused on school. There are just no opportunities where I live. Your school is brilliant. We don't have anything like that either. Windsor Knoll is the only place I wanted to get assigned, which is another reason it was so hard finding a family to match with. I read about your school two years ago and have been dreaming of it ever since."

"Yeah," I say through a breathy laugh as I look at Megan in the rearview mirror. "Please remember that when I try to wake you up in the mornings and you beg to stay home. It's a dream school."

I try not to focus on the fact that Eden is half focused on her phone, texting frantically to someone. I'm hoping it's her mother, updating her with positive feedback on what she thinks of us. But I see a few questionable emojis out of the corner of my eye and maybe the word bitch. It makes me have to gulp back some emotion. Does she think I'm a bitch? I brush off the fear and stop trying to get a glimpse at her phone screen.

"I'm a little bit nervous though," Eden admits, nibbling at her lip. "I know we're not in the same grade but will I be able to go around with Megan? At least at first."

"Definitely," Megan answers, the joy I've missed so much returning to her voice. "Right, Mom? I could show her around the first day?"

"We can arrange that." One of the things I enjoy most about Windsor Knoll is that it's all grades on one campus. Our kids will be there from kindergarten until they graduate. They call them lifers. "It'll be nice to have all three of you on the same campus." Eloise is so grateful to me for taking this on last-minute, I know she'll pull whatever strings I need. I mark it all down as a win so far. "And for dinner, do you like tacos?"

"Tacos?" Eden's voice is worried. "I usually can't..."

"I've got you covered." I beam. "Corn tortillas, and everything else is allergy-friendly. But if you don't like them, that's okay too. I also have—"

"I would love tacos. Oh my gosh, is it because it's Tuesday? Are we doing Taco Tuesday?" She squeals a bit. "That's so American. I love it." She shoots off another quick text and I definitely see the taco emoji and the little green face emoji that usually means something is gross. I force myself to look away.

For the rest of the ride home, Megan and Eden chat about music and school. The age gap is apparent but Eden is being kind and not pointing out every instance where they are different. Megan isn't allowed to wear makeup yet but she has some glosses and lotions from the brands Eden is asking about. She isn't allowed to listen to some of the music Eden brings up but once that becomes clear, Eden shifts to other artists that would be more appropriate.

I take deep, centering breaths as I try to process how good this is going and what I will tell Everett when he calls tonight from Japan. I will say Eden is gentle with Megan and silly with Ashton. She's thrilled to be here and endlessly grateful. I'll assure him that when he comes back, he'll think she's wonderful too. And maybe it's a bit too early to make that assessment, but I'm going with it. The new spontaneous Jo.

Eden opens her social media on her phone. She spins around to Megan and I want to tell her to sit forward and be safe, but I bite my tongue.

"What are your socials? I'll add you." Eden waits, her fingers hovering, ready to type.

When Megan doesn't answer, I take the hit for her. "Megan isn't old enough for social media. Not until high school. Lots of studies say it's terrible for your brain and your focus. And there are a lot of creeps on there who could get you into dangerous situations."

"Oh." Eden pulls a strange face and exchanges a look with Megan. It feels conspiratorial. Like they've just silently decided I'm the problem. "Are you twelve?"

"Yes, and before you ask, every single one of my friends are on social media." Megan's voice is sharp. "Everyone except me."

Eden hums some little noise before she speaks. "I was like ten when I got my phone and all my socials. That's how friends mostly stay in touch though, but maybe it's different here."

"It's the same here, my mom is just psycho," Megan snarls.

I watch from the corner of my eye and up in the rearview mirror as something forms between the girls. I can't name it and I don't dare call it out. But it's there. Eden spins back around and changes the subject, but I can feel the temperature around me change. I'd hoped Eden would be a sensible voice of reason. Now I'm worried she'll be the ally Megan has been waiting for.

FIVE

I'd planned to tell Everett everything had been perfect. Better than perfect. Amazing, really. The good news is I didn't have to embellish anything on my call with Everett because we played phone tag until the time difference made it impossible to connect. I'd forgotten to keep my ringer up while we were having dinner and then we went straight into making a list of all the things Eden wants to accomplish while she's here. I love that some are frivolous and stereotypical and others are deep and challenging. She wants to make the most of her time at school, but also dig into some of the indulgent opportunities being here offers.

With all the excitement and a deadline for Everett, we missed each other. It happens. And we've always done a good job of not taking it too personally. The life we have is because of the work he does and it requires sacrifice from both of us. I know we'll have a chance to chat when I'm in line to pick the kids up from school later. By then I'll have so much more to tell him.

"Breakfast," I call up the stairs to the kids and feel a flutter of excitement at the food I have laid out. It's safely prepared and

I was careful to listen to Eden's lists of favorite ingredients. Things she normally can't get for fear of an allergic reaction. I've gotten very good over the years at altering recipes for Ashton. I like the challenge, and this morning it's paid off.

"Oh," Eden says, her face filled with concern as she and Megan come clopping down the stairs, chatting the whole way. "Um, pancakes? Maybe I'll just have an apple."

"They're safe," I announce confidently. "It's an allergy-approved mix. Tapioca and rice flour. The chocolate chips are safe, too. I know it's probably scary to try new things but I feel very confident that you can trust the food I make for you here."

"I've literally never had pancakes," she replies, seeming emotional at the thought. "The syrup is okay too?"

"It is." My sing-song voice would usually make Megan cringe this early in the morning. But today she got up without a fight and seems genuinely excited to go to school. That would be enough, but the words that come out of her mouth next bowl me over.

"My mom is really good at doing this stuff. She can make food taste awesome even when she can't use the things you're allergic to."

I want to thank her but I know her well. That would be a bridge too far. I'd be *making a big deal* out of her compliment and like a spooked animal, she might retreat back into her emotional cave. Instead, I just hand them their plates and fill up their glasses of juice. Ashton is a step or two behind but soon takes his food over to the table too.

My mug of coffee is steaming as I walk over to join them. Without having to wage war over every detail of the morning routine, we seem to have a lot more time to sit and be together. My jaw isn't clenched. My posture is relaxed. Life is good.

Eden flips her hair off her shoulder and I watch Megan do the same a moment later. My daughter has found someone to model herself on, and after just a day together I can see the similarities. Little gestures like the hair flip and even Megan's posture. I love that Megan is at least willing to pay attention to someone in this house and adjust her attitude accordingly.

"Is there more coffee?" Eden eyes my mug. It's such a casual request but still takes me by surprise. It's odd to have this half-woman, half-child in the house. Someone who's life I know nothing about. When she's sitting next to Megan talking about pop music, she seems very childlike. But I suppose it wouldn't be that odd that she drinks coffee at her age.

"Uh, yes. Do you drink coffee?"

"Of course." She laughs. "I mean, only if I want to function. My friends and I have been drinking it for ages."

"Can I have some too?" Megan asks, giving me this desperate look. My gut is to say no. Children shouldn't drink coffee. I want to tell her that too much caffeine can increase anxiety, raise heart rate and blood pressure, cause acid reflux and screw up her sleep. I always hold the line on this kind of stuff. If it's a safety issue I'm perfectly fine being the bad guy. But the look she's giving me isn't disdain or frustration. She wants to be on the same team as me. She wants me to have her back in this moment.

"A little," I say, trying to make this no big deal. The good news is, I know she'll hate the taste and even if she chokes a bit down this morning, she won't be asking for it again.

"Me too," Ashton insists.

"No way. You're too little." Megan looks so pleased to be able to shoot him down.

"I'll make you some chocolate milk," I offer to appease him, and it works. That's a treat he rarely gets and is pleased to have as a consolation.

I prepare all their drinks in coffee mugs and carry them over as Eden gushes about the pancakes. They are filling their mouths and giggling about something as the morning minutes tick by. I try to remember the last time it was like this, and realize maybe it never was. Back when Megan and I were besties, Ashton was a wild toddler and then a rambunctious little kid. Even if Megan and I were getting along wonderfully he'd topple over a drink on the paper she was coloring and the morning would crumble into chaos. Eden, however, was like some kind of spell we could all fall under.

It's impossible for me to look away when Megan takes a sip of the very strong black coffee and winces. She expected something better. Something glamorous and delicious, considering how often the adults around her drink it. I don't react when she chokes that sip down and doesn't touch the mug again. Maybe saying yes sometimes isn't the end of the world.

"Have you heard this song?" Eden takes the wireless earbud out of her ear and hands it to Megan who instantly pops it in to listen intently. She nods her head along to the beat and I can hear the music's base bumping. It's too loud. Probably doing damage to her ears, but I try not to focus on that. I've never been good at choosing my battles. Everything feels paramount when it comes to my children.

I try to start a conversation that might bring an end to the music. "Eden, do you play any sports at home? Megan is really great at cheer."

"Like a cheerleader? Is that really a sport?" Eden asks, and I can see her mouth turn down a bit in judgment. Megan takes out the earbud, as I'd hoped, but the rest doesn't go my way. Or at least the way I envisioned.

"I don't really do it anymore. I stopped like six months ago." Megan shrugs as though the dream of being on the school cheer team didn't matter at all anymore.

"But you said you were thinking of trying out for the middle school team that cheers for the boys' basketball games." I let the confusion paint my face before I realize the trouble I'm causing. Megan shoots me a nasty look and Eden turns her silent judgment into something more vocal.

"We have some things like that at home but it's not really like you do it here. Aren't cheerleaders kind of vapid and a bit dumb? Or is that just what is on American television?"

"They're dumb," Megan answers before I can launch into any explanation about stereotypes and media. "I am not trying out for cheer. I'm not really into any school things anymore. I'm just doing my own stuff."

I take stock of Megan's time lately. Academics have been a bit more demanding this year and I realize suddenly that she has taken a step back from most of the fun extracurriculars she had been doing. I've been so busy arguing with her that I hadn't noticed how much she'd retreated into herself. Thinking of the books I've read and the warning signs of teen depression, I make a note to circle back to this when we are alone.

"What's your own stuff?" Eden asks, looking genuinely interested. "What are you into?"

"I like shopping and fashion. Music. I'm really getting into music."

Those are all hobbies Eden has mentioned as her favorites but I don't interject with how new they are to Megan's list of likes. As in, since she heard Eden say them.

"That's cool," Eden approves cheerily. "You should try some stuff with environmental science. If you like animals it's a very interesting thing to get into. I did that when I was about your age. I went through a major phase where I was going to be a veterinarian."

"Yeah. I'd like that. Mom, can you see if there is anything like that I can get into?"

"Sure." I let only that word slip out. I swallow everything else I want to say. I knew that Eden would have an influence on Megan but in such a short period of time, it's much stronger than I'd imagined. The positive news is that Eden has guided Megan toward an interesting field with a lot of potential. It could be far worse.

"You all go brush your teeth and then grab your backpacks and lunches I have ready. We should leave shortly." Not a single whine. No negotiating to stay home or pretending to have a stomachache. Just a little chatter about a body spray Eden plans to let Megan use. It's glorious. For six months Megan has been a nightmare every morning and now, it's smooth sailing.

Well, until I notice it. I was distracted a bit when the girls came downstairs and hadn't really taken in what Eden had picked for an outfit. The shorts are entirely too short and her top shows her midriff.

"Um, Eden, I love your outfit," I say tentatively from behind my coffee mug. "But Windsor Knoll has a pretty strict dress code."

"Dress code?" Eden asks, looking down at her outfit with confusion. "Like uniforms?"

"No, not uniforms," I edge out hesitantly. "I can print the dress code for you to see. Maybe that will help. I really should have done that to begin with. It's my mistake."

"It's oppressive," Megan groans and I'm surprised to know that word is even in her vocabulary. "The boys don't ever get dress coded and the girls do all the time. You can't wear those shorts; they are too short. And you can't have your stomach out."

"We have uniforms at school back home, but I got really excited when I thought here you can wear what you want. I didn't know there were rules."

"The patriarchy," Megan answers with a shrug and I let out a small giggle I can't contain.

I feel compelled to give Eden more context. "Megan, it's not that. The school just holds kids to a high standard, and they think that having a strict dress code helps keep clothes from being the focal point of anyone's day. They don't allow shirts with large logos or words on them either. Nothing political."

"Oh." Eden looks down at her outfit and frowns.

I hum as I think this through. "Do you have anything that

would work for today, and then we can make a plan and go over the dress code together to find some clothes? It was a total over-sight on my part. I should have thought of it."

"I have some jeans I can wear today. And I can put on a sweatshirt?" Eden looks disappointed to have to change the outfit she clearly thought would make the best impression on her first day.

"Do they have rips?" Megan asks, ready to break the bad news. "Are the jeans ripped?"

"Yes. Is that not allowed either?" Eden looks shocked.

"Nope." Megan sighs and shakes her head. "Seriously oppressive."

I roll my eyes at Megan, taking a page from her book. "The jeans will be fine today. I'll send an email to let the head of school know that it was a mistake on my part, then we'll pick up some clothes that will work this evening. At least we get some shopping out of it."

Eden looks concerned and I know exactly how to squash that worry. I put her at ease. "And the clothes will be our treat since we forgot to get you this information up front."

"No, you don't have to buy me clothes," Eden argues, but weakly. "That wasn't something you were expecting."

"We all get a trip to the mall." I wave her off. "And it's no big deal at all. I'm happy to do it. It'll make me feel better about my mistake. So you'd be doing me a favor."

Eden nods and looks to Megan, who is fluttering with excitement. "The shopping will be fun."

"So fun," Megan agrees. "Our mall has tons of good stores and it's a great place to hang. Lots of people-watching."

People-watching? It's another phrase I didn't realize Megan knew, which I find a little unsettling, to hear her tossing all this around so casually. More than that; it's the way she waggles her brows as if there is some code they're exchanging. A private joke. Or maybe a secret.

SIX

Crisis averted and clothes changed, we make our way out to my SUV as I check to make sure everyone has what they need. It's strange to have Eden up in the front seat but I like the company. When Everett is home, he always drives and when it's just me and the kids I'm up here alone.

"Do you have family here?" Eden asks, clearly trying to make polite conversation with me. She's obviously more comfortable chatting with Megan, but the seating arrangement in the car means she's stuck up front with me.

"Everett's family is back east. We see them for holidays and we spend a week there every summer together. Lots of family time. Grandparents, aunts, uncles and tons of cousins."

Ashton leans forward in his seat to make his awkward interjection. "We don't have grandparents on my mom's side because they're dead."

Eden winces and looks regretful for asking, but I put her at ease. "I lost both my parents when I was pretty young. But I've been lucky to have so much loving family on Everett's side. They really accepted me and made me feel like I belonged."

It's not entirely true but it's the version best suited for the kids to hear. My past is unfortunately littered with stories best left untold. I try to swallow down the awkwardness, but Eden clocks the redness in my cheeks and tries to change the subject.

"Can I play some music?" Eden asks as she pulls out her phone and reaches for the cable that hooks it up to my vehicle's speakers.

"Sure." All this saying yes is not as hard as I'd imagined. The music comes to life over the speakers and everyone is doing a little happy dance in their seat as we cruise along toward school. The first few songs are upbeat pop that I recognize. Soon the lyrics turn suggestive and the language not what I'd normally allow in my car. Megan is occasionally making eye contact with me in the rearview mirror, daring me to flash my badge as the fun police and shut this down. With every new curse word pumping through my speakers, I desperately want to. Instead, I try to play it cool.

"Did that lady just say ass?" Ashton asks through a giggle as he covers his mouth. "Did she, Mom?"

Eden answers before I can. "She's talking about her body but in an empowering kind of way. It's girl power." She flexes her muscles playfully and then Megan does the same.

I have so much to say about this, but only bite my tongue and try to ride out the rest of the trip hoping each song gets a little less vulgar. About two minutes out from the drop-off line I turn the music down and run through the list in my head for everyone.

"Ashton, you have the field day contest today, so make sure you drink your water and eat your snack so you've got energy to play. Also, if you're all eating outside on the field, what do you do?"

"Sit with Mrs. Lonnar." Ashton sounds a bit disappointed, but resigned to the idea. This is our life. He understands the risk of not following the rules.

"Right, we don't know what is in everyone else's lunch and

unlike the cafeteria that has an allergy table, eating out on the field isn't safe." I look in my mirror and wait for him to nod in agreement.

The memory of that terrifying day when Ashton was two years old flashes through my mind, a vivid and haunting reminder of why these precautions are nonnegotiable. It was a sunny afternoon, and we were at a friend's barbecue. I was chatting with the other parents, feeling relaxed and happy. That was my first mistake. I let my guard down. I'll never forget the frantic cry. I spun to see Ashton, his tiny face turning red, eyes wide with panic. He was clutching his throat, struggling to breathe.

My heart stopped. I rushed to him, my mind racing. I thought at first he was choking on a toy or something he picked up in the yard. Everyone knew of his allergies. No one would let him have any foods that weren't safe. Soon I realized we were in serious trouble. His lips were swelling, his breaths coming in short, desperate gasps.

I screamed for someone to call 911, my voice breaking. Someone grabbed their phone while I fumbled for the EpiPen in Ashton's diaper bag. My hands were shaking so badly I could barely get the cap off. It was Everett who came to the rescue, grabbing the pen from my hand and injecting Ashton. Time seemed to slow down as I watched it unfold, praying it wasn't too late.

The minutes that followed felt like hours. Ashton's breathing was shallow, his skin clammy. I held him close, whispering soothing words even as my own panic threatened to overwhelm me. The sound of sirens was the most beautiful thing I'd ever heard.

At the hospital, the doctors confirmed what I feared, anaphylactic shock. It was an intense reaction brought on by a brownie he'd eaten off another child's plate. Maybe two brownies. Both loaded with nuts. I had been watching him closely for most of the party. But someone had gotten my ear about an upcoming fundraiser and I'd been distracted by the promise of a fancy night. The dress I might buy. The people I might connect with.

I took my eyes off my child and he nearly died. It was the moment I became hyper-vigilant, determined to protect my son from a world filled with unseen dangers.

"Ashton," I say, my voice softer now. "I know it's hard, but remember that we do this to keep you safe. You're so brave, and I'm proud of you."

He nods again, more resolutely this time. "I know, Mom."

This exchange is met with something from Eden I can't name. Some kind of huff. An exasperated laugh that makes me instantly self-conscious. It's strange to have an audience to my parenting. I glance at her just after she lets the little noise out and she flashes me a disingenuous smile. Something to appease the crazy woman driving the car.

Moving on to the next item I glance back at the other side of the back seat. "Megan, you are going to be taking Eden down to the office and seeing Mr. Heinz. He knows you're taking her on a tour of the school first. Then you'll bring her down to the library in the upper school where she'll meet with Trisha. That's Tonya Spartan's daughter. You remember her from when you did that cheerleading camp?"

"A cheerleader." Megan is speaking almost exclusively to Eden this morning, and I'm annoyed at the judgment I hear in her voice.

"She's very nice. You'll like her, Eden." I don't let the catty lilt in Megan's voice win out. Trisha is a lovely girl and she'll be very sweet to Eden.

"Okay, thank you." Eden exchanges a sassy kind of look with Megan and it bothers me but I just press on. They are kids. School is sometimes a wild place and I can't control every bit of it. At least she and Megan are bonding nicely. I just wish it wasn't at the expense of a group Megan used to love being a part of.

"Eden, you've got your class schedule but don't feel too much pressure. It's just your first day. If you make it through without falling asleep from jet lag, that's a win."

"I can't wait," Eden exclaims, turning to share the excitement with Megan. "The Design Thinking course is going to be incredible. And then a whole lesson dedicated to drone technology. You are so lucky, Megan."

"I don't have those kinds of classes yet," she replies, looking disappointed. "Ours are just basic math and science stuff to get us ready."

"But you're going to have these classes," Eden answers breathlessly. "You have no idea how lucky you are. And your dad already works in tech. My mum works in a bar and it's fine, but it's not like I have some leg up when I'm ready to start a career."

"Yeah, I am lucky," Megan agrees, not looking at me in the rearview mirror. She might be willing to admit it to Eden, but she's not saying it for my benefit.

I pull up to the curb and watch the excitement grow in Eden as she steps out of the car. There is no eye rolling from Megan or near tears from Ashton. Everyone steps out, says a kind thank you and goodbye and heads off to the adventure that awaits them. I feel endlessly lucky that my children attend Windsor Knoll. I love that they come to the same campus every day and will for their whole school career, and now Eden gets folded right into that too. I'm ready to pull off but, of course, it doesn't happen.

Eloise is quick this time and even though I don't hesitate, she's at my passenger window.

"I see a lot of smiles," she coos with a haughty expression. "How's it going?"

"Really well." I don't go into detail on the little bumps in the road we've had, figuring they are normal things that happen in the adjustment phase. Instead I focus on all the things that are going great. "You were so right. Eden is adorable, and Megan and Ashton are loving the experience." I tamp down the few little moments that have irked me and stay focused on the positive. "I do have a few questions, though. Do you have a second?"

"Of course. You made me incredibly popular with the RAS program. They've never had such a hard time placing a child and you came through. I ended up looking like a real hero. What can I answer for you?"

"Should I be messaging Eden's mother more? Her phone number was on the application and I checked the box that she could reach out anytime, but I've only heard back from her once and it was brief. I sent her some pictures and let her know Eden was settling in nicely, but didn't hear back. Is that normal?"

"I've had both. Some parents are incredibly communicative and worried, and others are trying to give their children space. Things are different in other countries. Kids not much older than your Megan are riding the metro, helping out at family businesses, and living far more independent lives than our children. I'm sure Eden and her mother worked out what level of communication the two of them should have. But if you're wanting to get a little more response from her, come up with some questions to ask. Something she'll be sure to respond to. It doesn't have to be urgent, just maybe about Eden's preferences on food or if she minds you doing something over the weekend. Just to get her talking."

"Great. And what about rules? All my rules are for little kids. I'm assuming Eden will make friends here at school. She's a charming girl. I'm a little out of my depth when it comes to curfew and who she can drive around with. I feel this immense pressure to make sure she's safe. Caring for someone else's child this far from home, it's a lot."

"Take a breath, girl," Eloise chirps condescendingly. "I

promise I've done this many times over for exchange students and my own children. It all works out. You trust your gut when it comes to boundaries and it'll go smooth. The children in these programs are normally high performers, eager to please, and very independent. Just don't overthink it."

"For sure," I lie as if this is even a possibility for me. I think things to death. I worry circles around the issue until I wear a path. I will lose sleep. I underestimated the pressure of keeping another person's child safe. The food thing I can manage, but if she's going out with friends and driving in cars with kids I hardly know, I'm not sure how I'll survive that anxiety. "Thank you so much, Eloise."

"When I'm accepting the volunteer of the year award at the annual ceremony, I'll mention you in the speech." She holds up a pretend award and grins. "Just text me if you have any more questions."

"I sure will." I shift the vehicle into gear and pull away from the school.

My new task for the day is to connect with Eden's mother. I'll take Eloise's advice and send something that encourages a response. I can't imagine if it was Megan on the other side of the world with strangers. I'd spend every free second I had staring at my phone hoping for an update.

I pull into the driveway at home and give it some thought.

Hello Ivy. This is Jo. I'm sure Eden's been updating you but I just wanted to let you know she's off to her first day of school here and all is well. What does she normally pack in her lunch?

I include the picture of Eden standing in front of our home holding the sign I made for her first day of school. I know it's probably a very American thing to do and maybe a bit cheesy, but I want Eden to have as close to an authentic experience here as possible. If Eden found it in bad taste or annoying, she didn't show that at all. She seemed absolutely thrilled to pose.

I can see the bubbles come up on my phone to indicate Ivy is writing a response. I hop out of my vehicle and head into the house fully expecting to start a pleasant exchange. But the bubbles soon disappear. My message is read and then unanswered. As a woman with high anxiety, this is a nightmare. Did I say something wrong? Was the picture a bad idea?

I work to talk myself down from the spiral of emotions and remember that Eden's mother works. She might not have the ability to reply right now. We've done a wonderful thing by taking Eden in and Ivy isn't angry. It's hard for me to admit just how much people's hypothetical anger scares me. It sends my body into a tailspin. Flashes of my childhood flood back. If someone is mad at me, then I'm not safe. People-pleasing was never about being loved and accepted, it was about avoiding danger.

It's bothersome to me that my brain requires this much emotional extinguishing to the fires I set in there. I'm the arson and the firefighter when it comes to the ebbs and flows of anxiety. Some days I can let that controlled burn do its job and other days, I die in the smoke.

The bubbles reappear for a moment and I hold my breath. Write something, dammit. Put me out of this misery. Reply.

The bubbles disappear again and I let out a little scream.

SEVEN

Never in my youth would I have imagined a stack of bills would be a relief. That's all the mailbox held today. But every day that I don't find the threatening letters is a good one. I contemplate why someone would be so consistently dedicated to trying to ruin my life. As if it's some kind of hobby to call me a killer. To threaten my soul with eternal damnation. It's not that I don't deserve the menacing words and doom and gloom that comes in the envelope. I do. I made a choice many years ago that I can't deny or rationalize away. I should count myself lucky. Getting rid of a piece of mail every once in a while, before my family sees it, is a small price to pay.

And the good news soon overtakes those dark thoughts. Eden had a wonderful day at school, filled with new experiences and exciting classes. I soak in every word as she and Megan give more details about what's going on at school than I've gotten in the last six months. They giggle and whisper. I loathe the whispers. There really shouldn't have to be any inside jokes or secrets, but I like that they're bonding. So much so that Eden squeezed into the back seat between Ashton and Megan.

As I glance in the rearview mirror, I notice some looks pass between Eden and Megan that make me pause. There's something unsettling in the way Eden's eyes flicker toward Megan, a knowing look that seems to carry more weight than a simple school day anecdote. Megan, in turn, glances back at Eden with an expression that's hard to read—part admiration, part something else that sends a shiver down my spine.

It's not just the looks. There's a shift in Megan's demeanor that I can't quite put my finger on. She's been more secretive lately, more defensive. As they continue their animated conversation, I catch snippets of words that don't quite add up, references to things that don't fit into the narrative of their day.

"...and then, you know, like we talked about," Eden says, her voice dropping conspiratorially. Megan nods vigorously, her face lighting up in a way that both delights and worries me.

"What did you talk about?" I ask, trying to keep my tone light and curious, rather than intrusive.

"Oh, just some project we're working on," Megan replies too quickly. She shifts in her seat, her eyes darting away from mine. "It's nothing, Mom."

I try to believe her. Kids keep things from their parents. Silly things, just for fun. I put the worry out of my mind.

Now, as they walk through the bustling mall, Megan snorts out a laugh I haven't heard in ages. She beams as she and Eden chat animatedly, glancing at the stores they pass. It's like she has a big sister suddenly and the spark is back in her heart.

"Mom, can Eden and I walk around on our own for a bit?" Megan asks, her eyes sparkling with excitement.

The question is like an arrow through my heart. I'm completely torn. Normally, when Megan asks to go off on her own, the answer is an easy no. But now, with Eden here, what reason do I really have to keep them from going? Well, actually, I have a ton of reasons why I should say no. Malls are a huge target for trafficking young girls. Eden might be very independent at home, but things are surely different here than she's used to. There are strangers. Drugs that look like candy. Mass shootings. My gut churns with the choice. If I had a babysitter for Megan, she'd be Eden's age. And Eden has given me no reason to be concerned. Her judgment seems sound and her stories from back home are mostly sweet. It's her and her mother, and though she has a lot of freedom, it doesn't sound like she abuses it.

As Ashton pulls my arm in one direction, eager to look at some anime cards he collects down on the first floor, I feel pressure to say yes.

"You have an hour," I tell the girls, my voice serious. "Make sure the clothes you buy are dress code approved." I hand over two hundred dollars in cash to Eden.

Eden's eyes widen in shock. "That's way too much," she protests.

Megan, ever the opportunist, quips, "It's hardly enough at the stores I'm going to take you to."

I'm compelled to pull Megan aside and give her a stern talking-to about what to be careful about and how to act while we're apart, but things move too quickly and the girls are gone before I can utter another word.

As Ashton and I make our way to the anime store, my mind races with worry. I try to focus on Ashton's excitement as he picks out his favorite cards, but my thoughts keep drifting back to Megan and Eden. This is the part of anxiety I despise the most. How it locks me out of my own life. It transports me from the present into some far-off nightmare that never comes to be. While I'm off in my mind wondering if someone is talking to the girls into separating from each other, I'm missing the story Ashton is trying to tell me.

The hour drags on. Every minute feels like an eternity as I constantly check my watch and phone. Finally, as the hour mark approaches, we head back to the designated meeting spot.

I breathe a sigh of relief as I see the girls approaching, bags in hand and smiles on their faces.

"We found some great stuff," Eden announces, and I watch as Megan's expression turns dodgy and afraid. Something has happened. I know my child and this look is unfamiliar and worrisome. "And Megan—"

Megan sends an elbow into Eden's side to quiet her. "We should go to the car, I have homework," Megan says and quickly turns toward the door we came in at. I want to ask her what is wrong. I want Eden to finish her sentence but the tension is rising by the second and I want to handle whatever it is delicately. Maybe she started her period. Maybe she ran into a boy she likes and did something embarrassing. Or maybe Eden made her feel uncomfortable or unsafe. Either way, it's clear Megan doesn't want to say anything now. As hard as it is for me to wait, I let the car ride unfold, as awkward as it is, and try to focus on Ashton and the cards he bought. I make small talk with him and Eden and try not to draw attention to whatever is wrong with Megan.

When we pull into the driveway, I ask Eden to take Ashton up to his room so he can show her the cards he has and she could help him put his new ones away. She's painfully uncomfortable now and agrees, just for a chance to step away. My stomach is burning with anxiety as Megan makes a break for the stairs and I stop her.

"Honey, wait a minute, stay down here, please."

"I want to go to my room," she barks in that familiar and angry tone. I haven't missed that. "I just don't feel good."

"Did you start your period?" I'm trying to cut through the games and get to the heart of what might be going on. "Did you have your period pack in your bag? I know it can be overwhelming, I can answer any questions you have."

"Mom, just leave me alone. It's not my period. I'm fine."

"You obviously are not fine. Something happened at the mall and I want to know what it is. I can't help if I don't know."

"It's nothing. I just don't want to talk about it."

"Would you rather we call your dad and we can all talk about it together?" It's a veiled threat. I know she never prefers for Everett to be part of delicate conversations. "Did Eden do or say something to make you uncomfortable? It's okay, you can tell me."

"I'm going to my room," Megan screeches and she stomps up the stairs. I'm on the verge of chasing her when I think better of it. The books are clear on when to have the tough conversations and it's not in the heat of the moment, when I'm amped up with fear and she's flooded with some unknown emotion. But damn the books, something happened to my kid and I want to know what.

EIGHT

I'm ready to storm Megan's bedroom when a moment later Eden is in the kitchen with tears in her eyes.

"I think I mucked something up." She sniffles and I feel instantly terrible for her. Things had been going so well with her and Megan, but it was too soon for them to have unsupervised time. Eloise told me to trust my gut and I let the pressure of trying to make them happy overrule what I knew was true.

"What happened?" I gesture toward the table and we both sit down. "We can work it out, whatever it is." That's a lie. There are a lot of things I'll do to make the people around me feel better. But if one of those things harms my children, all bets are off.

The panic in Eden's eyes is what scares me most. "Megan told me you said it was all right and that she'd just been putting it off because she was scared. But that if I went with her, she would finally do it."

"Do what?" I ask, an atomic bomb detonating in my body.

"Get her ears pierced. I thought it was no big deal. Everyone at home has multiple piercings, like I do. And parents don't really care. But when I went to tell you and she reacted the way she did, I knew I'd screwed up."

"Megan got her ears pierced today?" The words come out choppy and I can see Eden's hands starting to shake. "How did that happen? I wasn't even there to give permission."

"I signed the paper," Eden admits with tears streaming down her cheeks. "I didn't know it was something you didn't want. I thought she was just scared and she was facing her fear or something. She made it sound like it was a good thing. I expected when we saw you, you'd be really excited for her plucking up the courage to do it."

"You're not even old enough to sign that paper," I counter, trying to keep the anger out of my voice. "We have a rule. She needed to wait until she was fourteen to get her ears pierced."

"They didn't really seem to care who signed the paper at the mall. The girl doing the piercing was pretty chill. They didn't ask how old either of us was. Megan told me—"

"Megan is a little girl." My voice rises a few octaves. "I can't believe this. This is permanent. It's holes in her body that I did not want her to have at this age." I feel the tears forming in my own eyes now.

"I am so sorry. What can I do?" Eden covers her face with her hands. She's crying, or she at least sounds like she's trying to. It sounds over the top and dramatic but I don't know her well enough to tell if this is genuine or an act.

"There is nothing you can do," I huff, feeling the heat in my cheeks blazing. "You should have known better than to believe her and do something so drastic. This is a very big deal."

"I didn't know it was drastic. At home we just pierce each other's ears. It's not something our parents even care about. I thought doing it at the mall was very safe and nice. I didn't know over here parents were so uptight about something so simple."

"I need to call Everett. Can you please go up to your room for a little while? I'll call you all down for dinner."

"Jo, I'm so—"

I just nod my understanding but make it clear with my expression that I don't want to talk about it with her any more now. I'd like to charge up to Megan's room and demand answers. Instead I pick up my phone to call Everett. If I have to, I'll call three times in a row. That's how he knows it's urgent and no matter what meeting he's in, he'll step out and pick up.

When I look down at my screen there is a message there. It's Ivy, Eden's mother. She finally texted back.

Sorry it took so long for me to get back to you. I worked a double shift today. Thank you for the message. I am glad Eden is settling in so well, and we are very grateful for all you've done for her already. She sings your praises and she can't believe her dreams are coming true. I will call her in the morning before school. Thank you also for the picture. She looks happier than I've ever seen her before. Anything you put in her lunch, she'll love.

I don't write a reply. I don't know what I'd say. *I'm glad Eden's having a good time. She just maimed my daughter without my consent and I'm furious.*

Instead, I call Everett and, luckily, I don't have to try three times before I reach him. He picks up after two rings and before he's done saying hello, I'm sobbing. Everett's voice is filled with concern as he answers the unplanned call. I don't cry often so he understands it's serious. Also, we weren't going to check in with each other again until tomorrow so his antenna is up. "Hey, what's going on? Are you—"

Before he's even done speaking, I'm cutting off his words with my sharp explanation.

"Megan got her ears pierced," I manage to get out between

short and frantic breaths. "Eden signed the papers. I had no idea. I wasn't there to give permission. She was not supposed to get her ears pierced until she's fourteen."

There's a brief pause on the other end of the line. "Jo, take a deep breath. It's going to be okay. We had already talked about taking her to get her ears pierced on her thirteenth birthday, remember? We weren't sticking to the original rule of waiting until she was fourteen. It was going to happen eventually. That's only eight months away."

"But, Everett," I stammer, still overwhelmed. "I wasn't even there. They did it behind my back. Megan lied to Eden about not having them pierced because she was too afraid but that she wanted to face her fears today."

Everett's tone is patient but slightly dismissive. "I've really got my hands full at work. It's almost midnight here and I'm still going. So, I'm not trying to be abrupt, but it's not the end of the world. She's the only girl in her grade without pierced ears. It sounds like Eden didn't know our rule. She thought she was helping."

"But Eden should have known to ask me first. It's a big deal."

"There are cultural differences all over the world with this stuff. Some people get their babies' ears pierced when they are just a few months old. There's no real clear rule on what is right here. And Eden obviously thought she was doing Megan a favor. She must feel terrible and shell-shocked now. Megan, on the other hand, needs to understand the consequences of lying and going behind our backs."

I take a deep breath, trying to calm myself. "I just can't believe her ears are pierced and I wasn't there. I had an image in my head about how we would do it and what we would do after to celebrate. I didn't think she would do something like this."

"Talk to Megan and make sure she knows how serious this is. But maybe the punishment can wait until Eden leaves. That way, they can still enjoy each other's company and Megan can learn a valuable lesson without ruining Eden's experience here."

Everett is so pragmatic. Everything is approached with logic. And in moments like this, I'm grateful for that. Or I should be. The tornado of anger in me is still spinning, I just have to pretend it isn't now. "Okay. That makes sense. Everything was going so well. I can't tell you how great things have been. I like having Eden here and I think you'll really like her."

"Just talk to Megan and make sure she understands the gravity of what she did. But also, let her enjoy the time she has with Eden. We can figure out the punishment later."

"Thanks," I say, clearing my throat as my feigned composure returns.

"Call me if you need anything else. I've got another hour of work ahead of me here. So I'm going to get going."

"Okay," I say, feeling a bit more grounded. "I love you."

There's a strange noise in the background on his end before he replies, "I love you t—" He doesn't even finish the last syllable before he ends the call. Was that a voice? Someone else talking? Or the television?

NINE

I sit for a moment, gathering my thoughts. I know what I have to do next. I need to talk to Megan, but I also need to reassure Eden. I head upstairs and gently knock on Megan's door.

"Megan, can we talk for a minute?" I ask softly. Being calm goes against all my instincts right now. But that's what the books say to do. It's the science of parenting and I am committed to navigating these tough times better than my parents ever did.

She opens the door, her eyes red from crying. "I'm sorry, Mom," she says immediately. "I was just so tired of being the only one without my ears pierced. You don't know how it is for me, and—"

I pull her into a hug. "I know, honey. But lying and going behind my back was not the way to do it. I called your dad and he agreed you need to be punished. But also that we should not let that impact the time Eden is here. For now, let's just focus on making things right with Eden and enjoying the time we have together. Then once she heads home, we'll figure out what punishment makes sense. But I need you to know this is very serious."

She nods, tears still streaming down her face. "I know. I'm

really sorry. I didn't think the place would actually let Eden sign the permission slip. It kind of happened fast. She asked me why I didn't have my ears pierced and I told her it's a rule in our family to wait. She said all her friends have their ears pierced when they are like ten. Eden said I should just do it because once it's done there really wasn't anything you could do about it."

The lie is more infuriating than the act itself. I'm tempted to call her out and tell her that I know she tricked Eden to get this done. I want to confront her about how she's been getting sneaky and distant for months. I can't believe she's willing to throw Eden under the bus just to keep covering her own mess. But I can hear Everett's voice in my head. We need to play the long game. This will all be waiting for us after Eden's trip is over and it's become clearer than ever that Megan's issues are growing. We'll need to take a more strategic approach once we have the house back to ourselves.

Instead of hitting her with facts, I kiss her forehead. "I love you. Dad loves you. Let's just make sure you know how to take care of those piercings so they don't get infected."

Leaving Megan's room, I head to Eden's. I knock gently before opening the door. Eden looks up at me, her eyes filled with remorse.

"Eden, I know you were just trying to help," I start, sitting down next to her. "Megan wasn't honest with you, and I'm sorry you were put in that position. I'm not mad at you, but we need to be careful with decisions like this in the future."

Eden nods, wiping away her tears, though to me her eyes look quite dry. "I'm so sorry, Jo. I didn't mean to cause any trouble. I can make up for it. Just tell me what to do. The washing-up? I can weed the garden. Mop floors." The affect in her voice seems rehearsed and disingenuous. I know my daughter well. I understand how gutted she was about what she did. Eden, however, I can't seem to pin down. Maybe it's my own bias, but though her words are apologetic, everything else feels forced.

I give her a reassuring smile, but it's a reflex. I smile to make others feel comfortable, not because I am comfortable. "No, that's not necessary. We don't expect anything like that."

Eden's hands are shaking; she bites at her nails and seems like she might jump out of her skin. This is the first thing I see that I can connect with. That's a fear rooted in experience. This is how I cowered in front of my parents. Not because I was weak but because they gave me real reasons to be afraid. I wonder if maybe Eden has experienced that too.

"I can wash the car. Seriously. I work really hard at home. I want to sort this." Her hands fold, begging for me to punish her properly.

"Eden, honey, it's okay. I promise. I know I reacted strongly but Megan is the one that lied and took advantage of the situation."

"But I don't want her to have to—"

"I already talked to Everett and we're going to hold off on her punishment until after you leave so she doesn't miss out on this time with you. After you go, she'll be grounded from some of her electronics for a period of time and maybe have to miss a couple of things with her friends. She seems to understand right now just how serious what she did was, and I don't think she'll take advantage of either of us again."

"Seriously? That's it? I thought maybe you'd want me to leave. I would have understood if you did." She looks down at the floor. "And Everett is going to have such a bad opinion of me now even before we've met. I'm so embarrassed."

"Trust me, Everett was in your corner on this one."

This seems to shock her. "He was? Really?"

"He's very logical and he understood quickly that it was Megan who screwed up. He wanted me to come in and reassure you that everything is fine. Megan is the one who created this situation, not you. She's been struggling lately. Everett will like you just fine."

"And my mum. She's going to kill me." Eden covers her face with her hands and begins to cry again. I watch her closely. Is her fear of her mother the root cause here? Is that genuine?

"I reached out to your mother earlier today and told her everything was going great. Because it is. This is just a hiccup. I don't plan to send her a message about this. If you want to share it with her, that's fine, but please let her know we're all okay. It's nothing to stress over."

"Why are you like this?" Eden looks up and blinks away the last of her tears. "Are you always this nice? I don't know anyone like that."

My soul, still shaking from earlier, soaks in this compliment. "I try to be calm and patient as often as possible, but to be honest it's been really hard with Megan lately. She's acting out and pulling away. Frankly, she hates me. I've been short-tempered with her and nothing I do seems to make her happy anymore."

Eden breathes out her astonishment. "She's so lucky. Just the fact that you try so hard is amazing. No one is perfect, but you care so much."

"And she already adores you," I cut in quickly. "I really like how well you two are getting along. That compliment she gave me about the pancakes this morning is the first one I've gotten from her in a long time. I think you being here is going to be great for her. We just had a rough start."

"Very rough."

"Why don't you clean up for dinner and come down when you are ready. I have a feeling Megan might be in to apologize. The guilt is eating her up too."

"Thank you, Jo," Eden says in a whisper as I leave and close the door behind me. The knot in my stomach has yet to untie but I've eased everyone around me the best I can. I'll figure out my own feelings later. Later, when I'm sitting in my room with a glass of wine. Then I'll decide if I'm actually okay with all of this. For now, everyone is stabilized. I've held them all together and propped them back up. I'm the only one left on the ground.

But I have to get up. There is food to prep for tomorrow's lunches and I have a school committee meeting coming up to address further changes to cafeteria protocols for safety. I was meant to be working on that agenda tonight. I check my watch to see how much time I have to get it all done. That can't be right. Is my watch wrong, or my brain?

Didn't Everett say it was nearly midnight his time? I do a quick calculation in my head. When your husband is a globe-trotting executive, you get very adept at time zones and doing the math in your head. It would be nearly three in the morning his time. Not almost midnight. My gut lurches with doubt but I try to push it away. He's overworked and exhausted. He misspoke. Yet there is one other thing you get very good at when your husband is a globe-trotting executive. Doubt.

TEN

Ashton insists we make a sign for Everett coming home, even though he's traveled all of Ashton's life and never had a sign held up for him in the driveway before. But I'm trying to say yes more. The last couple of days have been much improved since the ear-piercing incident. I'm trying to keep the good energy going.

I had a good cry about the whole thing alone in my walk-in closet the first night after it happened. That's the spot furthest away from the kids' rooms and a place without windows so I can make it perfectly dark. If I'm going to sob it doesn't count if I do it in the dark. My stomach still ties in knots when I see Megan's little stud earrings and the way she wears her hair up to flaunt them around at school. But it'll pass.

Trying to keep the good vibes is why I've also decided not to ask Everett about the mix-up of time zones. I could slip it in very casually, like it didn't matter at all. But he's stressed and tired and he'll take it as an accusation. I don't need that kind of tension in the house at the moment, so I put the thought out of my mind.

"How much longer?" Ashton asks, his arms clearly getting tired from holding up the sign.

"I warned you he was stuck in traffic. You've had us all out here for twenty minutes already. Maybe the girls should go in and you should put the sign down until we see him pulling into the driveway?"

"It's okay," Eden says with a bright smile as she directs her comments to Ashton. "I think it's nice that you're waiting for your dad like you waited for me at the airport. I bet he'll really appreciate it. I know I did."

"Okay, but I'll put the sign down for a minute." No sooner does Ashton drop his sign than Everett's car comes down the driveway. Ashton waves the sign over his head and both Megan and Eden stand up and start waving. I can't help myself and join the fun.

"Woah," Everett exclaims as he steps out of his car and pretends this greeting has blown his mind. Ashton is pleased with this and giggles loudly as he runs into his father's arms. Everett scoops him up and tickles his side as he walks over our way.

Eden looks tense but I can't blame her. It's tough meeting strangers, especially after having that awkward issue just a few days ago. Her shoulders sag and her eyes are cast down at her own shoes. I watch her gulp back her nerves, and though it's been a bumpy road between us, I do feel sorry for her. I know Everett will put her instantly at ease. That's what he does.

"And we have a new guest," he announces with a wide smile. "Eden, I'm glad to see you've settled in so nicely. Have you taken Megan for a tattoo yet?"

His humor is one reason I fell in love with him but as the years have gone by, I find him less funny. I don't know if his jokes have become less appropriate or if I've just matured past that humor. Everett believes there is no bad time for a joke. Nothing is too soon. On this point we disagree. But for Eden's sake I offer a laugh and she goes from looking horrified to relaxed.

"Dad, that's not funny," Megan says, taking the hug from his free arm. "You're going to make her feel bad."

"No, no, it's okay. I think it's a funny joke." Eden's cheeks blaze red and she blinks fast.

"You'll have to forgive him," I say as I drape my arm over Eden's shoulder. "He thinks he's hilarious. Can we all go in now and eat dinner? I've been keeping it warm for an hour and I'm starving."

"Sorry," he says as he plants a kiss on my cheek and puts Ashton down at the same time. "Traffic was a nightmare. But I am so ready for dinner."

"I think Eden's got about a billion questions about your job, Dad," Megan explains as we settle around the table.

"Didn't you all warn her how boring it is to hear about my job?" Everett loosens his tie and unbuttons his cuffs. There's sweat on his forehead and his jaw is set tightly, even though he's playing Joe Cool Guy for all the kids. I can see something they cannot. I can see how he's not really looking my way. Not fully. Just like Eden is gulping back her nerves, he's swallowing back some kind of stress. Or maybe it's guilt or a secret he's choking on.

"We tried to tell her you're boring," Ashton says with that comedic timing only a little boy can execute so perfectly.

"I think it's fascinating," Eden replies, her cheeks still pink and her hair a bit frazzled. She didn't believe me when I told her Everett would like her. I can see she's nervous, but settling in with every word. "You're a CTO of a global technology company. Are you still involved in the R&D?"

"The what?" Megan looks taken aback by how quickly Eden seems to switch from talking about the latest blush that just launched and from an actress they both like to this stuff.

"Chief Technology Officer and Research and Development," Eden says, but her eyes stay fixed on Everett. I know this feeling. I think things for Eden at home are probably limiting and tough. When your own life is so strangled by harsh realities, the alternatives are glamorous and fascinating. You can't be what you can't see, and Everett seems to be the first up close and personal look Eden has gotten at the world she wants to work in. The life she wants for herself. I can relate deeply to this. She's taken this enormous risk and adventure to try to open doors for herself. I only wish I'd taken the brave path instead of the dark and selfish one I'd taken to get here. If I had I wouldn't be stalking my mailbox every day intercepting threatening letters.

"Right," Everett says with an impressed expression. "I'm still fully immersed in R&D. I had it written into my contract. There was no way I was going to take on some executive role and then lose touch completely with the stuff I love about the job. I have to collaborate with other executives to drive business growth and innovation as well as represent the company at conferences, meetings, and with clients. But I make sure I still have plenty of time in the labs and working on new developments."

"Can I see some of it?" Eden asks, the courage growing in her by the second. "Like anything new you're working on?"

"Classified," Everett replies with an overexaggerated shrug.

"Oh." Eden looks embarrassed and I'm getting annoyed with his little jokes. Eden is still trying to get her feet under and he's unsettling and confusing her. I'd had to work so hard to navigate all the landmines around us this week, and he's out here just lobbing joke grenades around, blowing up her confidence.

"He's kidding," I groan and shoot him a look. "There's plenty he works on that he can show you. Trust me, he tries to bore us with it all the time. He'll be glad to have someone who doesn't pretend to snore when the presentations come out."

"Who's pretending?" Ashton quips and gets another great laugh around the table.

"I definitely will put some stuff aside for you to look at." He finally backs down and gets a little more serious. "Unfortunately, I'm not here much during your stay. You're already down to just five weeks and I've got some end-of-quarter deadlines that are going to keep me pretty busy. But I'll definitely put time aside to show you more of what we do."

"Thanks." Eden starts eating the meal I'd made for her. Tonight it's lasagna. This was a bit harder with her allergies but I'd worked on the recipe twice in the week before she came. Judging by the look on her face, she loves it. I sigh with relief. A win.

"This is delicious." Everett winks at me and smiles that cool smile. But it doesn't reach up to his eyes. I stand and pour him a drink and slide the glass his way.

"Eden could have wine." Megan looks pleased to make this announcement. "She's allowed at home. It's legal there for kids to drink."

"It's not legal here." My lips are tight and I give Megan a look of warning. "Juice for all of you."

"But don't you think that's interesting that it's legal for kids to drink there?" Megan is poking at me to make some point and I'm not sure where to begin.

"Thoughts on that, Everett?" I'm too burned out to deal with yet another verbal sparring match so I tee my husband up to deal with it. He hesitates for a moment before he jumps in. This is about the only way I can get him to engage, to leave him no choice.

"There's a lot of the world you haven't seen yet, Megs. Cultures. Ideas. Laws. All things that you can't even begin to understand at this point in your life. Yes, it's legal where Eden is from but it's not like kids are out just getting drunk in the streets. It's illegal for someone her age to buy alcohol. However, if you're sixteen or seventeen and accompanied by an adult, you can drink beer, wine or cider with a meal. But here we don't do that, so Eden wouldn't drink here."

"I don't really drink at home," Eden cuts in quickly. "My mum says that my dad was an alcoholic and there are clear studies that warn about the genetic component to alcoholism. I don't think it's really a cool thing. My mum works in pubs. I've spent so much time in them that I don't really want to be like any of the people I've seen there." She looks to Megan with a warm gaze. "It's not as great as it sounds."

Gratitude fills me. This is what I've been looking for. Eden has so many opportunities to be a good influence, and each one seems like a victory for me. I'm also secretly glad it's in front of Everett. I went out on a limb talking about how good this would be for Megan and I am trying to make sure that limb doesn't snap.

Ashton fills his fork with pasta as he makes his own announcement on the matter. "My dad drinks bourbon and my mom drinks wine all the time."

"Ashton," I scold, but Everett only laughs. "We do not drink all the time. That's not appropriate. Don't say that to people."

He points to our two glasses and waggles his eyebrows. "All the time," he teases and I huff out my exasperation. He's so much like Everett.

Eden and Megan are giggling and Everett looks a little impressed with his son's joke and timing. I'm usually the odd man out when the jokes start rolling.

We finish dinner and I'm careful not to pour another glass of wine for myself. Maybe it was a joke, but I worry if Ashton says things like that to people at school. I'll be more careful about it going forward. Eden is right, alcoholism can be genetic and my parents certainly carried the gene. I might drink a bit but I certainly work hard to make sure I don't resemble their parenting or lifestyle. I wonder about Eden's father but don't plan to ask. She hardly speaks about her mother who she lives with; I doubt she wants to share about her father who sounds like he's not around.

"We're going to watch TV," Megan calls over her shoulder as she and Eden run upstairs to the media room. I feel like I should ask more questions. Why can't they just watch down here in the living room? What are they going to put on? But before I can pepper them with queries, Everett is in my ear.

"They're fine," he whispers. "Just give them some space."

"The last time I gave them space our daughter put holes in her body. Maybe I'll just go up and watch with them after the dishes."

Everett rolls his eyes and huffs. It's infuriating. "Jo, please, let them be. It's good Megan is getting a little independence. It's overdue. I know you have this vision for her life and how to keep her safe but she's getting older. There's a lot of pressure in middle school to fit in and I think we're setting her up for failure if we don't let her breathe a little."

"Look at what she's already done to fit in. She lied and she did something serious." I wave my hand in the air and feel my body pulse with defensiveness. I field this kind of judgment from other parents and have to hear about it all the time from Megan. Everett sprinkles in his opinion on matters like this, but for the most part he acts like it's not his business to deal with. That's something I oscillate between being glad about and resenting. That moving target might not be fair to him but life's not fair.

Twisting my words, he makes his point. "Look at what she felt like she *had* to do in order to get what was important to her." His counterargument enrages me, but I don't show it. "Jo, you're a great mom and Megan is an awesome kid. She's going to make mistakes, but I think we need to start trusting her more. Not less."

"That seems very counterintuitive." My lips are pursed and

I'm trying to keep my voice level. "She broke our trust, therefore we should keep a closer eye on what she's doing."

"She's upstairs in our own home, not at some party." He folds his arms across his chest defiantly.

He doesn't realize what kids have access to through a Smart TV today. Megan is desperate to feel cool and she's clearly willing to take risks to do that.

I try to explain. "There's no parental controls on that television. I only have it set up correctly in the living room. They could literally watch anything up there."

"Jo." He sighs and wraps his arms around me. This doesn't feel like a comforting hug as much as an effort to keep me stuck here. "You can't always be thinking about the worst-case scenario. You'll drive yourself crazy."

He kisses my neck, trying to soothe my rising anxiety. But he doesn't understand. He has no idea what it's like in my head. His passing comment about my "worst-case scenario" thought doesn't even begin to scratch the surface of the madness I live with every day.

If only he knew about the intrusive thoughts that plague me. Every moment of the day I'm bombarded with worries. It started with Ashton's allergies. Discovering how life-threatening they were flipped a switch in me that I can't turn off. Every bite he takes, every new place we go, I'm scanning for dangers that could kill him.

But it doesn't end there. The fuel that keeps my anxiety running nonstop is plentiful. A half-hour watching the news. My phone alerting in the middle of the night with the spotty details of an abducted child not far from where we live. Social media feeds are flooded with new threats, horror stories, and school shootings. Childhood cancer. Everyone in the world seems to be suffering, and that fate feels like it's waiting around every corner for my family. The only thing keeping it at bay is my vigilance. Watching for threats. Checking for symptoms. Keeping them home. Keeping them safe.

Even that isn't enough. Home might feel better than them being out in the world but all it takes is a window being open upstairs. I have paralyzing and vivid thoughts of one of the children falling out. Even though neither of them is a toddler that would carelessly push the screen out any more. And it isn't just a fleeting, "Oh my gosh, what if that happened" thought. No, it's a full scenario in my mind. I see myself finding them outside, their tiny bodies broken and bleeding. I imagine their lethal injuries, planning their funeral, standing at the graveside. I feel the crushing weight of the loss and the emptiness that would follow.

The death of my children is the noose around my neck. It's what keeps me from being able to move freely. It tightens when they aren't with me. When I can't see them. It chokes me in a way Everett couldn't imagine. But I don't tell him.

How could I? How could I explain the constant terror that haunts me, the endless loop of horrific possibilities playing out in my mind? He wouldn't understand because besides his grandparents who died well into their eighties, he's never lost anyone. He doesn't know what I know. Death, the unexpected or premature kind, results in a metamorphosis of the people left behind. It's altered me. Maybe more than average because there is blood on my hands. Blood I can never seem to wash away.

Leaning back, Everett looks down at me with concern. "I know you think you can keep them both in a bubble, but eventually they need to experience things in the world. Megan is twelve. She's in middle school. We can't shield her from everything. She has to take some chances to figure out how to make her way in the world."

I have dozens of rebuttals. Horror stories of children Megan's age who don't just make little mistakes and bounce right back. Life-changing or life-ending things happen to kids. I could list a thousand scenarios I'm trying to protect her from. But I know when I won't be heard. When I can't make my argument without being painted as crazy or overprotective, I let him get his point out and then I offer a sweet smile as if he's calmed my nerves. He doesn't know that's an impossible task. And he'll be right back to work, busy and distracted. Too distracted to keep making this point. I'll take it from there.

"If they download porn, you can say I told you so," he jokes as he refills his glass and helps me clear the table.

I laugh, though I'm not feeling very giggly right now. Defeated, I pour another glass of wine and start on the dishes. I don't ask for help because I can't risk the cross-contamination of Ashton and Eden's dishes with any of ours. Everett doesn't take that task seriously enough. I fill both sides of the sink separately. Use different sponges. Different cloths to dry and then everything goes into its designated cabinet spot. Everett calls this overkill.

If Everett really knew what worry I carried around, he'd want me locked in a rubber room. As long as I keep this tucked away, just for me, it'll all be fine.

Just as I'm finishing up, Ashton comes into the kitchen. His face is pale, and his breathing is labored. I drop the dish I'm holding, and it shatters on the floor.

"Ashton, what's wrong?" I rush to his side, my heart pounding in my chest.

"Mom... I can't... breathe..." he gasps, his lips turning blue and starting to swell.

It's happening again. In the blink of an eye, I could lose him.

ELEVEN

There is nothing worse than seeing your child look sick or scared. I can feel my body shaking with adrenaline.

"Ashton, what's wrong?" I ask again, my voice trembling.

"Mom... I can't..." he gasps, the swelling around his mouth getting more prominent.

I sprint to the kitchen drawer where we keep the EpiPens, my hands shaking as I fumble to open the case. It's been over two years since he's had a reaction, but the routine is ingrained in me. I grab the pen and rush back to him, feeling the world narrow to this one critical moment.

"Hold still, sweetheart," I whisper, trying to keep my voice calm. I administer the injection, pressing the pen firmly against his thigh. "Just breathe, Ashton. Mommy's got you."

Everett is already on the phone, calling for an ambulance. "We need an ambulance immediately," he barks into the phone. "My son is having a severe allergic reaction."

Ashton starts to catch his breath, the medication taking effect. But we know from past experiences he is not out of the woods. He needs to be taken into the hospital and I need to know what triggered this. I'm certain there was nothing in his dinner that would have caused this reaction. Too much time had passed.

"Girls!" Everett yells, his voice echoing through the house. "Get down here now!"

Megan and Eden come running down the stairs. Megan screams in fear when she sees Ashton's condition, while Eden looks absolutely terrified.

"Does anyone know what Ashton ate after dinner?" I ask, my voice urgent but controlled. "There was nothing in his dinner that should have caused this."

Ashton, still catching his breath, pulls a wrapper from his pocket. It's a candy bar, something I don't recognize.

"It's... from Eden..." he wheezes, his eyes wide with fear and confusion.

Eden's hands fly to her mouth in horror. "It doesn't have nuts!" she exclaims, her voice high-pitched and panicked. "I brought them from England. My friend with a nut allergy eats them all the time."

I look at the wrapper, my heart sinking. The ingredients might be safe, but cross-contamination can happen so easily. It was processed in a facility that also handles many of his allergens. I pull Ashton closer, whispering soothing words as the sound of sirens grows nearer.

Eden doesn't say anything else. Megan is in Everett's arms, crying quietly as he comforts her. Fury and fear fight for the top position in my emotions and I'm not sure which one will win out. I'm even more mad at the little voice in my head that feels sympathy for how badly Eden must feel. The part of me that can't tolerate anyone's discomfort, no matter how much of myself I need to betray to comfort them.

The paramedics burst through the door, taking over with a practiced efficiency. They check Ashton's vitals and prepare to transport him to the hospital.

"We'll take it from here, ma'am," one of the paramedics says, his voice calm and reassuring. "You did a great job. Who's going to ride with him?"

I nod, indicating I will, my mind still reeling. Everett and I follow the paramedics to the ambulance, with Megan and Eden trailing behind, both of them pale and silent.

I hoist myself into the ambulance behind the stretcher. "You follow in the car. Bring the girls."

I don't leave room for debate or questions. The ambulance door closes and we speed off, lights and sirens blaring. The next couple of hours are going to be stressful and I want Eden to understand just what she's put Ashton through by being so careless. She has allergies herself. She should know it's not as simple as just checking an ingredients list. She should know the dangers. How serious this is.

The realization strikes my chest as I look out the small back window of the ambulance at Eden's unreadable expression.

She does know.

TWELVE

Ashton is finally tucked into bed, his breathing steady and even. We were cleared to be released from the hospital after five hours of close observation. The ride home was tense and quiet and everyone scattered once we got back inside.

Everett is sitting in Ashton's room, keeping a close eye on him just to make sure he's okay. If my husband thought it was unnecessary, he didn't bother putting up a fight. This was not the night to call me overprotective. It was not the night for Megan to give me attitude, or for Eden to be hanging around apologizing endlessly. Everyone seemed to understand that instinctively and went their own way.

There is only one thing I can do right now to regain control of my spiraling emotions. I call it a reset. I head to the kitchen, feeling the familiar surge of determination. This needs to be done. It's not just a compulsion; it's a necessity.

The first thing I do is wipe down every surface, scrubbing each inch with a disinfectant cloth. Counters, cabinets, and even the handles of the appliances. I can't afford any mistakes. It's not entirely logical since we know what Ashton ate to get his reaction, but I won't sleep until it's done. Not a single crumb or trace of contamination can be left behind.

The sink is emptied and scrubbed with a separate sponge, one that's only ever used for this purpose. Next, I move to the dishes. We have two sets, each in distinct colors to avoid any confusion. Red dishes for safe food, blue dishes for everything else. The silverware is similarly color-coded, with red handles for Ashton and Eden's utensils. Each piece is meticulously cleaned and placed in its designated spot. Any crossover could mean disaster, so I double-check everything.

The countertop convection oven is solely for safe food. It's smaller and separate from our main oven, ensuring no cross-contamination. I wipe it down thoroughly, inside and out. In the pantry, I clear out everything. All the shelves are emptied, and I disinfect them before placing the food back in its rightful place. I toss any foods that are not safe. I don't normally do that. Everett insists that there needs to be 'normal' food in the house too. Megan needs snacks she likes and it's not practical to keep Ashton's environment completely sterile and allergen-free. He needs to start learning how to advocate and protect himself too, and Everett believes that can't happen if I turn our home into a bubble. But tonight, I toss the unsafe food out. Everett won't give me trouble. He wouldn't dare right now.

I inspect the rest of the kitchen. Different cutting boards for different foods. A set of red knives for safe food preparation only. I even go as far as to have separate drying racks for the dishes. My adrenaline is surging as I move things to the furthest point on the kitchen counter to give even more physical distance.

I stand back and survey my work. It's spotless. Sterile. The boundaries between safe and unsafe fortified beyond question. This is how I control what I can, how I protect my family from the invisible threats that lurk everywhere.

"Jo." Eden lingers in the doorway of the kitchen. "Can I help with anything?"

I jump, not expecting anyone to interrupt this process. "No. I'm nearly finished up." I'm suddenly self-conscious of my appearance. My forehead is spattered with sweat. The curls in my hair are frizzy and my shirt is covered in cleaner and splotches of water.

"Is there anything I *can* do?" Eden's twisting her hands nervously and I feel that damn tug in the center of my chest. I can't cope with people's pain. I feel the immediate need to extinguish it instantly. I'm self-aware enough to understand where this all comes from. The people-pleasing sits deep in my soul, attached by the sharp talons of my childhood. I grew up unable to keep anyone in my life happy and I was certain that was my job. A job I took seriously and never succeeded at. Like a ghost haunting the familiar places of her past trying to complete some unfinished business, I keep trying to settle everyone else's soul. Setting myself ablaze so that they will never be cold.

But I'm too angry at the moment to let that knee-jerk reaction win out. Eden is not some stranger who doesn't understand the risks that Ashton faces. She's well versed in the process I use here at the house. For the life of me I don't understand how she could make this kind of mistake. Which makes me wonder if it was a mistake at all.

"My friend has a nut allergy and he eats those all the time..." Eden attempts, but her voice trails off when I don't look her way.

"It's late, Eden. You should get some sleep." I don't ask her why she gave my son candy without asking me, even though she knows my rules. Instead I turn my back and pretend the cutting boards need more attention.

"Okay," Eden whispers as she backs away. "I'm glad Ashton is better."

I can't let this casual assessment of Ashton's current state go unchecked. "You do understand that every time he has a reaction it makes the next more dangerous. Repeated exposure to allergens can increase the sensitivity of the immune system, potentially leading to more severe reactions in the future. Just because he's all right now doesn't mean there was no impact."

"I know. I'm so sorry." I can hear the emotion in her voice but it doesn't deter me from my anger. I will hold the line on this.

"Eden?" Megan asks gently as she comes up behind her. "We know you didn't do it on purpose. It's really scary. But don't beat yourself up about it. Ashton is okay and we're not mad."

She's using that word *we* pretty liberally but I don't interrupt. I watch as they embrace and Eden tries to compose herself. It's Everett who appears next and cracks some little joke. I don't even hear it, my ears still thudding with adrenaline. I just watch as their shoulders relax and Megan smiles. Everything is suddenly fine? We're all just moving on?

Tossing down the towel that's in my hand, the symbolism of throwing it in isn't lost on me. I want to give up on all of them right now. "I'm going to sit up with Ashton awhile," I reply coolly. "Everyone should get to bed soon. It's late."

Everett opens his mouth, likely to try to convince me to relax, but he catches my expression and decides against it. He wants to say that Ashton doesn't need a night nurse sitting vigil and that I should get a good night's sleep. I would rather he choke to death on those words than utter them.

"Come on, girls," he directs, sounding disappointed. "Off to bed." He begins to usher them away and I finally look at Eden again full on. Apparently, all of her guilt has evaporated as she and Megan start chatting about what they'll wear in the morning. Like it never happened at all. She glances over her shoulder at me as she loops her arm into Megan's and I swear she shoots me a menacing look. It lasts only a beat. A breath. And then she turns away, leaving me to wonder what I just saw. A shiver runs up my spine. I'm losing my mind.

I make a move for the door and Everett stops to question why. "Where are you going?"

"I forgot to get the mail today," I utter halfway out the door.

"Leave it until tomorrow. I'll grab it in the morning. Why are you always obsessing over the mail?" He doesn't turn fully around as he asks and I don't stop to answer. The air of the night hits my blazing hot cheeks as I head down to the mailbox.

I have such little control in this world. I can clean the kitchen. I can keep the EpiPens close by. I can keep Megan from sleeping at a friend's house. And no matter what else happens, I can get the mail before they do. I can protect this secret. I have to.

THIRTEEN

The hits just keep coming. I've managed to make myself the odd man out in my own home. Even Ashton seems to be turning on me. He's frustrated with the new restrictions. The more I push back, the worse I look in everyone's eyes. I've taken to just being as agreeable as possible as I count down the days on the calendar until things go back to normal around here. Eden's departure date is mentally circled in big red marker in my mind. This morning is just another battle I won't win.

"It's barely makeup," Megan protests as she flutters her overdone eyes at me. She looks like a little girl playing dress up. The sweater she borrowed from Eden hangs too low at the neck and the makeup is plastered on. But still she tries to make her case. "This is not concealer, it's a toning bronzer. And the mascara is clear, not that gunky black stuff. The lip plumper is a gloss with a little tint."

This argument feels well-rehearsed. No. Coached. Someone gave her this language to try to hit me with and I know it was Eden. I can practically see them sitting in front of the bathroom mirror practicing how to make Megan's case to get what she wants.

"We don't do makeup at your age," I say firmly.

"It's skincare, not makeup." Megan folds her arms defiantly across her chest. "Eden wears the real makeup. I'm not wearing any of that. This stuff is different."

"That sweater doesn't fit you," I argue. "It's too low-cut. You don't even look like yourself." In fact, she looks like Eden which I know is the goal. "I need you to go change."

"Eden is going to be down in like two minutes and you're going to embarrass me so bad. Why can't I do anything? Have you even been in middle school? Girls are wearing way worse than this and tons of makeup."

"Hey, sweetie," Everett sings to Megan as he steps into the battle zone that is our kitchen. "You look beautiful. Are you doing something different? I really like it." There is a see-saw in parenthood. You each sit on one side, and it's rarely level. There has to be a good guy and a bad guy. A high and a low. The lower I go, the higher it lifts Everett and he loves it. I know it feeds his ego. He adores being adored. Being fun. The prankster who thinks I take life too seriously and doesn't miss an opportunity to point it out in front of the kids. He makes them sound like jokes, but it's obvious what he's doing. He wants to keep himself high by pushing me even lower.

I could kill him. "Everett, she has makeup on."

"Oh, it's nice. And that sweater is new?"

"It's Eden's and it doesn't fit her. And we don't allow makeup, she's twelve years old."

"Oh sick, you're doing the jumper today," Eden says as she strolls into the kitchen. "That bronzer looks great, too."

I want to yell at the top of my lungs. If Ashton comes in and says he likes the sparkles over Megan's eyes I might just hop in my vehicle and start driving without a destination. I'll stop when I hit the ocean... or maybe I won't.

"Thanks." Megan gives me a desperate look. I'm biting my tongue so hard, I might need a new one after Eden leaves.

Everett doesn't answer my comment about no makeup and doesn't look at all bothered by what is happening. I have to choose my battles since I'll clearly be a solo soldier here.

I offer a compromise. "Megan, just do me a quick favor and run upstairs to put a tank top on under that sweater."

"Oh, yes," Eden agrees. "That's how I wear it too. It's kind of low-cut so you definitely need a tank top underneath."

"Okay," Megan replies, basking in her victory. I won a little battle, but she's winning the war so far. They all are.

Everett won't be home when I get back from dropping the kids off so I won't have a chance to explain just how much he undermined me this morning. It's at least the fifth time in the last three days that I've looked like a complete jerk because these three are in cahoots. Since Ashton went to the hospital and I've been slightly less warm to Eden, it seems to have unified them in the attempt to protect her.

Maybe it's unconscious but they are aligning, and I am doing a terrible job of being able to hold my ground. I hate when I'm right, when my logic is backed by science or data and I have to act like it's better to compromise. I have to bottle it up and find the middle ground when in reality there shouldn't be any.

I want to remind my husband that my rules are not random. He should know that studies suggest early use of makeup can lead to a reliance on external appearance for self-worth, potentially leading to body dissatisfaction and lower self-esteem in the long run. Girls may feel pressured to conform to beauty standards and believe their natural appearance is inadequate. I've got stats on smartphones, social media, and eating disorders. But at some point, the pressure to fit in outweighs the facts. And if I'm the only one holding my ground, I find myself standing alone.

"I can do school drop-off," Everett offers as he checks his watch.

"It's in the opposite direction of the airport," I remind him.

It's not as if he doesn't know where the school is, but he's certainly rarely there and definitely doesn't do school drop-off.

"I know, but I'm going to be gone this week. My flight isn't for four hours. I've got time to drop them off first. Take it easy this morning."

His words grate that part of me that hates to be seen as idle. Productivity is the currency with which I measure my self-worth. And the idea that he thinks I might just lounge around since I don't have to drop the kids off hurts, though I know it shouldn't.

"You don't have to." I wave him off. "You probably have calls to make before your flight. I know work has been stressful lately, just stay locked in and focused."

"Daddy!" Ashton wraps his arms around Everett's waist and looks up at him adoringly. "You're driving us to school? Can we stop for the good snacks?"

"Good snacks?" This is news to me.

"Dad stops at the gas station when he drops us off," Megan announces casually. "He lets us pick out a snack while he pumps gas."

The questions swirl in my mind. Does he let the kids go in the store alone while he's outside, pumping gas? What snacks is he letting them pick? Is he sure they're safe for Ashton? I swallow back the questions. The eyes on me feel piercing and united. I am the problem. I am the murderer of fun.

"It's not junk food," Everett chimes in quickly. "And I always make sure it's safe for Ashton." He leans in and kisses my cheek. "I'd really like to take them in today. I hate that I'm leaving again."

"Okay. That sounds great. I have to get over to the pharmacy and the grocery store. I appreciate it." I punctuate my lie with a smile. What I'd really like is to ask him *since when*. Since when is he trying to squeeze extra time in with the kids before he leaves? This will be the first time this year he's dropped them off at school. Even when I had the flu I had to arrange for a ride with some neighbors. He's just tipping the see-saw in his favor.

The excitement in the kitchen grows as they pack up their things. The things I meticulously arranged and cooked for them. Things Everett couldn't find in this house with a bloodhound and a GPS. It's the invisible labor. The things I do so consistently that no one even notices unless they aren't done.

They all laugh exuberantly and discuss who gets to be in charge of the morning playlist. What gas station he's going to stop at and if they can get drinks too. I don't get another kiss goodbye. The kids barely glance over their shoulders at me as they pile into the car. Everyone looks so relaxed. Completely at ease. I watch through the window as they laugh. The music is so loud the bass rattles across the driveway and I can hear it in the house.

I pour my full cup of coffee down the sink, my stomach too sour for another sip. Glancing out the window I see Everett and Eden in the front seat of his car, their smiles genuine and wide. They bop along to a song, both mouthing the lyrics in unison.

How does he even know that song?

I recognize the beat as it thumps through the windows. It's an anthem of young women. Not something Megan has ever been into. What young women does he know that like this song? The ease in Eden's shoulders doesn't bother me as much as the way she's looking at him. It's adoration. So easily won for Everett. I've done all the work trying to make Eden comfortable and included, and here she is staring at Everett the way most women stare at him. They can't see the flaws. The failures. The shortcomings. They only see the fun. The blue eyes and the punch lines. Damn him for being so easy to love.

The voice in my head gets crass and urgent.

Everyone is happier without you. You stress them out. You

rob them of the fun they deserve. You're a helicopter parent. A buzzkill. You overact. You overthink.

You don't belong here. You're impossible to love.

They back out of the driveway and Everett flashes Eden the sweetest smile as the song ends. That used to be how he smiled at me.

FOURTEEN

The only thing to replace the intrusive thoughts is the noise of what has to be done. What I must accomplish. This is how I survived all the years before Everett and this life we've built.

I would scrub the walls of the tiny apartment I grew up in until the paint would start to wear thin. Even though my father's car was rusty and the tires bald, I'd lug the vacuum down three flights of stairs and try incessantly and futilely to get the stains out. My mother would have called all my efforts an attempt to put lipstick on a pig. There was no amount of elbow grease I could apply that could make our lives look any better than they were.

Then as I got older it was the shame I tried to cover. The guilt of my choices that I tried to scrub away and paint over. I finally made my life shiny and pretty, but just underneath were the dirty secrets I had to carry. And on the days where my life looked pretty enough to forget all that, the words of those letters would whisper in my ear.

Blood on your hands. Damned to hell. Selfish. A killer.

I follow the urge to clean something so my soul can feel spotless. Gathering laundry, I move from room to room grumbling about how close these people can get their clothes to the laundry basket without actually putting it in. I walk into our spare room, Eden's room, and see she's at least a little better at keeping her dirty clothes contained. I reach into the basket and pull out her last few outfits. From the pockets of one pair of impossibly small shorts falls a vape pen. I know what it is because I've spent ample time educating myself on this new epidemic.

Dropping the laundry to the ground I lean down and pick up the pen. It feels like a big deal. Like something I'm supposed to address. Something that could impact my children, who are spending all their time following Eden around like she's some kind of hero to worship. Have they seen her vape? Do they think it's cool?

My cell phone is in my pocket. Everett would be alone in the car soon. I need to tell him what I found. What I'm afraid of.

Like a movie playing on the screen of my mind I can see his underwhelmed reaction. I can hear him dismissing me.

She's not our child. It's not our place to police everything she does, and vaping is not the end of the world. Why were you in her room anyway? You can't invade her privacy. She's a teenager. Teenagers screw up. It's not that big of a deal, but going through her things is.

I don't agree with a single one of his imaginary points I've conjured up but I'm tired of the tension growing between me and everyone else in the house. I wanted this to bring us all together but all it's done is give me a preview to how alone I will be parenting my children through the teen years. If I thought making my case for using only organic food was difficult, I had no idea what kind of trouble was ahead.

With a shaking hand I put the vape pen back in Eden's shorts pocket and place all her clothes in the hamper. It goes against what I believe to be right, but there is one thing I can hold onto. It's temporary. In a few weeks Eden will fly home and I can recalibrate my family to what I know is right. To what they need. I'll still be outnumbered but not by as much. I just have to wait it out.

Because if I don't, if I fight this battle, no one in my house will be smiling at me the way Everett smiled at Eden this morning. And I don't think I could survive that.

FIFTEEN

A week later I find myself sitting in the head of school's office, waiting to find out why I was called in. The room is brightly lit, with large windows overlooking the school courtyard. There are children outside playing and I look for Ashton but don't spot him.

The walls are adorned with motivational posters and pictures of smiling students. Mrs. Evans, the head of school, sits across from me, her expression apologetic and surprised. I expect Eden has broken a rule that needs to be addressed. To quell some of the issue I will play the cultural difference card. Dress code. Vaping. Whatever it is, I'll remind Mrs. Evans that this is temporary. The same thing I've been reminding myself. I'll take Eden home for the day and use the opportunity to talk with her about how the rest of this trip needs to go.

Mrs. Evans looks so reluctant. "Jo, I'm sorry to have to tell you this, but Megan is being sent home for the day." Her voice is gentle but resolved. "Suspension."

"What happened?" I ask, my stomach knotting with worry. Megan? I've never been called into this office in all the years we've had a child attending this school and I certainly didn't assume it would be Megan going home.

"She was overheard by a teacher calling another girl a 'ratchet bitch with buck teeth and no friends.'" Mrs. Evans shakes her head, clearly shocked. "This is so out of character for Megan. She's usually such a sweet and well-behaved student."

I'm stunned. It doesn't make any sense. "Are you sure it was Megan? This doesn't sound like her at all."

Mrs. Evans nods. "I understand your surprise. It's a trend we've been seeing more in high school, but not in middle school yet. Unfortunately, it seems to have trickled down. It's from a reality TV show called *Hate, Date or Destroy*. The women vying for a date with the man on the show have to berate each other and record it using a particular filter before posting it online."

"What?" I'm confused and let it show on my face. "Megan doesn't watch that show. She doesn't even have a smartphone to record or post anything."

Mrs. Evans sighs, looking even more sympathetic. "She was using someone else's phone to post to her social media."

"But Megan doesn't have social media," I insist. This doesn't add up. "We've been very strict about that."

"Kids are clever these days," Mrs. Evans explains. "They find ways around everything. It's hard to take such a hard line because they have access everywhere. I'm truly sorry to send Megan home, but we have to make an example so this trend doesn't become more prevalent in middle school."

I nod, my heart sinking. This is the last thing I expected to hear. "I understand."

Mrs. Evans offers me a small, thoughtful smile. "We're all trying our best to navigate this new landscape. In a lot of ways cell phones are a necessary evil. In my experience, trying to completely shut them out only makes them want it more. If you need any resources or support, please don't hesitate to reach out."

"Thank you," I say, standing up and shaking her hand.

I step out into the hallway, where Megan is sitting on a bench, her head down. She looks up as I approach, her eyes filled with tears. Those have no effect on me right now. We walk to the SUV in silence, the weight of what just happened hanging heavily between us.

Once we're in the car, I turn to her. "Megan, what the hell happened?"

She sniffles, wiping her eyes. "I'm sorry, Mom. It's not what you think."

"Why would you say something like that?" I ask, trying to keep my voice calm.

"It's this stupid show everyone's watching," she admits. "It's supposed to be funny. Ginny didn't even care that I said it to her. She knows it's a trend that's going viral and—"

"Going viral? On your social media accounts that you aren't supposed to have? The ones you've lied about and created on someone else's phone? You're suspended for the day. Do you understand that? Do you know how that looks? How it makes all of us look?"

"Is that all you care about? What people at this stupid school think of us? What about how I feel? That's what you should care about. Me. Just me. Not everyone else."

I take a deep breath, trying to process everything. "Megan, you know better than to follow what everyone else is doing, especially if it's hurtful. Social media is incredibly dangerous for someone your age. That's why you aren't on it. Because I do care about you. You and your brother are all I care about."

"You're living in this fake reality," she yells, and I look around to see if the people passing by can hear her raised voice. "You think you can keep us in this bubble but you have no idea what it's actually like in the world. You don't know what people think of me, what they do to me, because you don't let me have anything or do anything. I don't get to go to the sleepovers. You're ruining my life. And when I finally start trying to fix that and actually have a life, this happens."

She's not going to get away with playing victim on this one. "This didn't happen to you. You made choices and these are the consequences. You are going home, going to your room and I'm calling your father when his plane lands."

"He won't care," she bites back angrily.

"Excuse me? Your father won't care you got suspended?"

"Dad is on my side. He knows you are way too overprotective. He jokes around with us about how you are going to follow us to college. How we might be able to date when we're thirty. We have jokes, you know. Inside jokes about you. He does things for us when you're not around so we can be normal. He's going to be mad that I got suspended, but he gets it. He gets it and you don't. You're the only one who doesn't. Eden even—"

"Stop." I hit a volume she's never heard from me. The yell makes her jump and her eyes go wide and wild. "I don't want to hear what Eden thinks of my parenting. I don't need to be told that I'm the problem. You think you have the world all figured out, but you have no idea what is out there. What can happen. I know. I know what is out there because I've lived it and my job is to make sure you don't have to go through any of the things I did." I'm still yelling as I put the car in gear and pull away from the parking spot. "I'm strong enough to deal with your hate for me. I'm strong enough to deal with people judging me for being a helicopter mom. What I'm not strong enough for is losing you. Or watching you make terrible mistakes you can't come back from. So hate me. Judge me. Gang up on me. I don't care. But you don't get to list all the ways people think I'm wrong, because I know them by heart. Now you are going home. You are not saying another word. And I will figure out what we do next after I talk to your father."

I speed a bit, my grip on the steering wheel tight. I don't know what comes next. There is no perfect strategy to parent my way out of this situation. We are at an impasse. But I will figure it out. What I need is an ally. It won't be Everett. He clearly has more interest in making sure the kids like him than keeping them safe. He and I won't be aligned. That kind of fissure will be just one more thing Megan can exploit. I need someone on my side.

Eden. I need Eden. I've been doing this all wrong. I've been hoping that organically the influence would be good. I need to be more direct. Tell Eden exactly what I expect.

I've mapped my conversation out perfectly over the rest of the afternoon while Megan sulks in her room. I'll be able to sway Eden if I nail the conversation.

The problem is, she's not home yet. She went to robotics club after school so I did not pick her up with Ashton. I heard the roar of the activity bus lumbering up our hill and expected Eden would come walking in a few minutes later, but there's no sign of her. I try to keep my breathing steady, but the worry gnaws at me.

I dial her number, and it goes straight to voicemail. My heart skips a beat. Where could she be? My mind races through every possible scenario, each one worse than the last. This day has been horrible enough, and tracking her down is the last thing I need.

"Megan, Ashton, get your things. We're going to find Eden," I call, my voice shaking despite my efforts to stay calm. I want them both down in front of me, partly because I need to make a plan and partly because I need to see the two of them are safe.

"What's wrong, Mom?" Megan asks, her eyes wide with concern as she rushes into the kitchen with Ashton close behind.

"I don't know yet," I reply, grabbing my keys. "But we need to find Eden. She was supposed to take the activity bus home after robotics club. She's missing. We need to find her."

SIXTEEN

As we pile into the car, I call Eloise in a panic, explaining the situation. She tries to reassure me, but none of her attempts work. She calls me a worry wart and reminds me that cell phones die. Kids change plans. The little laughs between her jabs is what riles me up even more. The news is plastered with stories like this every day. It's not a joke. Eden is missing and her dismissive tone makes me want to scream.

The drive to the school feels like an eternity, each red light and slow-moving car adding to my growing anxiety.

As we pull up to the school, I scan the area, my heart pounding. I imagine all the terrible things that could have happened. What if she got lost? What if something worse happened? What would I tell her mother?

I take a deep breath, trying to push those thoughts away. I think of the trafficking issues at the mall. The stories of girls getting tricked into dangerous situations.

"Mom, are you okay?" Megan asks, looking ghost white with worry. "You look like you're going to be sick."

"We need to find Eden. We need to find her now."

"She's probably fine," Megan offers weakly. "You shouldn't freak out."

"I'm not freaking out," I snap. "This is the problem, Megan, you don't know a thing about the world. You don't know what could happen. I do. Eden isn't where she's supposed to be. She could be... anywhere."

SEVENTEEN

As I put my hand on the door to step out of my vehicle, my phone rings. I fumble to answer it, my hands trembling. "Eden?" I say, relief flooding through me.

"Yeah, it's me. I'm at the house. Where are you guys?"

I let out a breath that had been trapped in my chest under my thudding heart. "We're at the school, looking for you! Why didn't you take the activity bus?"

"I missed it by accident," she explains. "I was talking to one of my teachers about an upcoming competition and lost track of time. I didn't want to bother you, so I walked to the nearest bus stop and took the public transport bus home instead."

My relief quickly turns to frustration. "Eden, the nearest bus stop is a mile away from the school, and the closest drop-off is two miles from our house."

"I know," she says, sounding a bit sheepish. "I didn't expect it to be that long a walk, but I managed. I use public transport all the time at home. My phone was dead, but I just got home and plugged it in."

I feel the panic start to subside but the sweat dripping down my back hasn't gotten the message yet. Everything is all right.

"Eden, you should have used the phone in the school office to call me. I would have come to pick you up."

"I'm sorry. At home, I'm kind of on my own to sort these things out. I didn't think to call for help."

Her words make my heart ache. "Eden, you're not on your own here. We're a family. You can always call me, no matter what. I'll come pick you up, whatever's going on. I'm glad you are okay."

"Did you think I wasn't?" She sounds genuinely shocked by my worry. "I suppose I'm just used to my mum. She's going from one job to the next and I don't check in with her that often. I'll do better. Sorry."

The word sorry feels like it's losing its meaning, she's having to say it so much. And I in turn sound like a lying broken record. "It's no problem. Not a big deal at all." She doesn't realize I was just moments away from charging into the school and demanding to see the security camera footage of all of Eden's last movements. I was thinking of which picture of her to give to the police for the missing posters. My mind is like a row of tightly packed dominos; it takes just the slightest nudge for everything to cascade into chaos. And once they start toppling it's hard to get it to stop. But I grip the steering wheel and head for home. Crisis averted.

A couple hours later I've sent Megan to her room and Ashton is sleeping. I take the opportunity to try to make some kind of peace with Eden. I need a way forward for everyone's sake. We're sipping coffee out on the back porch. Eden looks uneasy. The miscommunication earlier today, and I assume she's heard from someone at school what happened with Megan getting in trouble.

"Eden," I start, trying to keep my tone light. "I've sent a few messages and lots of pictures to your mom, but I haven't heard back much. How often are you checking in with her?"

She looks down at her coffee mug, swirling the liquid inside. "Not very often. My mum's got two jobs. She's really busy."

I nod, trying to understand. "Tell me about your mom. I feel like you've hardly mentioned her at all."

"I love where I live. It's beautiful but struggling. The economy isn't great, and it takes a lot to stay afloat. My mum works hard to keep us going. She's the one who paid for me to come here. I'm so grateful for that."

"She sounds like a real hard worker," I say genuinely. "But that leaves you on your own a lot. Was it like that when you were younger too?"

"Yes. I learned early on that I had to take care of myself. If I wanted something, I'd have to work for it or find a way to make it happen. I'm not used to having someone ready to pick me up when I screw up."

"You didn't screw up. Missing the bus happens. I want you to know you can call me when you need something. You can talk to me if you need help with anything. I was really scared today when you weren't on that bus. I know you're capable but you're my responsibility and I care about you. Even if it's inconvenient, I'll drop everything to come help."

Eden shifts in her seat. "I really appreciate that. I know my mother would do that if she could. She tries her best, but she can't really put me first. Your kids are really lucky."

"I just wish I could get in touch with your mother more. I want to make sure she knows how you're doing here." It's neither a veiled threat nor an accusation. It's the truth. I'm uneasy with the idea of not hearing back from her mother more often. I'm falling into the trap of judgment. Comparison in order to make myself feel better. I could never go so long without hearing from my child. I'd never make them walk to the bus stop in a strange area just because they'd lost track of time. I'm better than that. I love my children more. It's hard to tamp that down but I know I'm coming from a place of privilege with these false equivalencies. Her mother is doing her best and in a completely different set of circumstances.

"You don't have to update her," Eden replies softly. "She trusts that I'm okay."

There isn't a cell in my body that relates to that approach, but I know I'm at one extreme and her mother must be on the other. I take a deep breath, deciding to dive into the real reason for our chat. "Eden, do you know what happened at school today with Megan?"

She nods slowly. "Yeah, I heard."

"Have you and Megan been watching that show together?" I ask, my voice careful not to start off too accusatory. Eden looks a bit defensive.

"Yes, but Megan knew all about the show already. She'd seen pretty much all of season one over at a friend's house after a football game. I assumed it was fine to watch it together. And when I talked about other shows that were the same and she mentioned she liked them, you didn't say anything."

"I understand." I'm trying to keep my tone calm. "I'm not upset with you, but I am worried. Megan is acting out, lying, getting suspended. I need your help. I need you to back me up and get Megan to understand the dangers of things like social media, the wrong kind of television, viral trends, and even vaping."

Eden looks taken aback. "I get that you're worried, but you have to understand, school is like a jungle. People are cruel when someone is different in any way. Especially at a school like Windsor Knoll. They are always competing for everything and paying constant attention to what everyone else has got or hasn't got. Megan is just trying to fit in. Watching a reality show isn't the same as vaping."

"Windsor has a no tolerance policy on that kind of bullying you're talking about. I know kids can be tough on each other but it's the top-rated school in the county. It might not be what you are used to, but Megan is in a very safe and positive environment in order to be herself and live by our rules."

Eden nods but is clearly unconvinced. She juts her brow up like I'm an idiot and she's got a better handle on the world than I do. "It is different to what I'm used to. My mother is very hands-off with me. She trusts that I can make good choices for myself and ask for help when I need it. Even when I was younger than Megan is now. She can't protect me from everything in the world. I've had to learn to protect myself."

I am trying to build a bridge here so I bite my tongue and come up with a more palatable answer than what I want to say. "I think that's really admirable of your mother. And I know that in other countries parenting is handled differently. But I'm not just making these rules up. There is ample science and data that show the long-term impacts of growing up too fast and getting exposed to things before you're ready. Trust me, I know. This is not the life I had growing up." I wave around at our lush backyard. "Things were hard for me. I don't want them to be hard for Megan. I don't want her to have the tough choices I did."

Eden laughs, a bit sarcastically. "With all due respect, Jo, what the books say and what actually happens are two very different things. Sheltering Megan from these things completely has its own dangers. She's going to encounter them one way or another. At least if she knows she can come to you, there is a way for her to figure out how to deal with it all."

"I'm trying to guide her." I feel a growing frustration. "But she needs to understand the consequences of her actions. That's where you come in. You're the most influential person in her life right now. I need your influence to be a positive one."

Eden looks thoughtful, then nods slowly. "I get it. I'll try to be more mindful and help Megan see the bigger picture. But you have to understand, she's just trying to survive middle school. It's not easy. But I'll help however I can."

I reach out and cover Eden's hand with mine. "Thank you.

For the reminder and the backup. I need someone in my corner here. Everett, he means well, but he's the fun parent. The one that gets to swoop in and make everyone laugh and hands out treats. I'm in the trenches here."

"Speaking of Everett," Eden says, sitting up a little straighter. "He said I could go into work with him one day next week. Do you think it's okay if I miss school for that? I am dying to see what he gets to do every day. We don't have anything like it at home and I feel like this is going to be my only chance."

The bridge is built but it needs to be shored up with some good will. "If he said it's an option, I can call the school and make that happen." I squeeze her hand a bit. "We've got to help each other out, right?"

"Right," Eden agrees with a smile but I notice it's forced. She's still dubious of my parenting style. But I don't need her to agree with me. I need her to help me. Those things can be mutually exclusive.

I nearly ask her about the vape. I consider pressing a few other issues that I've taken exception to. But I don't. Eden has already dug her phone out of her pocket and is texting someone with speed. I try to get a quick glance at who it might be without being too obvious.

"Is that Trisha? She's a sweet girl, right?"

"Uh, yeah." Eden tucks her phone away too quickly to be anything but an obvious attempt at hiding what she was doing. "I love Trisha. She's been so sweet, and I really like hanging out with her. We're making plans to get back to the mall tonight. Do you think you'd be able to drop me off? Her mum said she can pick us up and drop me back here after."

"Sure." I sip my coffee and feel a lightning bolt of intuition zap my spine. "I can always give you a ride. No worries."

Correction: Worries. All the worries.

And the uneasy feeling in my gut only gets worse when Eden goes two hours without answering my texts while at the mall with Trisha. Everett, back home from his business trip, kept telling me to stop checking my phone but I could tell he was feeling the stress too, even if he didn't want to show it. When she finally answered it was to tell us that Trisha's mom couldn't actually come get her and she needed a ride home. Since I'd just given her the lecture about asking us for anything she needed, I couldn't very well be pissy about it when she did. But I could send Everett. The cool one. The one who wasn't mad to have to put on his shoes and go out at nearly ten at night to pick her up.

"Want me to grab anything while I'm out?" he asks, trying to sound like this was no trouble at all.

"No, just maybe explain to Eden that she's got to set more concrete plans before going out. You've got to work tomorrow and it's late."

"I'm good," Everett answered with a dismissive wave. "She's here for such a short period of time, she's just trying to squeeze it all in."

The fifteen minutes it should have taken him to drive there and back has come and gone. It's now been forty-five minutes and I haven't heard a peep. It's like the old cartoons when one character gets lost and you send another to go in and find them and then you've got two people missing.

After nearly an hour, I finally watch as the car pulls into the driveway.

Maybe it was just a glance at first, but something keeps me there longer. Staring. There is tension in the front seat of that car. Like they seem to be arguing about something. Everett is a man who keeps his cool. I watch as his brow creases deeply and Eden seems to protest back with an animated gesture.

I look away as though I'm intruding on something private. I busy myself in the kitchen until she walks in and he trails behind. When Eden has gone up to bed, I can't help but ask.

"Everything okay?"

"Yeah, she wasn't where she was supposed to meet me and wouldn't pick up her phone. I was just—"

"Worried?" Something about this accusation gives me great pleasure. The guy who always thinks I overact got a taste of his own medicine tonight. "It seemed like you guys were having some words out there."

"You were watching out the window?" He rolls his eyes, playing into the crazy stalker mom accusation Megan always throws at me.

"It's scary when they aren't where they are supposed to be and you can't get in touch with them. I understand."

"I'm going to bed," Everett grumbled under his breath as he shuffled out of the kitchen. I want to follow him and rub it in a little. Remind him that it's not easy being responsible for children who don't think about how dangerous the world is or have consideration for our time. Instead I linger in the kitchen for a bit and let him pout in peace. He'll never say I'm right, but that little spat they had in the front seat speaks volumes.

EIGHTEEN

Sending Eden off to work with Everett puts a pit in my stomach. Mostly because I know she's going to love it. She's been following him around like a starstruck groupie all week, and I'm not petty enough to list all his flaws for her to hear, but the thought crosses my mind. Instead, I pack them both a lunch, remind them of the evening schedules, and wave them off for the day.

"Don't forget Eden really needs to be back here by the time Megan gets off the bus because I'll be at the allergist with Ashton. You can go back to work if you have to, but someone needs to be home."

Sullen Megan lets out a loud huff. "Because I can't possibly stay home by myself. Even though people my age are babysitting already, I still have to be babysat."

This morning Megan is mad about everything, not just that someone needs to be home this afternoon. She's mad that I didn't let her wear a crop top she picked out this morning. She's mad that Eden has actually been backing me up when she challenges me like I asked. And, maybe most of all, she's mad that she has to go to school while Everett and Eden leave together without her. She's never been to Everett's office, and she would hate it, honestly—she'd think it was boring. But today, in her young, no-frontal-lobe mind, it's because Eden is now the favorite. Which isn't true, but I don't have the energy to fight with her about it. Not now.

Eden's too busy bombarding Everett with questions about his company and their thoughts on AI to give me more than a half-hearted wave as they head down the steps to the car. I call after them, raising my voice because I need some kind of acknowledgment.

"Everett, seriously, you'll have Eden back here in time, right? I can't change Ashton's appointment, and I need to know you've got this."

He stops, turns halfway, and sighs, his shoulders slumping like I'm the one burdening him. "Yes. I've got it. I had it the first three times you said it. Don't stress. It'll all work out. Just chill, chill, chill."

Eden bursts out laughing as she sings along to the song I can't stand. "Chill like you've got ice in your veins. Chill, chill, chill."

"It's a song," Megan mutters from beside me as she finally steps outside.

"I know," I snap, not able to keep my frustration in check. "I've heard the song."

But what I've also heard, too many times, are the excuses. The way Everett forgets things and then blames me for not reminding him, in the same breath that he calls me a nag. I remind him too much, apparently, and not enough, all at once.

It's like I have to mother him through life, making sure everything is in place, but at the same time, I'm expected to be this carefree, easygoing wife who doesn't bother him with trivial things. I'm supposed to manage the kids, the house, the appointments, his schedule, all of it—but not be too demanding. I'm expected to meet all his needs, but not be needy.

This whole conversation feels like a script we've played out before. He hears me, but he doesn't really listen. Sure, he acknowledges the words, but he doesn't see the mental load I'm carrying, doesn't realize how much I'm holding together. To him, I'm just talking, repeating myself again. To me, this is what it takes to make sure the wheels don't fall off.

Megan slouches beside me, annoyed, impatient, but I can't even deal with her attitude right now.

Everett and Eden are halfway down the driveway, and I let out a sigh. I want to mutter under my breath, but I can feel Megan watching me. Waiting for me to be as annoyed as she is. I can't tell if she wants to blame me for this or commiserate with me.

I'm going to be the bigger person. I wave a goodbye to Everett and Eden. He's backing down the driveway so he doesn't see. But she does. Looks me right in the face and just blinks slowly. No smile. No wave. Just a thousand-yard stare and a cold expression. I drop my hand quickly, self-conscious and embarrassed. If Megan notices, she doesn't say anything. We retreat back into the house and finish getting her and Ashton ready for school. I've got a long to-do list, but the only thing I can think about is that stare. And why I thought it was a good idea to send her off with my husband.

NINETEEN

I spent the afternoon at the allergist with Ashton, going through the usual routine. It's become a ritual of sorts, these visits to ensure his safety. After the last issue that landed him in the hospital, I'm more on edge and assertive with the doctor than usual. I can sense their exasperation with me, but I don't care.

We're finally done and I'm feeling a bit more at ease. That is, until I get home and find the note. After four text messages from me I finally got confirmation from Everett that Eden was home waiting for Megan to get off the bus, since I couldn't pick her up from school that afternoon. But that wasn't the whole story.

Mom, me and Eden walked to the gas station. Dad said it was okay.

There is absolutely no reason to leave a note when Eden has a phone and plenty of ways to get in touch. Well, there is one reason – so they don't have to hear me say no.

My heart stops. I grab my phone and dial Everett's number, my hands shaking with rage and fear.

"Jo?" he answers, sounding distracted.

"What the hell, Everett? You let Megan and Eden walk to the gas station? It's over two miles away!" I shout into the phone.

"Jo, calm down. They wanted to go, and I figured it'd be fine. It's a nice day, and they're old enough—"

"Don't give me that," I cut him off. "This isn't about them wanting to go. This is about their safety, something you clearly don't care about. You keep undermining me and making me look like the crazy person. That store is right near the highway and it's basically a truck stop. People are in and out of there all day, passing through. It's not a place for two young girls to go on their own. I'm hanging on by a thread balancing everyone's issues and—"

"You're overreacting. I spent the whole day with Eden and she's incredibly mature. She has a good head on her shoulders and she's perfectly capable of walking with Megan for some candy from the gas station." His voice is firm but calm, which enrages me. "They're fine. They'll be back soon."

"Overreacting?" I can't believe what I'm hearing. "I'm the only one around here who hasn't gone insane. You're too busy trying to be the fun parent, the one they like more, instead of having my back. You're supposed to be their father, Everett, not their friend."

"Jo, I—"

"I've overlooked a lot of things over the years. You know I have. I ask nothing of you around here most days," I continue, my voice breaking. "You're never around, and when you are, you undermine everything I do. You have no idea how hard it is to do this alone because I don't ask you to—"

"I get it." He cuts me off. There's a long silence on the other end of the line. When he finally speaks again, his voice is low and remorseful. "I'm sorry, Jo. I didn't realize how much I've been letting you down. You're right, I've been distracted and probably trying to make up for that by overindulging the kids' requests for things. I'll make it up to you, I promise. How about we go out tonight? Just the two of us. I'll make a call right now and get our table at The Oak Barrel."

I'm too angry to feel appeased but I also know I can't keep being the only person trying to hold things together. Everett will feel reconnected after a nice dinner out, just the two of us, and he'll be much more likely to have my back when I need him. "Fine. But some of the night needs to be dedicated to talking about this stuff. I can't keep doing this alone. We're going to lose Megan if we don't figure these things out."

"Of course," he says. "I'll come home early, and we'll go out. We can talk about whatever you want at dinner. I'm really sorry."

When we get off the phone, I make a plan to hop in the car to go pick up the girls. I already know Megan will have something snarky to say about how Everett gave them permission. Eden will look at me like I'm an insane stalker. And I don't care. The gas station is not some hangout, and a two-mile walk for two girls is not some fun activity. I'll track them down and drive them home, no matter what they think about it.

Damn. With the busy afternoon I've almost forgotten. The mail was likely delivered while I was at Ashton's appointment. I grab my keys, planning to stop at the mailbox before I leave to track the girls down. But I see it and choke for a second. The pile of mail on the counter is half opened and splayed out. Two bills. One letter from the school about an upcoming event. And at the bottom, a familiar letter addressed to me. Everett must have grabbed the mail when he dropped Eden off this afternoon.

He's never home that time of day, and certainly doesn't think about a menial task like collecting the mail. I inch closer to the pile and shove the other things aside. He must not have read it. If he had, he'd have peppered me with questions when I called. Accused me of living a double life. If he'd have read this letter a nice dinner out wouldn't be on his mind. Divorce would be.

Picking up the envelope I see the seal is still intact. My life, still intact. I clutch it to my chest and realize I've been slipping. Getting too lax about collecting the mail. It can't happen again. It won't.

TWENTY

Hours later, after surviving the close call with the mail, and the girls' attitudes about picking them up from their walk, I'm dressed up and ready to go out, but, of course, Everett is nowhere to be found. So much for coming home early. My irritation is growing by the minute. I reapply my lipstick for the third time and move things around in my small clutch bag.

When he finally texts, he asks if I can meet him at the restaurant. Profusely apologizing, he tells me he'll come straight from the office and throw on a sports coat if I can bring him one.

I don't let the rage show as I finish up what needs to happen at the house. The kids are all in the living room, fed and given clear instructions on what they can do and watch. Everett is texting me another apology. One I don't bother reading because I've heard it all before.

I don't respond. Instead, I grab my purse and head for the door. The drive to the restaurant is mostly me gripping the steering wheel too tightly until my fingers hurt. I'm frustrated with how much effort I put into getting ready and now Everett will be coming from work. Putting in no effort at all. I wanted this to be something different. We'd attended plenty of events over the years for his work and then Windsor Knoll, but date nights like this were few and far between. With such a lack of trustworthy babysitters I'd had to be selective about our time out of the house. I'd spent the afternoon talking myself out of being too pissed at him. I was going to try to make the evening into something we could start building off of. Now I don't want to build at all. I want to burn it all down. And that's a terrible place to begin.

I arrive at the restaurant and don't valet. I'm making a point by parking in the back lot and walking in my heels across the gravel. I'm hoping Everett pulls in and sees this, feeling even worse for the delay. I refuse to text him asking for an idea of when he'll arrive. I want him to stew in the silence and know I'm mad.

The place is as lovely as I remember, but it does little to lift my mood. I let the hostess seat me at our reserved table, assuming Everett won't be long. I order my favorite very expensive bottle of wine, having a glass to take the edge off as the minutes tick by. The waiter doesn't seem to be worried about having to wait for my husband to arrive, mostly because my dress and jewelry give the clear message that we'll be big spenders.

"Jo, I really am sorry," Everett says forty-five minutes later as he rushes toward the table. "Traffic was awful. A huge car fire on the freeway." He's frazzled and his hair is out of place. The sleeves of his shirt are rolled up sloppily and he doesn't bother putting on the sports coat I brought him. Now I look like an overdressed fool. And he obviously thinks I'm a fool because what he doesn't realize is I ran the traffic in the GPS four times to get an idea of how long his trip here from the office would be. There had been no indication of an accident or a slowdown at all. At most it should have taken him fourteen minutes to get here from his office. I say nothing as he continues his explanation.

"I've been off my game lately. Big time. You've been carrying the load for our family for..." He looks away sheepishly. "Since we started a family. I hate when guys play the *I work full-time* card and try to make excuses for why their wives have it so easy. I know what you do is a twenty-four-hour role that takes up so much time and headspace. We would all be lost without you, and if I've done a bad job of telling you that, I'm so sorry. You are incredible. I can't imagine life without you. I don't ever want to."

The hardness in my chest softens a bit. "I love being a mother and all that comes with it. But it's intense sometimes. Especially with Ashton's allergies and the phase Megan is in right now. I just need to know that you and I are united on things. I can do the heavy lifting, but I need the kids to see us as a team first."

He reaches across and brushes my bangs out of my face and runs his finger down my cheek. "I've been taking the easy way out for too long. I want the kids to be happy and I'm always making up for lost time. I just wish I had the amount of time with them that you do. I get jealous of that. You get to see them at the birthday parties and field trips. You never miss a sporting event or art show. I'm never around for those special moments."

This is a first. From the outside it has always looked like Everett relished the time away. He seemed stressed by the noise and pace of the kids, and when it was time to pack a bag for work, he seemed relieved. But maybe I've read that wrong.

"I'll do better," he promises, reaching for my hand. "I'll be better. Tonight, let's just enjoy dinner, okay?"

I nod and sip my wine, trying to gain perspective. Yes, he's late but he's out working so that this bottle of expensive wine doesn't even register as an expense for us. The dress I'm wearing cost twelve hundred dollars and I've caught quite a few women at other tables checking it out. They're sizing me up. Everett, too. We're a young, attractive couple with expensive clothes and the best bottle of wine on the list. I fiddle with my diamond earring, spinning it so it catches the light. None of this works unless he works.

Back when I was young and I pictured the life I wanted, this was it. It's not about showing off or being better than the people around me. It's proving I'm worth the shiny things and the looks of adoration. It's success. Something I was told I'd never be able to achieve.

And doesn't success require sacrifice? I've had to trade away some things, some bits of myself, in order to get here tonight. I'm sure Everett has too. But we're here and his charming smile lulls me in. It feels good to be the one with the power. The ability to "let him off the hook." So I do. For now. I'll use this leverage to get him to back me up a few more times with the kids in the coming days. And there is still time to salvage a good meal.

"Can we get the caviar with blinis and crème fraîche? I've always loved those here." I cross my foot under the table and rest it against his leg. A peace offering.

"Anything you want." He licks his lips in that seductive kind of way that he'd always reserve for dates like this. Topping off my wine, he winks and I roll my eyes. This is an infrequent dance, but one we both still know the steps to. A date. A real date. And it feels better than I remembered.

When the food is served and the wine bottle runs dry, I see a shift in Everett. I'm a bit tipsy and Everett's demeanor changes slightly. He looks uneasy again. Apologetic, though I haven't given him any reason to think I'm upset at this moment. With a jumpy kind of movement Everett takes my hand across the table, his eyes earnest.

"Jo, I need to tell you something." His words are choppy and his eyes dart away.

My heart tightens and seems to stop beating for a long moment. He was waiting for the wine to be drunk. For me to have a buzz, and now he's got something heavy to say. Something to admit. I can tell. And any admission he's about to give isn't going to bring us closer together.

But before he can continue, his phone rings, cutting through the tension. He looks at the screen and frowns. "It's Megan."

A sense of dread washes over me as he answers. "Hey, Megan. What's up?"

His expression changes, growing more serious with each word. He looks up at me and starts relaying the information. "It's Megan. She says Eden has been missing since just after you left the house and she doesn't know what to do."

I grab the phone, my heart racing. "Megan, what's going on? Where's Eden?"

"I don't know, Mom!" Megan's voice is frantic. "She said she was going for a walk, and she hasn't come back. It's been hours. I'm really scared."

"Call the police," I order and start gathering up my clutch bag. I don't know all the details, but I can tell from the quiver in Megan's voice that something serious is going on.

"The police?" Everett questions nervously. "We don't even know what happened. Slow down."

I wave him off and gesture for him to leave cash on the table for the bill we don't have time to wait for the waiter to bring to us.

"I can't drive," I tell him as I hang up the phone. "We'll leave one car here. I had too much wine."

"Megan's calling the police?" Everett asks again as he throws too many hundred-dollar bills down on the table.

Pulling him by the arm I navigate the maze of tables until we're at the door. "Get the car, Everett. Get the car and get me home. The kids need me."

"But the police are going to come to the house and it's probably nothing. Do you really want the whole neighborhood talking about us tomorrow?" Everett clutches my elbow in an effort to slow me down but I shake him off. He knows me well.

The idea that we'd be part of the town gossip tomorrow does unsettle me. But not more than the thought of Eden being in some sort of trouble.

"It's late, she has no car, and she was meant to stay home and watch our kids tonight. If she up and left, then maybe something serious happened. We need to get the police involved."

Everett is ghost white as he fishes his keys out of his pocket. "Maybe she just went for a walk," he gulps out nervously. "Or someone picked her up. She's spending a lot of time with Trisha, right?"

"She left our kids home alone for hours," I remind him as I pluck the keys from his hand and slam them into his chest. "Get in the car, Everett. Drive. Get me home. Now."

TWENTY-ONE

"Mrs. Hargrove," Detective Treadway begins, his voice insistent, "we need to go over the details again. You said you left around six o'clock tonight and Eden was still here at the house?"

I nod, my hands trembling as I try to keep an eye on every member of my family. It's trippy with the lights flashing like a carnival ride. I see Everett looking stoic and Megan talking to another officer animatedly.

"Yes," I reply finally. "Eden was here watching the kids. My husband and I were at dinner."

The detective scribbles in his notebook, glancing up at me occasionally. "So she's a babysitter?"

I take a deep breath, trying to steady myself. "We hosted her through an exchange program. It's called the RAS Foundation. They match students from different countries with host families. Eden is from a small town in England. A woman from the school my children go to connected us to the program. Eden's been here for four weeks. She's got two more weeks before she goes home."

Detective Treadway exchanges a look with his partner and I

can feel something in the air change. "Eden was living here with you?"

"Yes." I look over at Megan, who is crying now. "Can I go talk to my daughter, she's very upset."

"Right now, we need to get all the information we can. It's critical to finding Eden.

Tell me, have you had any issues with her before today?" Treadway asks, looking inflexible.

"Nothing significant," I reply, my voice shaky. "There were some cultural differences, she challenged some of the rules, but we worked through it. She's been a wonderful addition to our family." It doesn't feel relevant to mention all the little speed bumps individually. They have nothing to do with her being gone. Missing. The word turns my stomach.

"Have you been drinking this evening?" He eyes me more closely, his flashlight coming up toward my face.

The question has my mouth snapping shut for a moment. "I, uh, I didn't drive. We had wine with dinner. Well, I did. But I didn't drive. We took two cars to the restaurant and left one there. I would never drink and drive."

He nods, jotting down more notes. "I'll assume she's made some friends in the last few weeks. Anyone she might have gone to see?"

I shake my head, feeling the tears welling up again. "She's made some friends at school, but I don't know of anyone specific she would visit without telling me. None live within walking distance. And she was watching the kids. We don't let them stay home without a babysitter. I don't think she'd ever just walk out and..."

"What about her family back in England? Have you contacted them?" Treadway asks.

"No," I croak, my throat clogged with emotion. "Her mother, Ivy, hasn't been very responsive to communication since Eden arrived. We've exchanged a few messages, but she's hard to get ahold of because she works two jobs. I didn't know what to say to her. I just don't know what's going on or what I should tell her. It's the middle of the night there."

Treadwell looks thoughtful as he bites at his lip. "We'll need the contact information for the RAS Foundation and any friends or acquaintances Eden might have made here. We're going to do everything we can to find her. We can reach out directly to her mother if you don't feel comfortable."

I nod, feeling helpless. "I should reach out to her. I don't want her hearing from detectives. That will probably frighten her more. Should I..."

"Is there anything else you can tell us about Eden?"

I take a deep breath, trying to recall every detail. "She loves science and technology. My husband, Everett, works in tech and she got to spend some time at his work with him. She's been attending Windsor Knoll with my children. She's... she's a bright, sweet girl. Where is she?" The idea of her being alone in the dark makes me feel ill.

"I want you to know that in cases like this it's very common for things to turn out just fine. Teenagers sometimes run off or change plans without checking in. Their phones die, or they make impulsive decisions. Most of the time, they're found quickly and are perfectly safe."

"But there are traffickers and drug dealers. What if she met someone online and..." I lose my breath for a moment.

He leans forward, his expression empathetic. "I understand your concern, but it's possible it's not as serious as it seems. Kids get minor injuries all the time and don't think much of it. Maybe she cut herself and panicked. We're going to look into it thoroughly, but I don't want you to jump to the worst conclusions just yet."

I take a shaky breath, wishing his words could lift some of the weight off my shoulders. But he has no idea just how good I am at worrying. "Thank you."

"We have officers out looking, and we're checking the places kids her age might go. We'll also review any surveillance footage from nearby areas."

"Can I talk to my husband?" I turn to make a move toward Everett and am surprised when the detective catches my arm.

"Wait here with my partner for a bit. I'll go check on everyone. Just try to stay calm and let us know if there is anything else you can think of."

Fifteen minutes pass, and the detective comes back. He looks at me intently. "Mrs. Hargrove, did you and your husband arrive at dinner at the same time? If so, when was that?"

I wipe away some stray tears. "Everett and I drove separately because he came straight from the office. He got to the restaurant late by about forty-five minutes. He said there was an accident and a lot of traffic on his route."

I don't know why I repeat the lie Everett told me. It just rolled off my tongue and it feels too late to take it back.

The detective's expression hardens slightly, but he says nothing further to me. He turns and walks over to Everett. Before I can process what's happening, I see them handcuffing him. They are putting my husband in handcuffs and pushing him against the side of the cop car. I open my mouth to beg them to stop but nothing comes out. I'm speechless. Breathless. And maybe I've been clueless, too.

"What are you doing?" I scream, rushing forward when my voice comes back to me.

Everett looks at me, his face pale and stricken. "Jo, it's okay."

"Ma'am, please step back," an officer says firmly, holding me by the arm. "We need to do our job here. The first few hours of an investigation are critical. I need you to step back."

"No! This is a mistake! He didn't do anything!" I shout, tears streaming down my face.

But it's no use. They lead Everett to a police car, and I watch in horror.

It feels as though they've tossed a lasso around my life and are dragging it forcefully away from me. Every dream. Every desire. All the plans. They are being yanked in a different direction.

"Call Merle," Everett says, the name of our lawyer sounding funny as he announces it from across our lawn. The man who usually reviews contracts and helped Everett get out of a speeding ticket is now supposed to be our lifeline? "Let him know what's going on and tell him to meet me at the police station."

"Everett," I shout as if we've just been separated in a crowd and I want him to come back to me. I nearly chase after them and throw myself across the hood of the police car they are loading him into, but I feel a hand slip into mine and squeeze. Ashton is suddenly at my side watching this all unfold.

The world around me feels like it's collapsing, and I'm left standing there on full display for all the neighbors as I'm buried alive. My designer dress doesn't feel like armor anymore, it feels like a straitjacket.

TWENTY-TWO

The female detective at my door looks sad for me, which is enraging. She's eyeing me like I'm some foolish wife who misjudged my husband and my life entirely. But she's the one who's misjudged everything. I'd been pacing around waiting for the police to finish searching every crevasse of our property and have finally gotten both kids to sleep when she arrived on my doorstep.

I'd guess that she's somewhere around her late thirties. Her brown hair is pulled back into a neat ponytail, and her skin is a blemish-free dark brown with a warm glow. I take note of her navy-blue suit that fits her like a glove. Her badge is clipped to her belt, glinting under the porch light, and her gun is bulging from her other hip. She's a beautiful woman, and I wonder how that must make her job harder at times. I also wonder if they've sent her in here, maybe one of only a few women on the force, to deal with "the wife."

"Mrs. Hargrove, may I come in?" she asks, one hand tucked into her pocket, the other holding a small pile of papers.

I nod, stepping aside to let her in. We move to the kitchen table, the room where just hours ago I sat with another detective, recounting every detail of Eden's disappearance for the tenth time. Now, it feels like a scene from a nightmare. My children are asleep and I want them to stay that way. Having this conversation again seems completely absurd.

"My children are sleeping," I comment coolly as I wrap my sweater tighter around myself as I sit down.

"I'll try to be brief. My name is Detective Delray. I just need to follow up on some details. We are working this investigation very hard and things are evolving quickly."

I don't wait for her to sit down before launching into my defense of Everett. "We can make this very brief. Everett didn't do anything wrong. He was at the office and then at dinner with me. He would never hurt anyone, especially not a child we're responsible for. This is a mistake. A terrible mistake, and you're wasting time."

The detective listens intently, her expression unreadable. My hands are trembling as I clasp them together on the tabletop.

"I understand this is difficult, Mrs. Hargrove. We're just following the evidence we have at the moment. Our number one priority right now is bringing Eden home safely. I can assure you the arrest of your husband is not something that was done lightly. He's been brought in to answer questions and hopefully he's forthright, which will help the investigation. But I'm here to talk to you about what you might know. Connecting those dots might help us tremendously."

The urge to bang the table nearly takes over but I control myself. The last thing I need is for Megan or Ashton to come down and see another detective here.

"I've already told all the detectives and officers everything I know. I've given them a timeline and told them what happened this evening, and what has that gotten us? You are focusing attention on someone who has nothing to do with this. You should be out there looking for Eden."

Delray nods, but it seems condescending since I know she doesn't believe me. Instead of offering any kind of verbal agreement to my statements, she presses on. "Can I share with you some information that we found that might help find some common ground to start from?"

"Please." I wave my hand in a challenge. There isn't anything she could tell me that would change my opinion on how insane this matter is. "Tell me why you've arrested my husband, who has an alibi."

"He told you he was in the office and came from there to dinner?" She doesn't cock up a brow or look pleased with herself. I'd prefer a little ego here so I could knock her down a few pegs. But instead her serious expression throws me off-kilter.

"Excuse me?"

"Everett led you to believe he went from the office to the restaurant without stopping at home?" She jots down a note in the pad in front of her.

"He didn't come back to the house. He came to dinner with me from work."

"Your daughter stated that she saw your husband's car in the driveway before Eden left for a walk. She just assumed you two either decided to drive together or that he came home to change quickly. But she states that before Eden left, he was here."

"That's not correct," I challenge, keeping my voice steady. "There was an accident on the freeway. He sat in traffic."

"So you don't know why he came back to the house? We spoke to his employer to confirm he'd been in the office today and they said he wasn't. He doesn't have an office in the building in the city anymore."

The air leaves my body as if it's sucked out with a vacuum. I know she's wrong and yet I can't grasp the loose ends of reality long enough to weave the truth back together and show her.

"My husband is the CTO of a global technology company. I've been in his very prestigious and well-decorated office dozens of times. Your people are a mess, and need to get the correct information before coming here and ruining our lives."

"We've been made aware of the fact that Everett is no longer the CTO of the company. He's now the district operations liaison for this area. The only travel he's done for the last six months has been in this region of the country. Primarily within two hours of home. That role doesn't have an office in the corporate building as his territory is local to this district now." She looks down at her notes and doesn't try to read my expression. "The demotion happened six months ago."

"He was in Japan a few weeks ago. Mexico before that." I feel like I'm living in some bizarre upside-down world where facts don't matter.

"He wasn't." She offers me nothing else. Just a blank stare and a long silence.

I think back to how Everett misspoke about the time and the noises I heard in the background. I blink fast. "He wasn't?"

TWENTY-THREE

I don't know if I've spoken in the last ten minutes. I can't seem to keep track of the time ticking by. When my confusion makes the moment unbearably awkward Detective Delray turns her notebook toward me and I see a list of dates and locations, all of which are fairly local. "Some of these meetings and conferences are so local that he was staying in hotels just thirty minutes from here."

"Everett wasn't demoted." For some reason I'm under the impression that if I just say things with enough conviction, they will be true. That I can will them to be so.

"We spoke to Human Resources and the CEO of the company. They all confirmed that Everett was asked to step down from his position as CTO and take on the director role. So you are saying you were not aware of this?"

"You talked to Mike?" I think of all the dinners we've had together with our families. How Everett and Mike have partnered on countless endeavors and always succeeded. Mike, his friend and CEO, would have no reason to lie to the police about this.

"Yes," she answers simply.

"I didn't know any of that." I straighten my back and level my eyes at her. Two things can be true at once. He can have lied to me and still be innocent. "I am sure Everett has a reason for keeping this to himself. If I could go talk to him..."

"Right now he's being held for questioning and we can't allow you to speak with him."

"Just because he was embarrassed about something at work and didn't tell me doesn't mean he would harm Eden. You don't have enough evidence to arrest and hold him. You jumped the gun completely."

Delray again glances down at her notes. "In a statement to another detective you mentioned that Eden had gone with Everett to the office today?"

"Yes. Eden is looking to someday have a career in tech. It's why she chose Windsor Knoll for her school placement through the exchange program. And Everett was kind enough to bring her into the office and give her a closer look at what they do." This feels like a terrible trap. One I could avoid if I planned to be evasive or even tried to be savvy. But the bait was too strong to turn away from. I needed to know where she was going with this.

"How did they say that went? Did Eden seem as though it went well?" Delray leans back a bit and bites the bottom of her pen as she waits for me to answer.

"Eden was thrilled. She was very grateful and said it was amazing to be able to see how everything operated. I only talked about it briefly with Everett at dinner tonight, but he agreed that it went great."

"Through speaking with his employer, we were able to validate that they have no record of this. As a matter of fact, they have strict policies against minors coming into the facility. There is liability of safety as well as proprietary information that they do not allow people outside the company to view."

"Mike wouldn't know if Everett brought Eden in," I

counter, happy to be able to make any possible point at all. "You'd need to talk to Janice. She runs everything there. Knows all the comings and goings. Everett would have introduced Eden to Janice."

"That's what Mike said as well," Delray explains, her eyes falling heavy with empathy. "So we did talk to Janice. She confirmed neither Eden nor Everett were in the office or the research and development center today. So, where do you think they'd have gone together for the day? Or why they would have lied?"

"What are you implying? Are you suggesting there was something going on between Eden and my husband? She's a child. Only five years older than our daughter. Everett would never."

"Has there ever been any infidelity in your marriage prior to this?" I can feel her eyes raking over me. Scanning like she's some sort of lie detector machine I'm hooked up to. If she was, I'd be setting off alarm bells with my nerves.

"No." I gulp and sputter. "Not that I'm aware of." The list of things I don't know seems to be growing by the second. "We have a great marriage." For a fleeting moment, I see a flash of Eden and Everett together. A kiss. A gasp. But I push the sick image away. It's not possible. That is not something my husband would do. "She's a kid," I remind Delray, and myself.

"Eden is a beautiful seventeen-year-old, Mrs. Hargrove. Things like this do happen. A young woman comes into your home, maybe your husband is feeling a hit to his ego about his demotion and he likes the attention. It might feel far-fetched, but I've been doing this job long enough to know it happens."

"I would have noticed something." I say this as much to myself as I do to Detective Delray. "You're not talking about an affair; you're talking about something sick. Eden came into our home as a child to be cared for. Everett is not a predator who would take advantage of a child in that way."

"It's important that you attempt to remember if there were any signs at all. Did you notice them sneaking off together or coming up with reasons for them to be alone?"

"They weren't alone at all besides the day they went to work together." I rack my brain to make sure I've got this straight. "He did go pick her up from the mall a couple times when it was late and I didn't feel like going back out. But I asked him to do it. He wasn't volunteering or scheming to be the one. And at most it happened twice. A twenty-minute car ride." What we both know but don't say is just how much trouble one could get into in twenty minutes. I was seventeen once. I remember.

Now I'm looking at those car rides through a new lens, wondering if the front-seat arguing I saw that night was something other than his frustration bubbling over about a miscommunication. I stiffen my expression so as not to give anything else away.

Detective Delray pushes on with her questions. "How was their relationship otherwise? Did you notice any dramatic shifts in Eden's behavior? Was she uncomfortable around him, or nervous?"

"No. They got along fine. Just how you'd imagine. We all got along well."

"So no trouble at all?" Detective Delray looks unconvinced, her poker face fading a bit.

"There were some bumps toward the beginning of her stay. It's strange trying to decide what rules to give a seventeen-year-old when you've never had one living with you before. But everything was fine. She wasn't scared or upset at all." I shake my head.

"Okay, okay." Delray takes a deep breath as if to center herself and turn the temperature down a bit. She's hit me with a lot and it must be obvious I need a second to get my bearings.

"I understand you're just doing your job but if you knew us, you'd never be asking any of these questions. Everett is a sweet and gentle man. He's never been in any kind of trouble before."

"Well, besides the sealed records." Delray gestures to a file in front of her. "I suppose he's been in some trouble."

"I've known Everett since college. He doesn't have a criminal record. Not to mention he'd never be able to have the clearance he does at work if that was the case."

"High school," she comments unemotionally. "Assault. The records are being unsealed. He got off with some community service and a hefty fine. But his family is wealthy, so that can tip the scales of justice at times. Apparently, the person he assaulted had life-altering injuries. They are still a wheelchair user. It was a serious offense."

"He has a record?"

"It was listed as a hazing incident but there are conflicting stories. Some say Everett had his eye on this girl who happened to be dating one of his friends on the football team. Everyone knew he had a crush on her and he was used to getting his way. When she wouldn't break up with the other guy, Everett decided it was time to make him look like an idiot in front of the whole school. He raced him up to the top of the retaining wall by the football field and then pretended to shove him off. But apparently, he pretended a little too hard. From the witness statements many people commented that Everett always found a way to get what he wanted. Has this been your experience with him? What is Everett willing to do to get what he wants?"

TWENTY-FOUR

The bait is tempting but this time I don't answer. I can't answer for something Everett did in high school or the statements of other kids who might have been there. I've had my fill of bombs being dropped on my head, and even if Detective Delray doesn't look as though she's enjoying this, part of me thinks she must be.

"And then there is forensics." She pulls another paper out of the stack and slides it toward me. I can't make sense of it so I wait for her to explain.

"It's not like the movies. We don't get DNA results back in a matter of hours or even days. We don't have a sample of Eden's to compare it to. Our team will try to collect something here in the house that might work, but it can be challenging. With that, the best we can do with the blood in the garage is get a blood type. Which we've done. It's a match to Eden's from her medical records."

"Okay." I nod to show I'm following along.

"With the warrant the officers brought back, you know they did more extensive forensic analysis of the home, the garage and your vehicles. While doing this blood was found in Everett's car. It's the same blood type that was found in the garage. Eden's blood type. Are you aware of any injuries Eden had prior to the day she went missing? Scrapes? Cuts?"

"No," I answer, before I've processed what she's asking. I answer truthfully because I shouldn't be afraid of the truth. My words shouldn't incriminate my husband. He's innocent. But something in my gut tells me to be more careful. "She may have. I don't know for sure. The kids did play outside quite a bit. Maybe she fell while running around."

"I know this is a lot to process. It is everyone's worst nightmare. Your family is in the middle of something horrific and it can be tempting to circle the wagons. To try to protect the people you love. I want to remind you that Eden has people who love her very much too. Bringing her home has to be our number one priority. I've been in touch with her mother and she's frantic. She's trying to get here as quickly as possible but she's struggling with customs and her passport."

"I... I haven't called her yet because I don't know what to tell her. Does she know Everett has been arrested?" The guilt chokes me to silence.

"She's been kept up to date on the investigation. I don't recommend you reach out directly to her, and we've instructed her not to reach out to you either. This has to be about more than self-preservation or the idea of protecting your husband. I came here today because I feel it's very important that you and I align on how to proceed. You're the primary caregiver to your children, right?"

"Yes." I take this question as some kind of a threat.

"They need you here, especially as things get complicated. I don't want to see you get caught up legally or punished for trying to shield your husband or withhold information. I hope this is all some misunderstanding. It would be wonderful if Eden is located and it can all be explained away. But if that isn't the case and something terrible has happened, your priority has to be your children. I don't want to see you become collateral damage and your children end up alone. Does that make sense?"

"Yes." I don't push any further on this. Maybe it's because she's right. I do need to think about my children first. "I'm going to ask to please speak to my husband. You're right. I do plan to protect my children, but I'm not going to let you use me against my husband either. Not when I know he's done nothing wrong. So, I want to talk to him."

"It's not possible right now."

"You're a stranger sitting in my kitchen telling me my husband is someone I don't even know. That he's full of secrets with a history of violence. I can promise you, someday not long from now, you'll be sitting at this table apologizing. Asking me to forgive you for what you put me through here tonight. And I won't. I won't forgive you because this was hell. So the least you can do is let me talk to him."

"Your husband can be held for up to seventy-two hours while he's questioned. At any point during that time he may be charged. Then a bail hearing—"

"Stop. Stop. There is no way. You do not have nearly enough evidence to get to that point. The things you've mentioned are not evidence of a crime. This tunnel vision, this witch-hunt, is costing Eden precious time. Wherever she is, whatever she needs, you're blocking that just so you can do some deep dive on my husband. Do your job. Find out what really happened to her. You're wasting your time here."

I stand and push my chair in against the table firmer than I intend to but she gets the point.

"I can see myself out." Delray gathers up her papers and heads for the door. "Get some rest, Mrs. Hargrove. You're going to need it."

TWENTY-FIVE

My eyes go blurry as I stare down at the untouched breakfast spread before me. My stomach churns at the sight of food. Everett's absence is a tangible void. I've made this breakfast for the kids like I would every morning, even though I don't intend to send them to school today. I can't imagine what people are saying and I don't want them having to bear the brunt of that. I'll let them sleep and reheat the food when they get up.

I pace the kitchen, my thoughts racing, when the doorbell rings, cutting through the silence like a knife. I open the door to find Eloise standing there, her face half-worry and half-anger. This is the last thing I want right now. I'm exposed. Disheveled. Vulnerable. And Eloise isn't here to comfort me. She's not my friend. She's a voyeur and I am on display for her.

"What's going on, Jo?" she demands, stepping inside without waiting for an invitation. Her voice is tight, and I can see the strain in her eyes. "I heard Everett's been arrested. They're saying all kinds of things. I thought for sure this was just some teenage angst gone wrong and Eden would be back by now. But this is very serious."

I lead her to the kitchen table, the same table where I sat

with Detective Delray last night. "It's a mistake, Eloise. They've got it all wrong."

She shakes her head, frustration evident in her every move. When her finger points in my face, I fight the urge to slap it away. "I put my neck out on the line for you. The police are pressuring the RAS Foundation on whether or not the background checks were done properly. Whether Everett was even interviewed, which he wasn't because we were desperate and I vouched for him. My standing with the foundation will be incredibly rocky after this."

"I think that's the least of our worries right now." I keep my eyes wide so she knows I'm shocked by her approach. "Eden is missing. She should be what people care about."

"You're damn right. Now there are rumors flying around that there was something going on between Everett and Eden. I need to know what's really happening, Jo. Were Everett and Eden sleeping together? That's motive enough to do something to her."

"Sleeping together?" I raise my voice and curse my eyes for dampening. They are rage tears but Eloise won't interpret them that way. "She's a child, not some sexy assistant at his office. It's not an affair you're accusing him of. It's violation of a child. And he would never."

"Oh, please," Eloise says, waving me off. "Men are pigs and idiots and they have no real self-control. They take what they want, and if she gave even the slightest indication that she was interested, I'm sure he'd jump at that."

Before I can respond, Megan walks into the kitchen, her eyes puffy from crying. She overhears Eloise's words and bursts into tears. "Mom, is it true? Did Dad do something to Eden?"

"No, Megan," I say firmly, pulling her into a hug. "It's not true. These are just nasty rumors from people who are looking for drama. Your dad didn't do anything wrong."

But Megan continues to sob. "Mom, I think maybe Eloise is

right. Maybe there was something going on between Dad and Eden."

"What do you mean?" Eloise asks, stepping forward so her large presence is felt. "You

saw something?"

"I don't know. Sometimes, when Eden and I would sneak downstairs for snacks late at night, Dad would catch us and send me back to bed. Eden wouldn't come back up for a while. I'd listen for her to go to her room and it would be a long time after. And on the car ride to school, when Eden was sitting up front, they would joke around, but it felt weird. Different. Like they had some kind of inside jokes or secrets or something."

"Why didn't you say anything?" I demand, my voice harsh. But not enough to deter Eloise from interjecting.

"Like they were flirting?" Eloise looks thrilled with this idea.

"Stop." I hold up my hand to silence her.

Eloise's face hardens. "You better get your house in order, Jo. If Everett's done something, he needs to admit it and tell us where Eden is. I vouched for him. For you. And now my reputation is on the line too. He's a sinking ship, and if you were smart you wouldn't go down with him."

She turns to leave, but I can't let her walk out like this. I follow her to the door, grabbing her arm and pulling her back. It's a hard grip. Judging by her face it hurts a bit. I'm glad.

"Eloise, you listen to me," I hiss, my voice low and dangerous. "You spread any rumors, you keep fueling this fire, and I will make sure you regret it. I don't give a shit about your reputation with some foundation. You think you know me? You don't. I'll fight for my family, in the bloodiest, dirtiest, fiercest way I have to. The ship isn't sinking, we're loading the cannons."

Eloise's eyes widen in shock, and she clutches at her necklace as if it's a string of pearls and she's heard someone curse in church. She pulls away from me, a look of disbelief on her face. Without another word, she walks out the door, leaving me standing there, breathing heavily. If she knew the things I am capable of, she'd never step foot in this house again.

TWENTY-SIX

What women like Eloise don't understand is, I have dreamed this family up from nothing. I have built this house with bricks of sacrifice. From a very early age, I spent nights lying awake, manifesting the life I knew I was meant for. I have willed every success and triumph we've had into existence. I have done unthinkable things to pull myself out of the hole in which I started. I have climbed here. Fingers bloody. Knees scraped. Sweat drenched and face dirty. I have climbed out of that hole, and I will be damned if Eloise stands at the top and threatens to push me back where I came from.

When Eloise and her fancy car are gone from my driveway, I turn back to the kitchen, where Megan is still crying. "Megan, listen to me. Your father is innocent. We're going to get through this. We're going to find Eden, and everything will be okay. I promise."

But as I say the words, I wonder if I'm trying to convince her or myself. The only thing I know for sure now is *I will talk to Everett.* I will look him in the eye and ask him what the hell is going on. There is only one play that will make that happen. If I want to get in that room with my husband, everyone has to believe it's because I think he's guilty. Everyone has to think, I'm ready to turn on him.

And maybe I am. Maybe the urge to believe Everett is rooted in the desire to keep what I've created intact. If he is a broken and diabolical man, then I will become the idiot who chose him. My children will be the damaged goods. This home will be labeled a house of horrors.

That's probably what I deserve. The karma that's been looming around every corner. I manifested the perfect destiny too close to the sun and I'm toppling down from hubris. The letters coming more frequently should have been a sign. My past was closing in on me. When you trade a life to save your own, what you're left with can't be a happy one. Sure, you breathe and your heart beats but your soul is wrecked. Not a single thing in my life today would exist unless I was willing to be permanently stained by the consequences of my abhorrent choices.

But still I had hoped the universe understood that it was never about the designer bags or the square footage of the house. I didn't plan, and work, and scheme so the soles of my shoes would be red. I know money doesn't buy happiness. But it can put a hell of a down payment on security. And that is what I've always been after.

Adequate childcare bought and paid for with Everett's money means my children won't have to spend their summers with an unstable uncle and cruel cousins. They will be riding horses and making memories at prestigious summer camps we've spent an absurd amount of money on. Because of what I've been willing to do, my children will not have holes in their shoes or their self-worth. They will be worldly and traveled. Educated and connected.

I rose far above my station, not to look down on anyone, but to hold close the people I love and make sure no one looks down on them. It shouldn't be this way. That people living on the fringes are just a minor disruption away from catastrophe. An unpaid speeding ticket turns to a revoked license and a lost job. An illness without health insurance is a prescription for bankruptcy. I didn't make these rules. This cycle that holds people down is cruel and unforgiving. But I also wasn't going to live by those rules any longer either.

Everett was more than a charming boy I saw in chemistry class in college who caught my eye. He may think it was some meet-cute and coincidence that we fell into each other's lives. But it wasn't just that I had *a man like Everett* on my vision board. It was Everett specifically I was after. He was ambitious enough not to foolishly squander away the wealth his family would hand him. There was ample ego for me to stroke and then ignore in a push and pull to win his attention. And the most important ingredient of all was his beliefs. Everett loved an underdog. A cause. He was vocal in his beliefs and willing to fight for what he deemed worthy. All I had to do was make him believe in me.

With just enough designer clothes, polished etiquette, and falsely obtained worldly knowledge I was accepted into his orbit. I made friends with his best friend's girlfriend. I was sure to show up in the places he would be. But always aloof. A mystery.

I didn't lie. Never. I wasn't one to make up stories about trips my family took to the Hamptons or discuss which of our many homes I preferred. I didn't speak of my family or childhood at all. I talked of things he loved. Politics. Ethics. Technology. I distracted him from all the dusty and dirty bits of myself by always keeping something shiny for him to focus on. Sometimes it was my interest in a budding technology I recently read about, and other times it was a short black cocktail dress with a deep V-neckline. Both were effective tactics. We made it months of falling for each other before he even bothered to ask anything about me.

And by the time people began to realize I wasn't of the pedigree a woman Everett should be with, he'd already chosen me. I was his, and anyone who wanted to make a case that I was not good enough would deal with his wrath.

It wasn't love at first sight for me, which might sound cold. I fell in love with Everett when he fell in love with me. When I realized he would fight for me, and one day our family, that's when I fell in love with Everett. No one had ever fought for me before. I'd done all my own battling up until then. I was tired and he let me rest. And my feelings run deep because of that.

The irony might be what kills me in the end. I was willing to twist myself, my morals and my judgment into a pretzel to fit into Everett's world. All with a promise of some comfort and safety for myself and my future children. And now I'm asking if he's the one who will rip it all away. If that's about to happen, it's not going to be a sucker punch I don't see coming. He's going to do it while he looks me in the eyes.

But first, I remember. I need to get the mail.

TWENTY-SEVEN

With a teary plea I convinced Detective Delray that if I could just talk to Everett, he'd share what he knew with me. I told them how much I cared about Eden; how desperate I was to bring her home. Maybe they couldn't get Everett to say much, but I could.

Detective Delray reluctantly agreed and set us up in a small, private room at the back of the police station. She assured me our conversation would be confidential, that we should speak freely. I don't believe her, but I know this is the only way I'll get to see him.

I walk into the room and see Everett sitting at the table, his hands cuffed in front of him. He looks tired, defeated. Unshaven and drawn. When he sees me, his eyes light up with a glimmer of hope. I rush to him, and I embrace him though he can't hold me with his hands cuffed. For a moment, everything else fades away. I feel my husband, not a stranger, not a dangerous man, just the same man I've always loved and known.

But then, everything I've learned about him over the past twenty-four hours comes flooding back into my mind. The lies about his job, the time he spent alone with Eden, the blood in his car. I take a step back, needing to see his face, to look into his eyes and find the truth.

"Jo," he says, his voice breaking. "I'm so sorry. This is all my fault."

"What do you mean?" I ask, my voice trembling. "Everett, you need to tell me everything. I need to understand. That detective—"

He sighs deeply, running a hand through his disheveled hair as the cuffs clink loudly. "I didn't hurt Eden. I swear to you, Jo. I would never hurt her. But I haven't been honest with you."

"About what?" I demand, my patience wearing thin. "What haven't you been honest about?" The problem with calling out someone for their secrets is suddenly your own feel like they're barely under the surface. It's like poker, and if you call, you have to be ready to show your own hand. And I'm not ready for that.

He looks down at his hands as if they are not even his own. "I lost my job as CTO six months ago. They asked me to step down, and I've been working as a district operations liaison ever since. I was too ashamed to tell you, so I kept up the lie about traveling for work."

"What happened?" I feel as though I'm cross-examining him in a courtroom. Staying level and neutral, like his lies are not a threat to my whole life.

"I took on too much. I fumbled a couple of projects and the clients were unhappy and vocal. I felt like things were getting stressful at home with you and Megan at odds all the time. It just all piled on. Mike pulled me in and asked me to take a step back. He told me to stay local to home. Regroup. We had Dale step in as interim CTO with the intention of me going back to it once I had my head straight."

"Why didn't you tell me?" I ask, my voice softening despite my anger. "We could have worked through it together."

"I didn't want you to see me as a failure," he admits, his

voice barely above a whisper. "I didn't want the kids to think less of me. I planned to do what I needed to until I was back in the CTO position. I was going to tell you. I just needed some time."

"Everett, that's not—" I start, but he cuts me off.

"I just need to know you believe me," he begs, his cuffs clanking against the table as he folds his hands to plead.

"Where were you when you said you were taking Eden to the office?" I bite the inside of my lip hard; the pain feels vital to keeping me grounded at the moment.

"I took her to work. Just like I said I would." The worry lines on his face are deepening. But he doesn't look guilty. I take note of that.

"The police talked to Mike. They talked to Janice. You weren't in the office. You and Eden were off somewhere alone all day together?" My eyes never leave his. I want to see if they flash with fear or dart away as he searches for a lie. But he doesn't flinch.

"We didn't go to the office. I'm really not allowed to bring her into the main building. There's security clearance needed and other protocols. I took her to our Bellbrook Drone Lab. Leon runs it and I knew he wouldn't care if I brought Eden in. We spent the day there and plenty of people saw us. All day. I wouldn't lie to you about something like that, Jo. God, what did you think we were doing?"

"They think you were inappropriate with Eden. That you were..." I reply flatly, still scanning his face for the truth. Truth... The word is so hollow now. It's morphed. Changed meaning. His truth. Their truth. They aren't the same.

"How could you even think that I would... I'm not some sick monster. You know that." He pinches the bridge of his nose and drops his head down. The cuffs catch the light and remind me how real this situation is. They are trying to turn us against each other. It's textbook. Sending you in here like you're going to get me to say something when I've been icing them out completely. They're pissed they can't get anything out of me."

"Icing them out?" My stomach lurches and I feel something sour in my throat. "Just tell them what you're telling me. Give them the people to talk to that can clear your name."

"Merle has instructed me to not say a word to them. They can only hold me about twenty-four more hours. I can hang in there. If I say the wrong thing here and they twist it up, the way they did with you, I could find myself in a lot of trouble. Trust me, this is the best play we have."

"Trust you," I whisper the words as I lean away from him. "There was blood in your car. Have they told you that?"

"Jo, please. I can't do this if you don't have my back. It looks bad, but you know me." He pounds his chained hands to his chest. "They aren't even investigating any other angles. I'm the easiest person to pin this on. The bad husband. The creep. The liar. You know that's not who I am. They are railroading me."

There is something I can't let go unanswered. Something that would change everything if it were true. "Megan told the police she saw you come back to the house before Eden left. She saw your car in the driveway when you told me you were coming straight from the office to the restaurant."

This has been the part I can't seem to silence in my own mind. He was so late coming to dinner. He lied about an accident and traffic. I've racked my brain trying to think of how he looked when he walked in. If he was normal, or if it seemed like he had just...

"I didn't go home. I'm not sure what Megan saw, but it wasn't me. She's a child, she shouldn't have been making a statement to the police at all. They could have gotten her to say anything. We should have stepped in."

"At the time we didn't exactly know that you'd be a suspect. I wanted us all to be open and honest because that's what will bring Eden home."

"It's bullshit."

I push my chair back from the table. "I think you should talk to the police. Tell them the truth about everything and explain what you can. Eden is out there; something may have happened to her. The longer they are focused on you, the longer she might be in danger. I know you want to protect yourself but we should be thinking about her."

"I'm not trying to protect myself." His eyes are wide and he's offended. "The kids. You. That's what I'm thinking about right now. You're all I care about."

"We need to care about Eden." I'm cold and I can see it wounds him. "The kids and I will be fine. We're right here. Safe. But Eden..."

"I know." He clears his throat and looks away.

"You should talk to the police. Tell them everything. Icing them out is wrong. Maybe then they'll start looking elsewhere."

I turn and knock on the door for the officer to let me out. I don't hug him goodbye or try to reassure him that everything will be okay. Not because I don't love him but mostly because right now, I don't recognize him.

"You're going?" He's astonished at the brevity of my visit. "You just got here."

"The kids need me and I don't know what to believe right now."

"Believe me. I'm your husband. We've been together for all these years. You think I would hurt Eden?"

"I think I can't be your wife right now. I have to go be their mother." The officer opens the door and I step out before Everett can protest. I'm angry that I haven't gleaned anything that settled my soul in the least. Everett's eyes gave nothing away. If I want answers, I'll need to find them for myself.

TWENTY-EIGHT

I can't sleep. I can't eat. Ever since my conversation with Everett, my mind has been in overdrive. His reassurances, though well-intentioned, didn't quell my fears or bring me any real comfort. The police seem to be at a standstill, and I can't just sit around waiting for something to happen. Waiting for the clock to run out on their ability to hold him for questioning. I have to do something. I have to find out what else might have happened to Eden.

It's early morning when I pull up to the house of the girl who showed Eden around on her first day of school. Trisha is a sweet girl. Popular and well liked. I only know her as a camp counselor for some summer cheer programs Megan attended. I was glad when they picked her to show Eden around and they hit it off. Teenagers have secrets, and maybe Eden shared some with her.

As I walk up the pathway, my steps crunching on the gravel, my heart races. What if this girl knows something? What if she's hiding something? I'm so far out of my depth. Weeks ago, before Eden arrived, the biggest problems I had were trying to get Megan to eat something for breakfast and stop changing her outfit thirty times a morning and making us late. Now I'm standing at the door of a practical stranger about to probe her for information to keep my husband from being charged with a crime.

I knock on the door, and after a moment, it opens and Trisha is standing there. She looks at me with curious eyes, her hair pulled back in a messy bun. She's wearing a tracksuit with a cropped top that shows her flat stomach, and hoop earrings, bigger than I'd think anyone would find comfortable to wear. Lips covered with gloss and eyes smeared with sparkling shadow, she stares at me for a long moment, waiting for me to say something.

"Hi, I'm Jo," I begin, forcing a smile. "I'm Eden's... well, I'm her host mother. I was hoping to ask you a few questions about her."

The girl furrows her brow but steps back, allowing me to enter. The house is quiet, the kind of silence that feels like it's waiting to be broken. We sit in the living room, the air thick with unspoken questions. I'm making her uneasy and I'm sorry for that. But I want answers no one else seems to be able to give me.

"I'm sorry she's missing," Trisha says, a little too casually for my liking. "It's so weird. Like something you'd see in a movie but it's happening right here."

Again, I find her tone prurient instead of worried. She doesn't seem bothered to have me here or concerned about any questions I might ask. Her friend is missing, and she's unbothered.

"I was glad when they picked you to show Eden around the first day of school," I say, trying to keep my voice steady. "And I appreciate you being friends with her. Can you tell me how she was doing? Did she mention anything that might explain why she left, or if something bad was going on?"

I brace for impact. What if Trisha knows some secret I don't want to hear? Something about Everett that I don't want to believe? But instead of spilling some gossip, Trisha's confusion is immediate and palpable. "I did show Eden around on the first day," she says slowly, "but after that, we didn't really talk. I mean, we weren't friends or anything."

Her words hit me like a punch to the gut. Eden had been so convincing about their growing friendship. "But what about the times you met at the mall? And the movies you went to together? Eden came over here after school sometimes too, right?"

Trisha shakes her head, looking even more bewildered. "That never happened. I don't know what she told you, but we didn't hang out outside of school. Even at school, after that first day, we didn't really talk. She made it pretty clear I wasn't the kind of person she normally hung out with. I think she saw me as just the stereotypical cheerleader airhead. She's super smart, obviously, and she didn't really miss an opportunity that first day to let me know."

My mind races. Why would Eden lie about being friends with Trisha? Then I realize, maybe that's not the case. What if Trisha is the liar? If she was friends with Eden and it went wrong in some way, she'd be trying to distance herself. Talk as if they were strangers. "Have the police been by to speak to you yet?" I ask, trying to keep my tone casual.

"No," she replies, her eyes narrowing slightly. "But is it true that your husband was arrested? That must be so wild. Was there something going on between them? Because I thought there was something weird about her."

I bypass her question, focusing on my own. "Who did Eden make friends with at school then? If you two weren't close, then who did she spend time with? The kids also on the robotics team?"

Trisha's confusion deepens. "Eden wasn't on the robotics

team. My boyfriend is, and I wait for him after cheerleading practice. I never saw Eden there."

My head is spinning. "She told me she was on the team, that she rode the activity bus home three days a week. If she wasn't staying after school for that, then where was she?"

"She wasn't on the team," Trisha insists. "I'm sure of it."

Desperation claws at my insides. "How was she doing in school?"

Trisha leans back, thinking. "She was really quiet. Everyone thought she was just incredibly shy, so they gave her some space. I thought, honestly, she was kind of cocky and rude. That's why I didn't really try too hard to keep hanging out with her. Mostly, when I saw her, she was on her phone. It was weird because she used a flip phone. I didn't even know you could text on those."

My mind latches onto this detail. "Eden had a smartphone," I say. "Not a flip phone."

"She had both. But she was always on that flip phone when we had down time at school. In between classes and at lunch. I think the teachers didn't say much to her about having her phone out because they knew she was not going to be around too long. She was obsessed with that phone. Everyone kind of joked about it."

"They made fun of her?" I feel a prickly heat of protectiveness. "She was new here and didn't know anyone. Maybe she was just struggling to fit in."

"We didn't make fun of her," Trisha corrects quickly. "She didn't hear us. It wasn't like we were picking on her or excluding her. She was excluding herself. The only person she cared about was whoever she was talking to on that phone."

"And you don't know who that was? Did she ever mention anything about who it might be?"

"I asked on the first day why she had a flip phone and she said so her mom wouldn't give her shit about something. I don't know what, but I figured it was a guy. Someone maybe she wasn't supposed to be talking to."

This is an idea I can get behind. Eden had a secret from her mother. From all of us. Someone she was in touch with that she was not supposed to be. Someone her mother would not approve of. And, most importantly, Trisha noticed this on the first day of school. Before Everett had come home from his trip and met Eden. Whoever she was clandestinely talking to could be exactly who the police need to find.

"The police should have spoken with you." I take my keys from my purse and stand up. "I'm going to make sure they do. Please tell them everything you told me. It's vitally important."

"Okay," Trisha says as I head out the door without another word. I know this will become some fodder for her friend group text chain. How crazy Mrs. Hargrove showed up at her house and started interrogating her about the weird exchange student they'd been making fun of.

It was amazing how my priorities had changed. For so long, how people saw me was more important than how I saw myself. The idea that someone might be talking poorly about me, that I might somehow be on the outside of this clique and not good enough for everyone at Windsor Knoll was crushing. I'd lost sleep over this. I'd changed the way I dressed. Upgrading the vehicle I drove. Making sure my bag was designer and in season. And what had it gotten me? What did it matter? Now I wasn't worried about fitting in. I was going to stand out. Be heard.

Getting home, I pace back and forth in my living room, phone in hand. I've called the detective back to my house, with the intention of demanding she do her job. She hasn't even talked to the other students at school. There is no reason I should be the one uncovering evidence while they keep my husband locked up and Eden is still missing. I'm buzzing with adrenaline ready to pounce and make my case.

The doorbell rings, and I rush to open it, expecting to see

the detective's familiar face. But standing there instead is a woman I don't know, though she looks vaguely familiar—an older version of Eden.

She's teary-eyed, with makeup smeared down her cheeks, her hair a messy tangle as if she hasn't brushed it in days. Her clothes are rumpled, and she clutches a worn handbag tightly, knuckles white from the grip.

"Ivy," I say, voice trembling. I'm face to face with the woman whose daughter I've failed. The girl who is lost and could be in danger. It's like standing before the firing squad, just waiting to hear the bang.

TWENTY-NINE

If it were me, I'd have thrown a punch already. If Megan was missing and it was Ivy's fault, I'd have clumps of her hair in my hands and my foot on her throat.

But Ivy seems to be showing some initial restraint. She looks as though she's in shock, her eyes fixed on something behind me as she speaks. Her accent is the same as Eden's and it rattles me to hear their identical inflection. "The police told me not to come here, not to contact you at all. They wanted to set me up in a hotel and arranged a rental car. But the second I started driving, I just felt so far from home. So alone. I just want my daughter. This is where Eden was last. This is where she'd come back to if she could. So, this is where I want to be."

I take a moment to process her words, then step aside to let her in. "Come in," I say softly, guiding her toward the kitchen. "When did you get here? The police said they were working as quickly as possible with customs."

"Just a couple of hours ago. It was torture waiting. I went to the police station first but they just had too much to say. I couldn't stay there. I couldn't listen anymore."

We sit at the kitchen table, the silence between us thick

and heavy. A bit later I put the kettle on, the sound of boiling water the only noise breaking the quiet. I make us both a cup of tea, though neither of us even takes a sip. It's just something to do, something to hold in our hands to keep them busy and steady.

Ivy's eyes are red-rimmed and swollen from crying. She looks at me, searching for something—answers, solace, anything. "The police arrested your husband?"

"He didn't do anything to Eden." I'm firm and unwavering, even though I don't know this for sure anymore. "They are not doing their jobs. Not investigating properly."

"They told me all sorts of things," she whispers, placing her tea down on the table as she finally looks at me head-on. "Did he hurt her?"

"No." I shake my head. "Ivy, I can only imagine what you are going through and you have no reason to believe me. But I promise you, this was not Everett."

"Utter rubbish!" Ivy slams a hand on the table and her eyes flash with a flame I think might burn my house down. "Women say that," she yells. "They stand by their men. But men always disappoint, don't they? Isn't this how it happens? Everyone thinks they're such upstanding people until the truth comes out. Until the man's base instincts come out. You really think your husband is some kind of saint? From what the police told me he certainly isn't."

I pump my hand in the air to slow her down. "That's not what this is. I called the detective to come over here. There is so much more to the story."

"It's not a story." She's speaking through her ground-together teeth. "This is my child. My only child. I did everything I could to make her dream finally come true and you turn it into a nightmare. She's gone. You were supposed to take care of her, and she's gone."

"They'll find her. She'll be okay. I think there is a chance she's with someone. That maybe she left on her own to meet up with someone."

"What?" Ivy looks stunned but it also squashes some of her growing rage.

"Detective Delray is on her way here. I thought you were her, actually. I have new information to give. Like how Eden had a flip phone in addition to her smartphone. And she lied about her friends and activities at school. There was something else going on."

Ivy looks up, surprise and confusion mixing on her face. "A flip phone? Why would she have that?"

"She told a girl at school it was to keep something from you. Someone she was talking to that maybe she didn't want you to know about. Trisha, the girl I talked to, said she was on it from the first day of school. That's before she even met Everett. She wasn't talking to him on it."

Ivy's shoulders slump, a fresh wave of tears threatening to spill. "Why would she hide that? What was she doing?"

"The police need to find that out. I don't know why they are only focused on my husband but—"

"They are trying to find out what he's done with her." Ivy is stone-faced and wild with anger. "That's what they are doing."

The doorbell rings again, and this time I know it's the detective. I leave Ivy for a moment to answer it, and as I return with the detective in tow, I see Ivy trying to pull herself together, wiping her eyes and straightening her clothes.

"Ma'am," Detective Delray says, looking shocked. "I thought you were advised not to come here?"

"We have nothing to hide from her," I cut in, standing for a moment between Ivy and the detective. "We all want the same thing. Ivy is welcome here. She can stay as long as she likes."

Detective Delray doesn't address my comment. "You said you have some information for me, Mrs. Hargrove? That conversation with your husband didn't seem to pan out very well. So what is it?" Her gaze shifts between Ivy and me, her expression somewhere between disappointed and grim. I take a deep breath and start to explain everything Trisha told me.

"I spoke with Trisha, the girl who showed Eden around on her first day," I begin. "She told me that Eden had a flip phone, in addition to her smartphone. She was always on it, from the very first day she started school here. Trisha said Eden claimed it was to keep something from Ivy—someone she didn't want her to know about."

Ivy's eyes narrow in confusion. "Why would she have that? What was she doing on it?"

"I don't know," I admit. "But it makes me think that maybe Eden was in touch with someone here in the States before she came over. Kids can be impulsive, and the dangers of the internet are real. What if she planned to meet up with whoever she was talking to? It could be some kind of trafficking scheme or a catfishing scenario."

Detective Delray listens intently, her eyes narrowing slightly as she processes my theory. "It's possible," she says warily. "But I need to caution you about getting involved with witnesses in the case. You could be compromising the investigation."

I feel a surge of frustration and anger. "Compromising the investigation? Someone needs to investigate! I'm the one finding these things out while you keep my husband locked up and Eden is still missing."

The detective's face hardens. "Mrs. Hargrove, I understand you're upset, but this is a delicate situation. We have protocols for a reason."

"Protocols?" I shout. "What good are your protocols if they're not helping us find Eden? If you're not talking to the people who might know something, what are you even doing? You need to go to the school and talk to all the kids who spent time around Eden. Maybe she opened up to one of them about

who she was talking to. We were dropping her off at the mall for
hours at a time. She wasn't meeting the people she told us she
was, so then who was she meeting? Maybe there is surveillance
video. I can give you the dates and times. And the phone, there
must be some kind of way to find out what the number was on
the phone. Then you can—"

"Mrs. Hargrove, I know on television they make all this
seem like it just falls into place between commercial breaks, but
it doesn't really work that way. We have been to the school but
we will follow up more specifically with Trisha. The cell phone
was not recovered here or in her locker at school but..." She
trails off and the room falls silent, the tension thick in the air.
Ivy's eyes dart between me and the detective, her expression
one of helpless desperation.

"What about her gym locker," Megan says, edging her way
nervously into the room. "The upper school has gym lockers too.
I know the girls hide stuff in there sometimes because the P.E.
teachers don't really pay attention or check things."

Detective Delray looks taken aback. "I'll look into all of
this."

I want Megan to head back to her room but I don't want to
be obvious. I'm afraid she'll say something similar to what she
did in front of Eloise. Something incriminating about Everett.
But I don't want to appear to be hiding anything either.

"Megan, this is Detective Delray and Ivy, Eden's mother." I
gesture to each of them and Megan gives a little awkward wave.

Detective Delray excuses herself. "I should be heading out.
There is a meeting in a half-hour for updates on the case. Ivy,
I'll call you shortly if there is any news. Otherwise, I'll work on
this information you all provided."

Walking Detective Delray to the door, I stop short when she
turns quickly to whisper something to me. "You should not let
Ivy stay here. It's not appropriate. If your husband is not
charged, he will be released soon and you don't need to all be

staying under one roof. If he is charged, you're opening your family up to some serious conflict. We have made housing arrangements for her."

"I appreciate your perspective but I think we can manage fine all together. What I need from you is to go to the school. Talk to people who saw Eden. Find out who she'd been meeting at the mall. The last time she went was Thursday. I dropped her off at the entrance by the frozen yogurt stand at six."

Detective Delray nods and steps out, offering one more warning. "Go back in there. Don't leave your daughter to talk to Eden's mother. Don't let Megan see that kind of fear and grief before she has to. You're putting your kids in a terrible position."

I want to argue with her, stand my ground that what I'm doing is right. But the sudden image of all of this going sideways and Megan having a front row seat has me rushing back toward the kitchen.

They aren't saying anything to each other when I walk in but the tension is palpable. It's awkward and I'm tempted to tell Megan to go back to her room. But Ivy looks like she wants to talk to her. Like that might bring her some comfort. Don't I owe her at least that?

"Are either of you hungry?" I ask, fiddling with some food in the pantry. "I can make something, or we can order some takeout."

"Not hungry," Megan says, staring down at her shoes and a moment later, Ivy agrees.

"We should be doing something," Megan announces more forcefully than I expected from her. "Don't you think, Mom? We should be looking for her or something."

"Yes. Where is everyone?" Ivy asks in a far-off voice. "Where are your friends? Where are the people trying to help?"

I open my mouth to answer but just shake my head like I don't understand. She continues to try to ask this difficult question.

"If this were happening at home the kitchen would be over-flowing with food that neighbors had dropped off. There would be people coming to light candles and comfort you. To walk the streets and look for my daughter. Where are the people? Don't they care?"

Ivy's words hit me hard, and I feel a pang of guilt deep in my chest. She's right. Very few people have reached out, and those who have, keep their distance. They likely see this situation, especially with Everett being arrested, as radioactive—something they don't want to get involved in. The friends I have are all part of this world I've wedged myself into, and the thing about forcing your way into a place you didn't belong is just how easy it is for them to push you back out.

I turn away from them, busying myself with the pantry items, trying to mask the turmoil brewing inside me. The reality is, this neighborhood, these people, they're not my friends. They're acquaintances, people I've socialized with out of necessity and proximity, but not true friends. The isolation is suffocating and never more apparent than in a moment like this.

Ivy looks at me with a seriousness that pierces through the fatigue. She gives me a pass on having to answer for the lack of people here to help and instead hits me with something even harder to face.

"Jo," she begins, her voice low and strained. "I need you to promise me something."

I've never been looked at this way before. The grave desperation in her eyes tugs at that part of me that always wants to fix. That needs people around me to feel whole and happy. She's the furthest thing from that right now and I am compelled in some other-worldly way to change that.

I nod, willing to promise her whatever she needs. "Of course, Ivy. Anything."

She takes a deep breath, her eyes locking onto mine as if

she's about to cast a spell or tell a fortune. "I know you don't think Everett did this—"

"I know he didn't," I interject quickly, my voice firm. I want Megan to hear me say it as many times as I can.

Ivy looks momentarily put off but continues, her tone unwavering. "All I want is for you to promise me that if there comes a time when you change your mind, when you think maybe Everett was involved somehow, that you won't protect him. That if your trust in him falters, you won't let loyalty or the preservation of your family be more important than finding Eden. You'll do what's right even if it feels impossible."

Her words hang heavy in the air, and I feel a lump forming in my throat. Megan is watching us intently, her eyes wide and filled with concern. This is a promise that goes against everything I believe about Everett, but how can I deny Ivy this request? After all she's been through, doesn't she deserve at least this assurance?

I swallow hard, forcing myself to meet her intense gaze. "Ivy, I promise you," I say, my voice trembling slightly. "If there ever comes a time when I doubt Everett, if I think he had anything to do with this, I won't protect him. I'll do whatever it takes to find Eden, no matter what."

Ivy's eyes well up with tears, and she nods slowly, seeming to take some comfort in my words. "Thank you, Jo," she whispers.

Megan's voice cuts through my thoughts. She's not willing to sit here and just wait for her father to be charged or some bad news to come in about Eden. "Mom, we should at least try to do something. Maybe we can put up flyers. If we're out there actually handing them to people they'll care more."

I nod, swallowing the lump in my throat. "That's a good idea." I turn to Ivy, who's watching me skeptically. "We'll organize something. I'll call around, get some people together. They are probably just waiting to be told how to help."

"And Everett?" Ivy asks, the word seeming to turn bitter in her mouth. "He'll be back here? And then..."

"Then he can help too." My answer is swift. "We all want the same thing. We want to find Eden and understand what happened. Getting Everett home is a key part of that."

Megan takes a seat by Ivy and I panic at what she might offer up but she doesn't disappoint. "My dad will know what to do."

Ivy's expression sours. "You have such faith in your father. More than I could in a man who's been accused of something terrible."

"She's a child," I cut in quickly, trying to quell the simmering, yet understandable anger in Ivy.

"So is my daughter. What would you do to protect yours?"

The question is unanswerable. It can't be spoken in a civilized conversation. I know how far I would go to give my children everything they need. To keep them safe. I've already done it, and part of me wonders if Ivy can see this written on my face. She sees the animal in me and I recognize it in her. I can't keep strong under her gaze, and I'm the first to look away. She sees it. I've done unthinkable things. She knows.

THIRTY

Sometimes timing is perfect. And occasionally, it's the direct opposite of that. Megan's suggestion and some phone calls had helped get the community involved. It was mostly people with a morbid fascination and those looking for more rumors to spread. But I could see Ivy was lifted a bit by the appearance that people cared.

The problem was, just after everyone had their flyers and were ready to head to their assigned locations in and around town, the police car pulled up. It could be news about Eden. Or just an update from the detective. But everyone seemed much more excited to realize it was Everett being driven home. Apparently, they weren't able to charge him and the time they could hold him for questioning was up.

I use the word excited loosely. It wasn't as though people thought he was innocent and they were pleased justice had prevailed. They were glad they were here to see the show. The local news had set up in the driveway this morning to help get the word out and I saw the on-air reporter nearly topple over to yank her cameraman in the direction of the car Everett had just stepped out of.

So yes, sometimes timing is perfect. Other times it's terrible. But I realize suddenly, worst of all, occasionally timing is planned and manipulated. The police were aware we were gathering here this morning. They knew about the flyer distribution and even the local news being here. Dropping Everett off now was no mistake. Pressure mounting on us is their goal.

I rush to meet him, ignoring the whispers and the flashing cameras. Everett looks weary, shadows under his eyes and his usually impeccable hair disheveled. He sees me and forces a tired smile. I don't know exactly what is driving me toward him. The unwavering belief I have in his innocence, the depth of our years of love, the eyes of our children on us, or my desire to make sure the world knows we're united. Either way, I'm the first one to him and the urgency to hold him grows.

"Jo," he says softly, his voice rough.

I embrace him tightly, feeling the tension in his body. "Are you okay?" I ask, pulling back to search his face. "You look like you've been through hell."

He nods, glancing around at the crowd. "Let's go inside," he murmurs. "I don't want to do this out here."

As we make our way to the house, the reporter intercepts us, microphone in hand. "Mr. Hargrove, can you tell us what the police questioned you about?" she asks, her eyes bright with curiosity. She's genuinely perfect and I'm captivated by her. Unblemished skin. No hair out of place. Flawlessly symmetrical features and a beaming white smile. Maybe you have to look that good to get away with being this cold and intrusive. "Do you know where Eden is? Were you having an inappropriate relationship with her?"

Everett stiffens but keeps walking. "No comment," he mutters, not even glancing her way. I on the other hand am fascinated by her, unable to look away. This gives her some hope as she turns to me next. "Mrs. Hargrove, how do you feel about your husband's release? Do you believe he's innocent?"

I grip Everett's arm tighter and shake my head. "Of course he is," I snap. "They know that, which is why he's home now. Hopefully the police will now start looking into what really happened and where Eden is, instead of falsely accusing my husband."

"Jo," Everett scolds me and tugs me toward the house. "It's no comment. Every time. No comment. Do not talk to the media."

I lower my voice but not my conviction. "People need to know I'm standing with you on this. They need to know you're innocent."

"People hear what they want and twist things around. The only way to keep them from doing that is to give them nothing. Merle will be here later today. You can hear it from him if you need to."

We push past the throng of onlookers and reporters, finally making it inside. Megan follows closely behind and I feel guilty for not thinking to wrap my arms around her too and usher her in. The irony of this terrible situation, which should have made me grip my family tighter, is that I'm forced to have to let go. Ashton is staying with his friend Micah. His mother Rachel is someone I met in the allergy and anaphylaxis support group I joined after Ashton's diagnosis. She's one of the few people I trust with him, but this is also the longest amount of time I've spent away from my son. He can't be here for this. The police cars. The news. His father looking like death. I want to hold him and read him his bedtime stories and smell his fruity shampoo in his hair as I kiss him goodnight. I want the life I had before all this.

Ivy stands in the doorway, her expression indecipherable. She is great at not giving away her next move with some preemptive look of anger or sorrow. This kills me. I am a professional at reading nuance and detecting people's moods and feelings. All so I can react in a way that might help. Ivy doesn't give me the signals I need to manage the situation and it makes the anxiety in me rise and boil.

"Ivy," Everett says, the same pained look I know I must have had the first time I saw her. She doesn't say a word and he looks away from her intense stare. Suddenly I can feel the terrible mistake I made. We do not belong in this house together.

THIRTY-ONE

"Is there an update?" Everett finally asks when Ivy's eyes move away from him.

I hadn't thought of how in the dark Everett had been. Police don't loop in their main suspect on the current status of the search. If they were telling anyone anything, it would be Ivy.

"Nothing." Again, Ivy's expression is flat. She's analyzing him. Trying to decide if he's capable of something terrible or not. I can't tell where she lands on this.

Megan's hopeful voice cuts in. "We have people handing out flyers all over town. The news is going to talk about how everyone is coming together to find out what happened to Eden."

"That's good, sweetheart," Everett says as he pulls his daughter in for a hug and kisses the crown of her head. I can't take my eyes off Ivy, who can't take her eyes off Everett. She's dissecting his interaction with our child, looking for some sign of something nefarious or inappropriate.

"What do you need?" I ask, unsure exactly how you support a person who's been held for intense questioning by the police for days.

"A shower." He pulls at his clothes as if they are toxic.

Megan is still the only optimistic voice in the room. "Then after that maybe we should meet up with some of the groups handing out flyers. They will be at the football field at school after lunch to check in, and—"

Everett's voice is harsh. "We can't, Megan. We can't be seen out like that. The news is going to be breathing down our necks for statements. People are going to be looking at every single thing we do, trying to make connections that aren't there. We have to lay low."

Ivy's face finally falters, a flash of disappointment that morphs into disdain. "Your daughter is trying to help find my daughter. And you're worried about your reputation?"

"No," Everett corrects quickly, rubbing at his temple. "I'm sorry. That's not what I meant at all. I actually think us being out there is a distraction. It'll take away from the investigation and slow the process down more. We have to stay out of the way so the police move on to what might really have happened. If we keep giving them new sound bites and sightings of us, it'll have the momentum going in the wrong direction. I want to find Eden. I want to know what happened. You have my word – everything I do will be in pursuit of that."

"I think you've done plenty in this situation, haven't you?" Ivy's stare is icy.

"If you're accusing me of—"

"The *police* are accusing you," Ivy counters angrily. I was so stupid to think I could keep this tension from reaching a boiling point. I underestimated how on edge Everett would be. I'd been able to make some headway with Ivy, but, of course, seeing the man who was arrested in her daughter's disappearance investigation would be a heavy thing to bear.

"Megan, go upstairs." I wave for Megan to leave the kitchen but she doesn't.

"No, stop treating me like a baby. I can hear what's going on. I should. I want to know when something happens."

"Megan," I reply, more firmly this time.

"She's right," Ivy interjects. "You can't hide her away from all of this. Her father is a suspect in my daughter's disappearance. You can dress that up any way you want, but it's reality. Sending her to her room won't change that."

Everett is stoic, grinding his jaw closed, clearly trying not to say what is truly on his mind. He doesn't want Ivy's opinion on what we do with our daughter, but he also must understand how little ground we have to stand on.

I hold up my hands, maybe in defeat, but also in an effort to calm everyone. "We have to keep pushing in the direction we were heading yesterday. Eden was keeping something from you. From us, too. She was talking to someone and meeting with them. We have to find out who that was. I'm calling the detective soon to get an update to see if they pulled the footage from the mall. That's who they need to be looking for."

I take Ivy gently by the shoulder and lead her into the living room. We sit on the couch next to each other as Everett walks upstairs to shower. My hope is that when he comes back down, we can truly all unite. That the tensions and feelings subside and we are a comfort to each other rather than a danger.

"I made you that promise," I whisper as I take her hand. "Please give Everett a chance. He wants what we want. For Eden to come home safe. I know it's difficult but we can't all turn on each other. We have to stay strong and stick together. Let me get you something to eat. You've barely eaten at all."

"I'll make something," Megan announces from the doorway of the kitchen and I nearly laugh. This is the child who mere weeks ago would throw a fit if I asked her to help carry in a single grocery bag. I make all her meals and she argues about putting a glass in the dishwasher. But she looks so serious about this.

"No, honey, it's okay. You don't have to."

"I can make grilled cheese," she insists. "Just let me do something."

What a turn. It's a little early to look for silver linings, and it would be in terrible taste to celebrate such things, but my child is feeling empathy. She's seeking out ways to help when things get hard. Something I thought her incapable of. Not because Megan is some terrible kid. It's the environment. Wealth and ease breeds an entitlement I've struggled to know how to parent. Every single opportunity for frustration or roadblock is cleared. We push away difficult things for our children with good intentions but terrible results. I'm more guilty of it than Everett. I struggled so much as a child, and the idea of my kids being even mildly uncomfortable has made me the snowplow that clears the way in front of them every day. Logically, and with everything I've read about parenting, I know it's a disservice to make their lives too easy. But my heart doesn't seem to want to listen. So to see Megan rise to the occasion suddenly, even if that occasion is horrific, I feel a pang of pride.

"Okay," I say warmly, trying to positively reinforce her kindness. "Do you want me to help?"

"Jo," Everett calls impatiently from upstairs. "Jo, can you come up here?"

"I'll help with the food." Ivy looks relieved to have a task and Megan seems happy it's someone besides me who will help. Mostly because my help usually looks like taking over completely.

The shower isn't running yet and he's still dressed, though he's slipped his shoes off. The look on his face is that of betrayal and it feels ironic considering the lies he's told. I rack my brain to try to get ahead of what might be wrong. He's in my face before I can sort it out.

"What the hell is the matter with you?" His voice booms in that way I've heard rarely but fear often.

I jump and lean away as he growls out his question. The flash in his eyes scares me and I gasp. He flips his hand in the air. "You're going to sink our family. You're insane."

I draw in a breath, shocked by this fury. For a split second I think he might grab my arm and shake me like a rag doll. We stare at each other waiting for something to happen. Waiting for him to do something he can't take back.

THIRTY-TWO

"Calm down," I whisper as I put a hand on his chest. I don't push him backward, but I hold him at arm's length. "What's your problem?"

"Why didn't you tell me Ivy was here?" he demands, his voice low but intense. There is a little girl still residing in my soul that trembles when Everett is angry. My body has grown to believe that someone's unhappiness is dangerous for me. It can't be convinced that I'm not being chased by a lion or hanging dangerously off a cliff. Yelling is a warning sign that danger is imminent. It doesn't seem to matter how long it's been since I was a scared child. The reaction has not diminished.

"When exactly should I have told you? It's not like there's some playbook for this. A girl goes missing, your husband gets arrested, and the mother shows up at your doorstep. I'm doing my best here, Everett." Though there should be, there is no malice in my voice. I am talking him back to calm. Or trying to.

He runs a hand through his hair, visibly frustrated. "Merle should have been notified about Ivy being in our home. My lawyer needs to know these kinds of things. The police talked to her, you know. She made a statement. We should have discussed this. I feel blindsided."

"Blindsided?" I say, incredulous. All my desire to keep this calm is being pushed to the limit. "I've been dealing with all of this on my own. Finding out bits and pieces of the lies you've been telling for months. Finding those things out from strangers sitting at my kitchen table. I'm the one who's been blindsided."

He turns his back on me. "I told you why I'd kept it from you. I just needed time."

"No, you needed to get back to your old job and hope I'd never find out what happened." My emotions had been mixed since I found out. There was fear and sadness. But no real estate in my mind for the anger to move in. Well, it's here now, with all its baggage. "You think I'm too stupid to ever find out what's going on, so you felt perfectly comfortable lying to me. Is that a trend I should worry about?"

Everett grits his teeth as he spins back around. "I just couldn't bear to deal with the fallout. That look in your eyes you get when any of us don't live up to your standard. Can you imagine if I sat you down and told you I was demoted? That my pay was cut and my last few projects failed miserably?"

"We'd have gotten through it," I answer soothingly. "I would have been there for you. With you."

"Bullshit. You'd have been asking me why it happened. What I could have done differently. Picked apart all my choices leading up to that moment and tried to look for some spin to tell everyone at school. The only lens you look through is the one pointing at us. The one outside looking in. You wouldn't have cared that I was gutted by having to take a step back. You wouldn't have understood that some of the project failure points were well outside of my control, and you would have looked at me like..."

"Like what?" I demand.

"The way you're looking at me right now. Like I'm the

person who stands between you and the perfect little life you're trying to project. A speed bump. Something to run over and leave in your rearview mirror."

"That's not fair." I don't feel any self-reflection or allow his words to penetrate my mind. My anger only grows. "I'm so terrible that the only way to deal with me is to lie?"

"Don't you see a trend?" He laughs humorlessly as he throws my words back in my face and paces around. "Look at the kids."

The lioness in me roars. "What about the kids?" *My kids. The kids I raise and care for and keep safe.* That's the unspoken part. The thing I want to yell back in his face. If he has a better way to raise them, let him put his hat in the ring. I want to dare him to try to do this for a week on his own. He wouldn't make it a day.

"Jo, they're tired of having to bend to your will constantly. You're not even a helicopter parent. A helicopter wouldn't be a close enough distance for you. Are you really surprised Megan is pulling away like this? You've got a chokehold on her and people will fight against being choked. Where does this obsession come from? What happened to you? Why are you like this?"

It's the veil I don't want lifted. The secrets I don't want found out. This is the argument we don't have, and suddenly I remember why. I can't probe too deeply on his failures if I don't want him spotting mine. Why do I want to protect my children so desperately? Why am I obsessed? We can't go there.

"Everett. Stop. You're tired and you're angry. Lashing out at me isn't going to get you what you want. I love our children and I've dedicated my life to making sure they have everything they need. I'm not perfect but I'm not going to take parenting advice from someone who's barely here. You do nothing to educate yourself on what's going on in the world and what the experts say is the best way to help your children. I don't need a life coach; I need someone willing to actually parent with me. Which is not what you want. So then I don't need the feedback."

"Even if I was here, you'd never let me anywhere near the parenting decisions anyway. You want control. Control of everything and how everyone feels. Life doesn't work that way. Things go wrong."

"I've noticed." I level my face, not willing to give him a reaction. I draw a very deep line in the sand when it comes to him criticizing what I've sacrificed for our children. I'm not going to be told I love them too much or watch them too closely. My children aren't the ones missing because I have made sure they understand the dangers of the internet and have not given them free range out in the world. Our kids have me protecting them. I'm not going to apologize for that. Or for Ivy being here. She wants to stay here because she wants to be here for when Eden is found.

Everett draws in a deep breath. "We need to do what Merle advises us to do. He's our legal counsel. I need to talk with him."

"I don't care what he says, we are not putting Ivy out on the street just because your lawyer thinks that's better for you. I feel like we owe her that much."

"We had nothing to do with what happened to Eden. The police need to look into the lead you dug up. It's not our fault Eden was talking to someone secretly and went off with them. Maybe Ivy shouldn't have sent her daughter to the other side of the world if she was sneaky and impulsive."

"Lower your voice," I warn, glancing toward the door. "I know you've been through hell, but you're saying a lot of shit you're going to regret. We don't know that this is just some kid stuff. She may have run off with someone who tricked her. She may be in real danger."

Everett's shoulders slump, and he sinks onto the bed. "Jo, we are in danger too," he says, his voice breaking. "Nothing is going to be the same, even after this is over. You think I'll ever get back to my old position? I'll be lucky to have a job at all. Being questioned like that for so long, being all over the news as a suspect. No matter how it turns out, our family will always be tied to this. Everyone reads the headline news, but no one reads the retractions. You need to understand, things will never go back to the way they were. The best shot we have is listening to the advice of our lawyer. I'm taking a shower and then I'm calling him. If he thinks Ivy should go, then that's what's happening." He steps away from me and into the bathroom where he closes the door firmly. If I have more to say, he's not willing to hear it.

Folding my arms around myself, I feel a chill. It's not the temperature but the sudden draining of the adrenaline that was coursing through my body. Everett thinks this is for him to decide, and I'm prepared to tell him he's wrong. I don't care what Merle says. If he doesn't want to be in a house with Ivy... I'll pack his bag for him.

THIRTY-THREE

My bed feels as if it's made of nails tonight. Everett snores softly beside me, his presence both comforting and alienating. He hasn't apologized for his earlier anger, but he hasn't doubled down on it either. We stayed mostly silent as we went through the rest of the day and then readied for bed.

There is nothing more infuriating in the world than arguing with a man and then watching him be able to fall asleep easily. My mind is like a whirring mess of his words pummeling me from the inside out. And he's off in some REM sleep recharging for tomorrow. They are truly simple creatures, and I envy that.

Merle's advice plays over in my mind. He actually thought having Ivy stay in the house was a positive thing. A bullet dodged for Everett and I to have to sort out. Merle's point was, if the mother of the missing girl wasn't afraid to be sleeping under the same roof as Everett, it was an endorsement of his innocence. He encouraged us to keep Ivy close and stay united if possible. As my eyes grow heavy, I can't help but think of how manipulative and calculated that is. Ivy is the mother. She's the one hurting the most and we're still trying to make ourselves look respectable.

But I don't wake him. There is no good to come of that. The room grows darker as I drift off to sleep. My thoughts blur and twist into disturbing images. I'm no longer in bed, but in our garage. The space feels colder, the air heavy with an unspoken tension. I see Everett and Eden standing near the workbench, their voices raised in an argument. I can't make out the words, but the anger is palpable.

Eden's face is contorted in fear and frustration. She turns to leave, but Everett grabs her arm, pulling her back. His grip is tight, almost too painful to watch. Suddenly, there's a flash of movement, and I see a wrench in Everett's hand. He swings it with a force that takes my breath away. Blood splatters across the garage floor, and Eden crumples to the ground. I try to scream, to run to her, but I'm rooted in place, my legs heavy and unresponsive.

The scene shifts abruptly, and I see Everett and Eden in the kitchen. Their interactions are clandestine, filled with whispers and stolen glances. The air between them is thick with some-thing dark and secretive. Love. Lust. Sexual tension.

The scene changes again, and I'm at a grave. Not at the cemetery but deep in the woods. Ivy is there, her face streaked with tears. She's sobbing uncontrollably, her body shaking with grief. There is no headstone, just a mound of freshly moved dirt, but I know it's Eden's grave. In every scene I am voiceless. I open my mouth to cry out but nothing comes. Powerless, I fall to the ground and instead of hitting the forest floor, I am back in my bed. Back next to Everett, but his hands are covered in dirt. His pajamas sweat-soaked and muddy.

I jolt awake, my heart pounding and my breath coming in ragged gasps. Everett's arms are around me, heavy and suffocat-ing. I feel trapped, like I can't breathe. Panic claws at my insides, and I shove him away with all the strength I can muster. He grunts in his sleep, barely stirring as I scramble out of bed.

I stand in the middle of the room, my body trembling. The

dream was so vivid, so real. The images of Everett harming Eden, of their secret interactions, and of Ivy crying at her grave haunt me. I can't shake the feeling that something terrible has happened, that we're missing something crucial.

Everett stirs, rolling over and mumbling something incoherent. I stare at him, my mind racing. Do we ever really know anyone? I certainly have held my secrets close to my chest. No one would ever look at me today and realize the horror I've inflicted on other people. The cruelty it took to get me where I am today. So how can I assume Everett isn't just as likely to be harboring secrets? If I've lied right to his face since the day we met, why do I deserve anything different in return?

THIRTY-FOUR

I tiptoe out of the bedroom, needing some distance, some clarity. The house is quiet, everyone else asleep. I make my way to the kitchen and pour myself a glass of water, trying to steady my nerves. The dream has left me shaken, but I know I can't let it cloud my judgment.

I think about Ivy and the promise I made her. If there comes a time where I think Everett might be involved, I won't protect him. I'll do whatever it takes to find Eden and bring her home. But the promise feels heavy on my soul.

I sip the water slowly, trying to calm the storm inside me.

"Bad dreams?" Ivy asks as she steps ominously into the kitchen. I jump the same way I had when I awoke from the nightmare.

"Just thirsty," I lie as I gesture toward the glass of water. "Ate too much grilled cheese, I think."

"I need something stronger than water," Ivy comments as she rubs at her own shoulder. "I heard you and Everett arguing. Maybe I should go. They've got a place for me to stay and—"

"Please don't go," I plead. "Eden is going to come home and

I want her to know we were all working together to make that happen. I think you should stay. Everett thinks so too."

"You're so sure of that?" Ivy tips her head down but her eyes up as she stares at me. "You know what he wants?"

"I do. I know my husband."

"How well?" Ivy folds her arms across her chest and waits as I fish for an answer. My mouth opens and closes a couple times before I come up with something.

"He wants you to stay. Everett and I have been together for a long time. You get to know someone deeply over those years. I can look in his eyes and see—"

"What you hope to be true." Ivy shakes her head. "I may not have been married to someone for decades, but I know what men can be like. I know how they split into two people like a worm cut in half. How they justify their lies and compartmentalize their feelings. The duality doesn't keep them up at night. I bet he's up there now sleeping like a baby."

How do you argue with someone who is so on the nose?

She continues and I appreciate the fact that she's not looking smug just because she's right. "You're too smart a woman to pretend you don't know this about men. About how they've acted through all of human history. Do you really think you ended up with the one man who deserves complete and unwavering trust?"

She doesn't know how wavering my trust is at that moment. "I want what you want," I remind her. "I want Eden home safe."

Ivy doesn't press further, seeming to sense I won't openly disparage Everett tonight. "They want me to make a statement on the news tomorrow," she explains, closing her eyes for a long beat. "Some plea for Eden to come home, or for anyone with information to come forward. It feels useless."

"A plea." The word hits my ears funny and gives me an idea. "A reward. We should offer a reward for her safe return."

"I can't—"

"We can. Everett and I can," I reply boldly. "Fifty thousand dollars? That would get someone talking, right? If Eden has made some terrible mistake and gone off with someone she shouldn't, maybe that would be enough to get some information the police could action. Someone else could have seen her. A reward might help, don't you think?"

Her expression is like a drug fix I've been sober from too long. Hope. There is hope in her eyes. The incredibly broken woman looks like she can breathe for a second. "That's too much to ask."

"When we signed up to take Eden into our home, we did so accepting she'd be our responsibility. We'll do whatever we need to do for this to be solved and for her to be brought home safe. I'll make some calls in the morning before you give your plea on the news and I'll find out how something like a reward would work."

Ivy hugs me in a way I've never been hugged. Like she's been stranded at sea and I'm the dry land she's finally made it back to.

"Thank you," she chokes out. "You are a good woman."

We part ways in the kitchen and when I get back to my room, I'm relieved to see Everett still sleeping. I don't want to lie to him but I don't plan to give him too much notice about the reward I've offered. He's on edge and I have to be the one to think clearly for both of us until he has his feet under him. I know this is right.

Lying back in bed, my eyes close again, the exhaustion finally overtaking me. But this time, there are no dreams waiting for me. I won't sleep like a baby, apparently, as I listen to Everett snore lightly; I'll try to sleep like an untroubled husband.

THIRTY-FIVE

"What part of *we need to seek legal counsel* do you not understand?" Everett asks in a gruff whisper as Ivy walks to the table they've set up in front of our house. She takes a seat first and then Everett and I join to her left. Someone lets Ivy know that she can speak whenever she's ready. I can feel Everett pulsing with anger as he processes what I've just told him about the reward we'll be offering.

The internet was a wealth of information and our bank account can more than accommodate this type of offering. I don't need Merle to run it through the machine of manipulation to help us decide if it's favorable or not for us. Statistics show rewards can incentivize people who might otherwise be reluctant to come forward with information. The promise of financial compensation can motivate individuals who have valuable evidence to speak up. It's the right move for Eden, and that's what matters.

Ivy takes a deep breath and begins to speak, her voice shaky but determined. "Thank you all for coming today. My daughter Eden has been missing for five days, and we need your help to bring her home. Eden, if you can hear this, please know that I love you so much and I want you here with me. If there is a way to get back to me, please, please do it. I'm waiting here for you. I won't go anywhere until I've got you back with me." She sobs out the last few words and then tries again. "Today, we are offering a cash reward for any information that leads to safe return. We hope this will encourage anyone who knows something to come forward."

I watch her, my heart aching for the pain she's enduring. I try to maintain a supportive posture, but I can't help but worry about how our body language is being perceived. Are Everett and I sitting too far apart? Can they tell we've argued? Do we look guilty or sincere? The weight of the public's scrutiny is almost unbearable as I stare into the camera and the crowd.

Ivy continues, her voice breaking. "I want to thank Jo and Everett for their generosity in offering this reward. It means the world to me to have their support at this difficult time."

She loses her composure, tears streaming down her face. I step in, placing a hand on her shoulder.

"We want Eden home," I say, my voice steady. "We will do whatever it takes to bring her back safely. If you have any information, please come forward. Help us bring Eden home."

The conference ends as a flurry of camera shutters rings out. Press has already been told we wouldn't be answering any questions, but that doesn't stop them from trying as they shout them out to us.

Ignoring the instinct to answer, we head back into the house. Ivy tries to compose herself, dabbing at her eyes with a tissue. Merle is waiting for us in the kitchen, a satisfied look on his face.

"That played well on the cameras," he says. "The reward was a great idea. Impressive strategy, Everett. You'll gain some public support that way. We'll get it set up in the appropriate trust and manage any tips that come in."

Everett looks taken aback but then nods, not correcting that it was my idea. He goes to speak but is cut off by the sound of the doorbell.

Merle advises, "If it's a reporter, no more comments."

I'm surprised that Everett doesn't make a move for the door. He still seems shell-shocked by being led off in handcuffs from our front lawn. He clearly doesn't want any surprises. Instead, I step forward and open it to find Detective Delray standing there.

"Detective Delray," I say, trying to keep my voice steady. I feel confident about how we handled the press conference and won't let her disparage us. "Come in."

She steps inside, her eyes scanning the room, taking in the scene. "I have some updates," she says, her tone serious. "We've been following up on the leads you provided about the mall footage and the flip phone. We're making progress."

I can feel Everett tense beside me, the unspoken question hanging in the air until he musters the courage to ask it. "Is there any news? Anything concrete?" he asks.

Detective Delray shakes her head. "Not yet, but we're getting closer." Reaching in her bag she pulls out a notebook that's in an evidence bag, opened to a page with writing on it.

"Ivy, can you confirm that to the best of your knowledge this is your daughter's handwriting?"

With squinted, tear-blurred eyes Ivy comes in close to the bag and nods. "Yes, that's Eden's handwriting. Where did you find it? What does it say?"

"It was in her gym locker at school," the detective explains. "Mrs. Hargrove, I need you to come down to the station with me. I know the timing is not ideal because there are still cameras out front. I've got my car pulled around back. We don't have to make a scene leaving here."

"What?" Everett asks, finally pushing himself in front of me. "You aren't arresting Jo. This is insane. Haven't you done enough to our family?"

He raises a hand like he wants to throw a punch and my heart freezes in my chest.

"Everett," I whisper, pleading with my eyes for him to cool it. "The kids."

If I'm going to jail right now, he can't go too.

THIRTY-SIX

"This isn't a vendetta against your family, Mr. Hargrove. I'm looking for a missing girl," Detective Delray corrects. "And I need to speak with your wife down at the precinct about some new evidence."

"New evidence?" Ivy asks with a gasp. "What is it? What have you found?"

Merle steps forward. "Is she under arrest?"

"No, right now I'd like her to come voluntarily to clear some things up and answer some questions." She waves for me to come with her toward the back door.

My body tingles with fear. How can these people have so much control over our lives? The ability to pull us out of our home and keep us like animals, caged. "Have you followed up on the footage at the mall? Who was she meeting there? That's who you need to talk to."

"She wasn't meeting anyone," Detective Delray explains. "Eden was alone at the mall."

I interrupt, knowing something must have been overlooked. "She was there for hours on end. Coming home and telling stories about how she was shopping, going to movies, eating in the food court with friends. She wasn't just sitting there alone."

"Actually, she was." Detective Delray is unmoved by our demands for a better answer. "I saw the footage myself. She looked despondent. Lonely. As if she was just killing time. Trying to be away from the house."

I take this as an accusation. "And the flip phone? She was talking to someone, and pretty incessantly. Maybe obsessively."

"We haven't found a record of the cell phone. It must be a burner. She may have bought it here soon after she arrived."

"Or someone bought it for her," I correct. "Someone trying to keep track of her, keep in touch with her. Maybe lure her away."

"It's not a lead we can follow up on until we know more." Detective Delray waves for me again but I don't move.

"We're offering a reward." I gesture to the front of the house where we have just given the press conference. "It seems like we're working harder than any of you on this."

"I really don't want to do this here," Detective Delray explains firmly. "And neither do you, trust me."

Everett sets his jaw in the way that always precedes anger. "I get that this is a tactic. You're trying to turn us against each other, create doubt. Fluster us. But it would be more helpful if you treated us like people trying to bring Eden home rather than suspects."

Merle steps in. "If you're taking her in, then no handcuffs, no perp march in front of the cameras. Show your intentions are not to sensationalize this. If you're just after the truth, then do it without the fanfare."

"That works for me," Detective Delray answers with a cool shrug. "Like I said, I'm parked out back. This is just you coming down to answer some questions about new evidence."

"Don't say a word," Everett demands, catching my arm and

spinning me toward him. "Merle will be right behind you, and all you have to do is sit there and say nothing."

"I'm not hiding anything, Everett." My face shows confusion as I look down at his tight grip on my arm. "She can ask me what she wants."

"It's not about the truth, Jo. This is a game. A story. Whoever tells it better wins. And it can cost the loser their freedom."

"I'm not afraid." I tug away gently and straighten my back.

"Do not say a word." He's so serious I have no other option than to nod my agreement. It's a lie. I have no intention of standing my ground and zipping my lips. Whatever Detective Delray can ask, I can answer. My conscience is clear.

We step out the back door together and I walk to the car. She lets me in the passenger seat and I crane my neck to make sure the media hasn't noticed. I want to get this over with. My kids need me. My life is waiting for me. Detective Delray can come at me with whatever she wants. I'm not afraid.

Except... maybe there are a few things I don't want her to ask me about. A few things I hope no one knows.

THIRTY-SEVEN

The ride to the precinct is mostly silent. I don't know the rules. It seems like her silence is intentional. Like she doesn't want to start our conversation until we are on her turf. For me, I'm just not feeling very chatty with a woman trying to ruin my family.

When we arrive, I'm not in handcuffs. She's not holding me by the arm. We just walk in like two old friends who might be meeting for coffee. And there is coffee. Two Styrofoam cups of sludge on the table between us. She slides hers aside as she pulls out the journal in the evidence bag and some other files.

"We had to make a call about foster care." Detective Delray looks neither arrogant nor compassionate. Just all business. "We have to explore placement for your children in case for some reason both your husband and yourself were not able to keep them in the home. It's protocol when parents might be arrested or unavailable to care for the children. Part of the process is to line up foster care."

"You are not taking my children into foster care." I punctuate my words with a hardy laugh. This woman is insane. "You've questioned Everett for seventy-two hours and decided he's not involved. If you need to do the same to me, that's fine. I can take it."

"We let your husband go because the law states we can't hold him longer than that. Not because we've excluded him as a suspect."

"My kids are not being put in foster care. My son has life-threatening allergies and can't be plopped in just any home. He could die and that would be on you."

"I know that. I remember you mentioned it multiple times when you and I have spoken. And I did consider that. So I knew I better do the extra work on this. If for some reason due to this case your children needed immediate placement, I wanted to be ready with the allergy and medical information. I reached out for his medical records."

"You what? Can you even do that?"

"It's pretty standard when it comes to a case like this. I called his pediatrician and they sent over his records. I didn't really see what I needed." She flips open one of the folders and looks at her notes. "So I reached out to his allergist. He's seen four in the last six years."

"Yes. We have been to many allergists. His case is complex."

"Your son is allergic to tree nuts," Detective Delray says flatly.

"Yes, and he ended up in the hospital when he was two and nearly died. He had another reaction recently. It's life-threatening."

"And you have him on a diet that restricts many other categories of foods." She raises a brow and dares me to answer.

"To save his life. Is that a crime?" I let the words draw out slowly, trying to give the detective time to realize how insane this all sounds.

"There are notes in his pediatric file that say he's been diagnosed with failure to thrive twice because of the diet you have him on."

"It's hard to keep on weight when there are foods you can't eat. But we meet with a nutritionist to make sure we're compensating with calorie-dense foods that are safe for him. It's a tightrope, but we walk it."

"Well, you walk it, right? You make all of his meals. Advocate for him at school. You've made significant changes to how Windsor Knoll operates based on your advocacy." Pursing her lips, I can tell she's pausing for me to walk further into the trap she's set. I don't back down.

"There are dozens of children in the school with food allergies. Policies needed to be changed in order to keep them safe and for them to feel more included. I did work to help educate people and make those changes." Whatever angle she's taking, I don't care. I'm proud of that work. It's saving lives. It also has nothing to do with Eden missing.

"You have your kitchen set up in a very rigid way. No cross-contamination. Making different meals in different spaces for everyone." She's glancing down at her notes, but I have a feeling she's worked out exactly what she wants to say to me. The notes are not needed.

"That's pretty standard when you're caring for a child like Ashton."

"When you're caring for a child with tree nut allergies?"

"With many allergies," I correct.

"Not medically diagnosed. In all the records I read none of the allergists or his pediatrician say that he is allergic to anything besides tree nuts."

I roll my eyes at her ignorance. "When you leave the office after some of the testing, there can be a delayed reaction. This has given us the information that we go on to keep him safe."

"Who is *us*? Because the allergists don't feel this way. There are notes in their files as well that there is some concern for how you are caring for Ashton as it relates to the diet he's on. That perhaps your anxiety is dictating how you choose to do things and what you feed him."

"Parents are anxious after they see their child nearly die. The decisions I make for his care are based on not wanting to lose him. I think that's pretty reasonable."

"I think there is reasonable care you offer to your child after a scare like that, but by looking at these records I don't think the care you're choosing is very reasonable. If I were to talk to your husband, what would he say? Is he aware?"

"Aware of what?"

"That your son is not allergic to the five other food categories you've stopped feeding him. Is he aware that the only diagnosis your son has is a tree nut allergy? A pretty common allergy that is normally manageable. Is your husband aware of that? Because I got the impression from the records, this is kind of a *you* thing. I don't see his name on the notes for any of the appointments. You manage it on your own? Do you keep this information hidden from Everett?"

Detective Delray folds her arms across her chest and for the first time since I met her, looks smug. And for the first time since she's met me, I'm ready to kick her ass.

THIRTY-EIGHT

I cock a brow up at the detective and lean in. My family might be a disaster right now, but my devotion to my children cannot be questioned. "You really want to destroy my marriage, don't you? My husband trusts me and appreciates that I have a broad understanding of allergies. That just because they don't pop up on an allergy test right away doesn't mean food isn't a risk to Ashton. I make decisions for our child, and Everett trusts that."

"I spoke with Ivy briefly this morning on the phone. I wanted to get an understanding on how things were going and caution her again about staying at the house with you. She mentioned she overheard a fight between you and Everett on the night he came home."

"Can you imagine the pressure we're under? You don't think we'd argue?" I lean back and sigh.

"It was what she said she heard that is important. Apparently, Everett didn't exactly agree with your parenting choices, with how you treat the children."

"That's not at all what we were discussing. She misheard—"

"The words controlling and manipulative both came up. Is that something you hear him say often?"

"Where are you going with all of this?" I slap my hand to the table and demand an answer. "This is about Eden. She's missing, and you can't seem to stop attacking my family instead of looking for her."

"Are you familiar with Munchausen by proxy?"

I laugh, this time my eyes wide, not wanting to miss her joining in. This must be a joke. But she remains stoic. "Of course I am familiar with it. I've seen movies. Crazy mothers making their kids sick so they can get attention. I don't make my child sick. I keep him from being ill."

"I would count failure to thrive as sick, wouldn't you? And that came directly from you and the food you withhold from him."

"Failure to thrive can happen when you are trying to figure out what is safe for them. We are always under the care of a doctor. I do not make my son sick for attention."

"But part of this allergy journey is your identity, right? There is a lot of attention paid to how you take care of him and how you advocate for him. Do you get some kind of pleasure from that attention?"

This is the first lie I tell in this room. "No. Of course I don't."

"There is a lot of attention around this thing with Eden, too. Media attention. Concerned friends. Press conferences. It would be natural to feel some comfort by that care you're receiving."

"The leap you're making is absurd. You think I hurt Eden for attention because you don't agree with the way I am caring for my son?"

"I think that you were not honest with us about how much tension there was in the house." She touches the journal that's lying on the table.

"Things were busy with Eden at the house. Our schedules were different. It was hectic sometimes. Life was crazy."

"The journal that we found in Eden's gym locker, the one that Ivy just confirmed is her daughter's handwriting, paints a picture of how hectic things were. It's interesting that you use the word crazy because that's a word Eden uses quite a bit to describe you in the journal."

"She calls me crazy?" I put a hand to my chest. "*Crazy?*"

"When you and I first spoke, you told me that there were a few bumps in the road getting Eden settled in. You made them sound pretty non-eventful."

"I expect any family who's taken an exchange student into their home has some amount of adjustment to do." I don't let her throw me off-kilter. I know what is true.

"In her journal, Eden described it as more than just an adjustment period. She felt pretty uncomfortable. She interpreted what was happening as more than bumps in the road. It apparently was significant conflict. She described you as..." She pauses to look down at her notes. "Manipulative. That you attempted to get her to persuade Megan to do what you wanted. A way to control your daughter. She said you didn't let your children have any oxygen. You smothered them every minute of the day. The kids had no freedom. No friends over. That you had no friends over. A house of isolation. They couldn't watch what they like on TV or do anything you didn't approve of. The food was controlled and restricted."

"The food was not restricted. It is separated and handled safely. Eden has allergies too. She should understand the process of preparing food. You know she gave Ashton a candy bar that sent him back to the hospital, right?"

"She did write about that. She made a mistake and you were furious. You spent hours scrubbing the house and being manic. Eden described it as something out of a movie, like you were possessed and no one else in the house dared to approach you."

"Eden is a teenager that's clearly been given excessive freedom and has grown up in a different kind of household. Of course she's going to come into my home and feel restricted. I'm not raising a seventeen-year-old, I'm raising smaller children. Their rules will be different. Do you know I barely heard from Ivy over the last four weeks? I reached out to her multiple times and she could hardly be bothered to comment on a picture of her daughter or inquire how things were going. When I'd ask Eden if she'd heard from her mother, she'd say they texted a few days ago. It's clear her mother is hands-off. That's not how things go in my house, and if Eden interpreted that as something other than just a mother's love, maybe it's because she's not accustomed to how a real mother should act."

"Is there anything you wouldn't do to protect your children?" Her eyes bore through me as she awaits my answer.

"You're twisting this around. This was a temporary arrangement," I counter with a sigh. "I don't know why Eden wrote all those things in her journal but I can tell you I think I was incredibly fair with her. I flexed on many of my rules to try to make her feel comfortable. And there was only two weeks left before she went home. I had everything under control."

"Just the way you like it?" Detective Delray asks.

"Are you arresting me?"

"Did Everett do something to Eden?" Delray blinks slowly as she asks this heavy question. She's taken a quick turn in her questioning and I'm completely thrown off. This was about me a minute ago. How I was crazy and seeking attention. Now we're back to Everett.

I don't answer. Not at first. My silence isn't calculated. I'm just truly at a loss for words. "This entire situation is—"

"Do you think he's capable of it? When you really look at your life, and your husband, what do you see? Not the superficial, social media anniversary posts. Not the Christmas card family photos. When your head hits the pillow, is there even a moment where you've had to wonder about something he's said or done?"

"You were asking about me..." I trail off for a moment. "You thought I did this for attention."

"Now I'm asking about Everett. What does your gut say?"

I don't have them tallied up. Those little triggers to my woman's intuition that I've ignored over the years. When he'd be away on business and "fall asleep" before calling me back at night, only to apologize with a text in the morning. The dinner receipts, where I could only see the totals, looked like they were for two people instead of just his bill at the hotel bar. I sniffed his shirts for perfume sometimes and can't be sure if there was really any there. A cheating, traveling husband is a stereotype but it's one for a reason. I knew the risks as Everett rose to power in his career but my strategy had worked so far. Don't dig too deep and you won't find anything. But this is an entirely different situation altogether. I can't make the leap she's asking me to.

"Marriages are complicated. So are people." I tip my chin up so she understands she's not breaking me. Delray came out swinging. Attacking me. Throwing me off my game and now she's circling back to Everett. She wanted my head spinning. "My husband isn't perfect. Neither am I. But he didn't harm Eden."

Merle makes his way into the room, huffing and tired. "Nice job blocking the parking," he grumbles as he wipes sweat from his brow with a handkerchief. "I had to walk from four blocks away. Have you made a statement?" He looks at me apprehensively.

"She's said plenty." Detective Delray stands just as Merle takes a seat. "I'll let you two confer. When I come back maybe your client will have more to share."

Merle tucks the handkerchief away and waits for the door to close. "You weren't supposed to talk with her. The best defense until Eden is found is to use that right to remain silent."

"I've done nothing wrong. I'm not afraid to stand up for

myself." I fold my arms across my chest and narrow my eyes in anger. I feel like there have been shots across my bow and I need to fire back.

Merle closes his eyes as he speaks. "Prisons are filled with innocent people who wanted to shout that from the rooftops and ended up accidentally changing a detail of their story, or putting themselves close to the crime scene. Talking does you no favors. Let them keep investigating. Let Eden come home safe. And keep quiet until that happens."

I nod even though I'd like to keep arguing. That conversation has sucked the life out of me and I have no fight left. There was a part of me that thought Everett had been weak in staying silent. As all the adrenaline leaves my body, now it made sense. If you didn't answer a question, they couldn't hit you with the next one. The gotcha moments. I close my eyes and realize if they want to keep me here, there are seventy-one more hours to go.

THIRTY-NINE

After several more grueling hours, I am finally released. There was a condition though before they let me out. Detective Delray had arranged for me to meet with a psychologist, a quiet, empathetic woman who asked questions about my parenting, my relationship with Everett, and the events leading up to Eden's disappearance. I answered everything, feeling exhausted but resolute. By the end of it, I was drained but a little unburdened too. Maybe it was just a different tactic but the psychologist, Dr. Lisa, wasn't interrogating me. Her questions were gentle, her follow-ups understanding.

When I explained my side of everything to her, she smiled. Not once did she jot down a note or look concerned. It was a kindness that I needed and I must have done something right, because I'm free to go.

Everett is waiting outside to drive me home. The car is pulled in to the first parking spot and he hops out with an urgency. Ushering me to the passenger seat, he hurries back to his side and quickly starts the engine. I feel more like he's breaking me out of prison than just driving me home.

"Are you okay?" he asks, his voice gentle. "It's good they let you out of there. That's a good sign. Merle said you did well."

Merle was a liar. He'd scolded me pretty harshly when he realized how much of a conversation I'd had with Detective Delray, and thought talking to the psychologist was a risky move. But obviously it does him no good to pass that worry on to Everett. I let my husband enjoy the false optimism for the moment.

"I just want to get home." I shift uncomfortably in my seat and he takes my hand. It feels like it's been ages since we've held hands like this in the car. But it's a welcome comfort.

"They play crazy mind games in there," he murmurs, squeezing my hand. "Whatever they said, just put it all out of your mind."

I hate to diminish his hope but I feel like a dose of realism is important. "It's not going to be that simple. We have a target on our backs. What needs to happen is Eden comes home safely. That's the only way this will ever be over."

He nods and I can see him gulp back some emotions. "What did they ask you?"

"They showed me a journal," I say, my voice barely above a whisper. "Eden's journal. She wrote about me, Everett. All these things... how controlling I am, how suffocating I am. Detective Delray seemed to think maybe that was motive enough for she and I to fight. Maybe something terrible happened and I panicked. I'm such a monster. Such a mean mom. Everyone agrees." It's clear by the expression that takes over his face he makes the connection to our last argument and his words.

He pulls the car over to the side of the road and turns to look at me, his eyes filled with anguish. "Jo, you're an amazing mom. If you doubted that for even a moment in that room, that's on me. I'm sorry for what I said the other night. I was completely screwed up after those hours in there. I was just lashing out. You have sacrificed so much for our kids. For our family. No one can say otherwise."

The part Everett didn't know was people were saying otherwise. There is truth to what Detective Delray has found but not in how she has spun it. The doctors do likely feel that I am too overbearing when it comes to the management of Ashton's allergies. But I find them too passive. They are willing to "wait and see" or take risks with my son's life that I am not prepared to sit by and watch. There is science to back up what I am doing, it's just not completely aligned with what these doctors believe. I try to put my focus back on Eden. On her journal.

"But why would Eden say those things about me?" I ask, my voice shaking with the threat of tears. I don't do well with criticism. I take it to heart like an arrow. I'd been stretching myself so thin trying to be agreeable and understanding with Eden and she still saw me like some wretched, mean monster.

"It might be a lie," he suggests, his voice steady. "The police can lie when they're questioning you. They can do a lot of things to get you talking. The journal might not have even been real."

"They can lie?" I shake my head, not believing our justice system could allow that.

"Yes. Police can use various forms of deception, like pretending they have evidence they don't have, or telling suspects that they have eyewitness testimony or forensic evidence that implicates them. It's messed up, but it's legal."

"A suspect. Is that really what we are? Suspects?" I pinch the bridge of my nose and think of the implications. "Our kids. Do you know what our kids are going to go through in this town? And Eden. Where is she? Was she really just upset with me and took off? Or did something terrible happen?"

"I don't know." Everett lets my hand go and slowly pulls the car back onto the road. "The only thing I do know is that we have to stick together. Maybe they'll keep trying to turn us against each other, but we can't let them. It's a game. It's all mind games. We have to treat every new accusation or bit of evidence like it's a lie."

The word Munchausen is on my tongue, but I don't speak it. It's a wild accusation and something Everett will reject completely. He'll chalk it up to a tactic they were using. But it's a box I don't want to open. One not everyone will understand if they look inside. Instead, I draw in a deep breath and straighten my back with a confidence I don't truly feel.

"Let's pick Ashton up on the way home. I can't stand us all being away from each other. I want us under the same roof."

"Okay," Everett agrees and offers me a weak smile. "We'll close the blinds and shut the world out. Just watch a movie like we used to. Do you have safe food for him at home, or should we stop at the store?"

"There's food at home," I say, knowing my voice sounds far off. He can assume it's the exhaustion because I can't seem to form the words to explain what's really triggering me right now. All I want is my kids safe under my roof. I'll fight anyone who tries to get in the way of that.

We only get six hours of peace. Just six. Enough for a movie and to try to act as though everything is going to be all right. No one mentions how Ivy has retreated upstairs and has barely said a word since I got home. I find it telling that she doesn't try to pepper me with inquiries about why they took me in for questioning. I don't think that I'd feel any different if I were in her shoes, but it's still unsettling to know she's upstairs, hurting and thinking the worst of us.

It's when I hear her coming down in a thunderous stomp that I know whatever little respite we've gotten is over.

"Megan, take your brother upstairs," I say, trying to usher them out of the kitchen before Ivy can storm in. I'm too late. She's there, arms folded across her chest as she glares at me.

"They should stay to hear this. Have you watched the

news?" She's not sad, she's angry. There isn't some terrible update about Eden; it's clear this is about some scandalous new tidbit the news has decided will make the story more sensational.

"We've kept it off." Everett is moving toward the children and I'm grateful he's got his head in the game again. "They are just looking to stir things up, not actually help find Eden. Look what they did after the press conference. They picked apart the way we were sitting. The clothes we were wearing. I don't think it will do any of us any good to watch it."

"They know you were questioned today." Ivy ignores Everett's comments and stands in the path of my children, keeping us all captive there in the kitchen. There is something rough in her eyes that makes me feel the tingle of danger run up my spine. It's one skill I've mastered as a hyper-vigilant anxiety freak. I can sense something looming that others might dismiss.

"Everett, take the kids upstairs to get ready for bed." I keep my eyes fixed on Ivy but she doesn't budge.

"You know they've just said she saw a psychologist today?" Her finger points at me like she wishes it were a gun. "They found evidence of 'conflict' in the house." She puts the word in air quotes as if it's not strong enough for the context.

Everett's voice deepens. "Ivy, they're doing whatever they can to try to drive a wedge between all of us. They think that they can shake something loose. But there is nothing to find here. None of that should have been leaked to the press, but obviously it's another tactic to try to break us."

"They said she's not mentally well." Ivy's nostrils flare. "That there are signs of medical child abuse in the home. My daughter was placed in an abusive home and now she's gone."

"They said what?" Megan asks, breathlessly.

Ivy turns and stares at my daughter with a fire in her eyes. "Your mother is crazy."

FORTY

"Hold on." Everett's voice is a shout as he steps between our children and Ivy. "There is no abuse in this house. The police do not think that we are abusive. I was there for days and I can assure you that was never a line of questioning."

"Not for you," Ivy replies coolly as she glares at me. Everett's presence in front of her does not seem to be intimidating in the least. "They say she makes your son sick. Fakes his allergies. Like a crazy person. Just for attention."

I watch the betrayal and confusion twist Everett's features as he stares at me, grappling with the realization that I hadn't been completely honest with him. His voice is raw when he finally speaks, cutting through the thick silence like a knife.

"Why didn't you tell me they'd accused you of that, Jo?" he asks, hurt lacing every word. "We agreed we'd be in this together, honest about everything. The only way we can stay ahead of their nonsense is if we tell each other what they are doing."

I swallow hard, and it's like sandpaper going down. "I didn't want to worry you. It's not like that, Everett. It's all a misunderstanding."

Ivy's eyes are ablaze with fury and disbelief. "A misunderstanding?" she spits, snatching the keys to her rental car off the counter. "My daughter was here with all of you. In this madness. Did she know? Did she catch you, and you just had to do something about it?"

"We all need to take a breath and talk about this." Everett holds his hands up, trying to pump the brakes on this runaway train.

She turns to leave, her movements sharp and decisive. Everett starts to reach for her, but I grab his arm, my grip firm. "Let her go."

"If we explain to her that—"

"It doesn't matter anymore, Everett," I whisper, my voice cracking. "The news has their hooks in us. Everything we built... it's gone."

He steps closer. "We can come back from this. People won't believe the trash they saw on the news. We have proof of Ashton's allergies. You've dedicated your life to his care. We'll call the news tonight, show them his medical records. Get Merle involved, it's slander."

He's ready to fight, to mobilize, but I hesitate. My heart pounds as I try to find the words. "It's not that simple, Everett. Some of what I do for Ashton... it isn't in his medical records. It's based on my reading, the online groups I'm in. It's complicated."

Everett's face falls, the determination draining away as he sees my eyes dart to the floor. He turns to the kids, his voice rough. "Go upstairs. Now."

"But, Dad—" Megan starts to protest, but he cuts her off, raising his voice.

"Now, Megan."

She takes her brother's hand, ready to lead him away. I can't bring myself to look at either of them, but I feel Megan's eyes burning into me. The weight of everything crashes down, and I realize there's always further to fall. Just when you think you've hit rock bottom the ground disappears beneath you again.

"What the hell is wrong with you?" Everett doesn't even wait for our children to be out of earshot before he shouts in my face. "You want us to fail, don't you? You are rooting for the destruction of our family. That's all I can think of. Because otherwise there would be no reason for you to keep this from me."

"I didn't think it would make the news," I counter, understanding how weak an argument that seems like now.

"Because the police are so upstanding and in our corner? You didn't think they'd leak it the first chance they got? Now you're the insane mother and I'm the devious father. We're a house of horrors. You see that, right? I told you not to say anything."

"What kind of strategy is that? It worked so well for you? They know you're a liar. And even our own daughter thinks there was something strange between you and Eden. That's what you should be worried about. Who cares what the world thinks about us? Your child saw you here when Eden disappeared. She saw you acting strange around Eden well before that. I saw you arguing with Eden in the car after you picked her up from the mall. What was that about? She wouldn't keep your secret?"

I didn't plan this conversation. It had been boiling in me for some time, but there was no benefit in accusing Everett. If he had done something he wouldn't sit here and admit anything to me, no matter what accusation I threw at him. Everett's best defense was always the same. Blustering frustration that made me emotionally cower. I don't do well against a raised voice. It's not as if Everett spends his days yelling his way around the house. He's normally affable and fun. It's when he's pressed. When his back is against the wall. That's when he knows how to back me down. A little shout. Some intimidating body language. I'm out.

"You've been married to me for all these years and suddenly you think I'm some kind of monster?" His veins pulse with anger. "You're going to turn my daughter against me? Not a chance. Look at how she looks at you. How she can barely stand to be around you. You're the problem. Everyone in this house knows that." His earlier apology is obviously forgotten. It was fake, and I'd felt it then; now I know it for sure. Just an attempt to put a coat of paint over the cracks in our marriage.

I open my mouth but no sound comes out. The thing about knowing someone so well is that you don't just know how to love them, you know how to wreck them too. You get the cheat codes on their weaknesses and in all the wrong moments you have the ability to use them. Everett took his shot, and it hit me square in the chest.

"I did see you," Megan shouts, careening into the room like a runaway train. Her finger is pointed at his face. She's bold in her body language and her voice doesn't shake. "Your car was in the driveway right before Eden left. Don't tell Mom that she's turning me against you. I know what I saw. And I know you and Eden weren't acting right the whole time she was here."

Everett isn't wounded by this in the way I thought he might be. His daughter doubting him isn't heartbreaking. He's angry. "Little girl, you—"

"No, don't yell at me." Megan doesn't move an inch. She doesn't cower. Her eyes are unblinking and her tone strong. "I don't know what happened to Eden but you're not going to stand here and yell at me or Mom about it. You lied about your job and where you've been and instead of begging us to forgive you, you're yelling? Mad that a liar is being accused of lying?"

I see something light in my husband. An epiphany. A frightening one. A father realizing his daughter isn't as forgiving as his wife. She is unafraid. Or if she's scared, she's at least undeterred. I don't know what I've given my daughter over the years, but I hope it is this strength I've not been able to find in myself.

"You two think I did this?" He's snarling through gritted teeth. "You have no idea what I've done for this family. You have no idea the sacrifices I've made. So you can accuse me of hurting Eden? I'm supposed to sit around and listen to this in my own home?"

"Or go," Megan replies coolly. "Just don't stay here and yell at us because you don't like hearing the truth."

Everett turns and punches the wall with a force that sends powdered drywall up in the air. I shriek. Megan glares. Everett leaves. The world stands still.

FORTY-ONE
EDEN

The night presses in on me from all sides, thick and impenetrable. The small shanty cabin offers no real protection. It's just a few wooden boards nailed together, barely keeping the outside world at bay. Every creak and groan of the wood puts my nerves on edge, and the sounds of the remote surroundings—howling wind, rustling leaves, distant animal cries—haunt me, keeping me awake through the endless nights.

I've lost track of time. Days blend into nights, and everything stretches out in an unending blur. I can't remember the last time I felt safe, the last time I wasn't constantly on edge.

Food is scarce. I nibble at the little I have, rationing it carefully, but my stomach still growls in protest. Each meal is a meager offering, barely enough to keep the hunger at bay. The ache in my belly is a constant reminder of my circumstances. My lack of control.

Safety is even scarcer. I jump at every noise, my heart racing with every snap of a twig, every distant howl. The nights are the worst. The darkness outside the cabin feels alive, like it's watching me, waiting for me to make a mistake. I lie awake, straining to hear anything that might signal danger, my eyes wide open but seeing nothing but shadows.

Sanity slips away a little more each day. The isolation, the fear, the uncertainty—they chip away at my mind, leaving me feeling more and more unmoored. I try to hold onto my thoughts, my memories, but they feel slippery, like trying to grasp water with my hands. I talk to myself sometimes, just to hear a voice, even if it's my own.

I pull my knees to my chest, trying to make myself as small as possible, as if I can disappear into the corner of the cabin. Tears prick in my eyes, but I force them back. Crying won't help.

The only thing scarier than being alone for so long is the sound of the approaching car. I can hear the engine from a distance. It bounces off the trees and the thin walls of the cabin. Like a deer in headlights I feel frozen, but I know lying on my side curled into a ball is not acceptable. Chanting quietly, I will myself to stand. To brush some of the dust off my clothes and try to flatten my hair, though I know it's in knots.

The car comes to a stop, and I hear the crunch of footsteps on the gravel. My heart races, pounding in my chest like a drum. The door creaks open, and before I can draw in my next breath, I feel the slap. Hard and stinging, it connects with my cheek, the force of it turning my head sharply to the side. Pain explodes across my face, a fiery burn that spreads outward. My knees buckle, and I collapse to the ground, the impact jarring my already weak body.

It's far from the hardest hit I've ever had, but it still knocks the wind out of me. I gasp, struggling to pull air into my lungs, every breath a painful effort. The taste of blood fills my mouth, metallic and bitter. I can feel the imprint of the hand on my cheek, a throbbing reminder of my helplessness.

"Get up!" The pull to my knotted hair is torture but I drag

myself to my feet. I feel some hair come loose and it's a relief as I stumble upward.

"I'm sorry," I whimper. "I'm up. I'm sorry."

With unblinking eyes filled with familiar fury, my mother stares at me. I've been in the dark, physically and metaphorically, for so long I don't know exactly what's made her this angry. I also know that doesn't really matter. The why is usually irrelevant.

"What have you done? You've screwed everything up. We were so close." She raises her hand to slap me again but I step back.

"I haven't done anything. I've been here. I've been here the whole time like we planned. You didn't come. It was taking so long. I was running out of food, but I stayed here, waiting."

"They arrested him. Everything we did to make that happen, it happened. We had him right where we wanted him. The money would have followed. I was just about to lay it all out to him. Once I'd have got him to agree to that, you'd have walked out of the woods and told the story of how you went for a walk and got lost. How you cut your hand in the garage as you were trying to find some boots that fitted. You found your way up to this cabin and did what you had to until the ankle you twisted started to heal. It was going to work. Until you screwed it up."

"I did everything," I say, just above a whisper, knowing something must have gone off the rails if she's this upset.

"I was in their home. Making headway. Getting to the point where I would tell him what was on the line and what he needed to do to make all this go away. But you had to bring *her* into it. Muddy the water. Things are a mess now. I needed Jo on my side. I needed the secrets to be piling up on Everett so he was desperate. I was going to be in her ear, turning her against him, and then I would give him his only way out. Why did you leave the journal? Why did you point the police toward Jo?"

"I just thought—" She slaps me again, but this time I move with her hand so it hurts a bit less. "I'm sorry," I correct.

"You'll stay here until I can fix this. Did you not realize the kind of person Jo is? She'll never pay us. She's too hung up on right and wrong like it's some perfect world if you play by the rules. Everett is the one we could extort. He is the way to get what we want."

I don't bother explaining to her why I left that journal to be found. I know she only sees what she wants. Never deviates from the plan she puts in motion.

"There isn't enough food here for me to stay much longer." I take a step back and fold my arms in around myself. "Can you bring me some more?"

"It's not like I can just go out for a joyride whenever I want. I had to put on quite the show of righteous indignation so I could peel out of that place and come up here. Sorry I didn't get a chance to get some shopping." She pinches her fingers and puts them in my face. "We were this close. This close. I had other moves I could make. Other things that would point the police back at him. The pressure would be so unbearable he'd have paid and you'd have walked out of these woods explaining it all away."

"I can't stay here without food. I can't stay up here much longer. I think if you told him now what we want and how I'd come home and make all this go away, he'd pay. I really think he would. I spent a lot of time with them and—"

"And weren't they great?" Ivy laughs. "Such wonderful people. A lying husband. A crazy wife who makes her son sick. Just stay put until I give you the signal to come out. Keep that two-way radio over there on and don't you dare start heading back down to town until you hear the signal on it."

"It's fourteen miles," I remind her. We'd used satellites on the internet to map out where I could hide. We watched to see if the road looked traveled by anyone or if this shack was inhabited. I'd been squirreling away snacks and food left over from meals and out of the pantry since the first week I arrived. It had all been planned so perfectly.

Go missing. Stay missing. Raise suspicion. Extort. Get money. Come back. Go home. But now it seems far more complicated than that. My mother is motivated by two things. Money and hate. That's all I've ever seen drive her over the years. I can't stand in the way of either of those two things or I won't be standing long.

"This is our chance." Her voice is gentler now but I know it's not out of compassion. She needs me to calm down in order to get me on board with staying here longer. She reaches into the bag on her shoulder. "I've been keeping these in the car in case I came up here." She pulls a small soft blanket and a brush out for me. "Don't be too clean. It needs to look convincing when you come down off this mountain. Like you've been through hell. Okay?"

"Yes." I pull the blanket into my chest and hug it tightly. "You'll use the radio as soon as you can, right?"

"The second I have the money. It's going to change our lives darling. All of this will. It won't just be the money I get from him. People will love this story. A girl lost and hurt, surviving alone in the woods. People lap that up. They'll probably pay for your university. Give you a job in the tech stuff you want. This will all be worth it in the end."

You can get whiplash if you try to keep up with my mother's moods. But the best lesson I've ever learned is that nothing, no emotion, supersedes the agenda. My mother knows what must be done and is willing to do whatever it takes to make it happen. I can't really begrudge her. It's how we've kept food on the table and the leaking roof over our head. How can I judge how many black eyes my mother had to dole out in the fight for our lives?

"I can do it." I stiffen my posture and let her know she can count on me. I can forage a bit if I need to. I think there were raspberry bushes not far from here. I'll look when light comes in the morning.

"It'll actually be good if you've gone without food for a bit. You'll need to look like you've struggled up here. And that ankle." She looks down at my bare foot and sighs. "You'll have to bang it up when the time comes."

"I know." The idea turns my stomach.

"I just have to make sure this family is fractured. Is there anything else you've done that I need to know about?" She narrows her eyes at me while scanning my face for lies. "Any more surprises?"

"No." I bow my head in the way that sometimes disarms her. "No more surprises."

FORTY-TWO

JO

Words have escaped me since Ivy left and the news started splashing my picture and name up for everyone to see. The phone hasn't rung. No one has texted to see if I'm all right. The court of public opinion would have already ruled on my guilt. Everett was right. I am the crazy mother, he is the depraved father. What a pair we make.

I called Micah's mother Rachel and asked if she would look after Ashton again. He must have overheard what was said about me and his allergies and has been unusually silent. Rachel came to collect him, her veiled glances letting me know that she had seen the news, but I knew she would take care of my son.

Megan and I have spent hours without another sound since they left. Without passing each other in the hall.

We're at a stalemate when I hear the front door open. It's Ivy. Her eyes are red-rimmed from crying and she's standing stone-still in the doorway. It's as if she's been battling with herself on whether or not to return. When she finally speaks, I hold my breath.

"This is destroying your family and it's making things harder on me. I'm already devastated, and I don't need a front row seat to your destruction. I don't know what is a lie and what is the truth, but I know I need to be here. Being alone is doing me no favors. This is still the place Eden would come back to. Still the last place she was."

I walk over and hug her. "We are so sorry for all of this mess. The lies being told are distracting from what matters." I know we need Ivy here to help keep us all in the right frame of mind. "Eden is what matters."

Megan hears our voices and comes down from her room looking concerned. She peeks around the corner and waits for me to give her a reassuring look.

"Ivy, are you okay?" Megan asks, clearing her throat nervously.

"I'm just losing it, I think," Ivy says, rubbing at her tired eyes. "It's the not knowing. Is my daughter cold? Is she alone? Is she crying out for me?" She sniffles and her face crumples with emotion. "I just need to know."

Megan instinctively walks over and hugs Ivy. They cry. They cry because they're scared. Because they're tired. They don't know who to trust and what might happen next. I've never wanted my daughter to worry. I never wanted her to know this kind of fear.

When they finally let each other go, I lead them both to the living room. We'll sleep here tonight. I grab a few extra blankets and pillows and turn on the television. There's an old sitcom on and we all stare through the show, clinging to our blankets and waiting for sleep to take over.

Megan is the first to start snoring quietly as she rolls onto her side on the love seat. I think maybe Ivy will be next, but instead she sits up a little straighter on the couch and looks at me.

"You love your children?" her whisper is pained.

"More than anything in the world." I feel like I owe her an explanation to the accusations against me. The science of why I do what I do. The research that drives me to be as cautious as I am. I want to explain why the police are wrong and I am right. But I know that's not what she's asking.

"That's what I was thinking about when I left. I've done things for Eden that people judge. I love her so much, and there is nothing that would stand in the way of me doing what it took to save her."

"Like staying in the house of people accused of hurting her." We exchange a knowing look.

"Exactly." Ivy hangs her head. "It's not easy to be here. But until I know for sure that he didn't..."

"I understand. I can't imagine how hard that is."

"I have to be here, even if it's uncomfortable. Even if it's hard. I don't know what is true and what is a lie, but I know that what you're accused of isn't the same as what they think he might have done. I think there is a difference between doing something extreme for your children, and doing something extreme to your children. I've heard how he talks to you. How he spoke to Megan when she was looking for ways to help. The fact that he wouldn't answer a single question by the police. Even his own daughter says something was off between him and Eden. You promised me you wouldn't stand in the way if the time came when you believed he knows more than he is saying. Has that time come?"

I think of Megan's finger wagging in Everett's face. The way she demanded he stop yelling and start being accountable. I think of the anger in his eyes where there should have been heartache and fear.

"I'm with you," I whisper. "Just tell me what you need."

FORTY-THREE

EDEN

Nothing felt crazy about this plan before it started. That's the scary part. It's not until I am alone, without my mother's constant reframing and retelling of what we must do, that I am starting to have doubts. This plan is more elaborate than any of the things we've pulled off in the past. Before this, we've mostly just targeted tourists in our dying little town and got whatever we could, while dodging any consequences. This has been our long game. The con to end all cons, and I assumed maybe there would be some tough bits. But I didn't anticipate this.

I sit in the dimly lit room, my eyes fixed on the radio. The tension knots in my stomach, cold sweat on my palms. The silence is deafening, each second stretching into eternity as I wait for the message to come through. Doubt gnaws at me, a relentless whisper in the back of my mind.

I think of the Hargrove family. My mother's plan was supposed to be quick, efficient. Get to Everett, the weakest link, and extort him. Bargain his freedom and reputation back for some money. Enough money for us to finally be able to live. But it hasn't gone as planned. It's dragging on, and every moment it does, their pain and my desperation grow.

The faces of the Hargrove children flash into my mind. Their innocence, their unknowing involvement in this scheme. I hate myself for it. For putting them in the middle. It isn't supposed to be like this. My mother has always promised me a better life, but at what cost?

I shift in my seat, glancing again at the radio. The static buzzes softly, mocking me. I clench my fists, fighting the urge to smash it against the wall. The plan is crumbling, and with it, my resolve.

Twenty-four more hours. That's all I'm willing to give. This time tomorrow I'm walking out of here and back the way I came. Whatever my mother is in the middle of trying to sort out won't be my problem anymore. I'll stick with her story. Phone broken. Ankle twisted. Lost in the woods. But everything else she'll have to figure out how to handle. And I'm sure she will. No one thinks faster on their feet than my mum. She's nimble when it comes to taking advantage of people. It's an art.

From bad to worse has always just been a saying. Maybe one I used from time to time but it only holds real meaning now. Detective Delray is back in my kitchen and it's not to apologize. Her words are floating around me like cartoon bubbles but I'm too frantic to catch them and make sense of what she's saying.

"Find my daughter," I beg, tears staining my cheeks. "Just find her."

"You saw her this morning?" Delray asks as uniformed officers flutter around our house.

"Yes. Just after breakfast she was heading upstairs," Everett answers, when I can't seem to. He stayed out all night and rolled in as we were waking up. I didn't bother to ask where he'd been. The only reason we're speaking again is because our lives have been thrust into a fresh hell.

"And how did she seem?" Delray presses, looking back and forth between us. "Was she upset?"

"Oh, I don't know," I finally chime in. "Maybe she'd seen the news where you were accusing me of abusing my children. Or every email message she's gotten from her friends about her father being a pedophile and dating Eden. I can't imagine why she'd be upset."

"I know this might be unconvincing," Delray begins. "But I did not leak any of that information to the press. We understand it's an issue in our office and one we're trying to address, but I would never jeopardize the case or share information with the press about an ongoing investigation."

"And you want me to believe that?" I'm blinking my stinging eyes at her. I've cried so much I feel them swelling. "My baby. My daughter. She is missing. I want her back. I want her back right now. I don't care if you leaked it or not."

"I didn't."

I breathe out a laugh. "It's not that comfortable for people to think you're a liar, is it? Question your integrity when you know you've done nothing wrong. So, to answer your question, yes, Megan was upset. We slept in the living room last night. I went upstairs to get showered this morning and when I came back down, she was gone. Vanished. Find her. Find her now."

"Do you have any idea of places she might go when she's upset?" Delray asks, sounding like the wind is out of her sails. Whether it was her or not that leaked all the details of the case, that is the reason Megan was upset. Upset enough to run away.

"She was overwhelmed. We all are. We argued last night." My words are laced with venom. "She knew it wasn't going to just get better. Not with all of you working so hard against us."

"What were you fighting about exactly? Was it just about the news story?" Delray questions.

I look to Everett. Let him recount the argument. I'd love to see how he twists this to make himself look innocent.

He gulps before he answers. "She was upset with me. I was losing my cool and she didn't like that."

"Losing your cool?" Delray looks over at the hole Everett punched in the wall. "Was there an altercation here last night? Was it physical?"

"I hit the wall," Everett says with an exasperated sigh. "You think I did this too? Did I kill Megan last night and hide her body somewhere? Gosh, I'm a busy guy."

With an unrelenting wave of anger I lean over and slap my husband's stubble-covered cheek. The room falls silent and all the officers freeze, waiting for someone to tell them what to do. Everett's hand flies up to his cheek and his eyes are wide with shock. I don't scold him for the brutal sarcasm that has no place in this moment. I don't need to. Some things are just so obviously wrong they don't need to be called out.

Delray clears her throat. "Everyone, just take a breath. Where have you checked so far? Could she have gone to friends?"

"I've driven to all of their houses," Everett explains, regaining his composure and seeming to focus on what actually matters. Our child. "I've knocked on every door. I don't know where she is."

"We're going to find her." Delray looks resolute but also a little queasy. "Where are Ivy and Ashton?"

I cover my face with my hand which is still stinging from the slap I delivered. "I sent Ashton back to his friend's house last night. It's too chaotic here for him. Ivy is out looking." I laugh out a humorless gasp. "The irony is insane. When we noticed Megan was gone, she's the first one out there driving around and looking. When her daughter goes missing you can't even answer the questions the police are asking." I shoot Everett a disdainful look.

Delray stands and makes her way over to me. I'm throwing verbal punches at Everett but she doesn't look as though she plans to deter me.

"Can't we put out an Amber alert or something?" Everett demands. "This is your fault. You should be doing whatever you can to make it right. My daughter is upset and trying to prove some point. I want her back here."

"I understand." Delray tucks her phone into her pocket and bites at the side of her mouth, deeply considering her options. "We can't issue an Amber alert as there must be a confirmed abduction. This typically means that we've determined that a child has been taken without permission and there is a credible threat to the child's safety. It sounds as if Megan was upset and left on her own. I think our best option is to keep speaking with her friends, canvasing areas she might go and continue searching. If you have friends and family willing to come together and search then I would start calling them now. Many times in situations like this—"

"Stop calling these *situations*," I demand, punching my fist into my palm. "Stop acting like this is something that just happens. It doesn't just happen. You *made* this happen. You and your people with your bullshit investigations and leaks to the media. You've imploded my family and done nothing to find Eden or comfort Ivy. You expect us to just rally the troops here and say, oops, we've got another child missing from our home? You've put this target on our backs and now you want to look surprised when we start getting shot?"

"Please." Delray's voice is almost a whisper, a crack in her professional facade. "We are doing everything we can. I understand your frustration, your anger—"

"No, you don't understand!" I snap, the rage boiling over. "You can't understand what it's like to feel so helpless, to have the people who are supposed to protect you tear your life apart."

Delray takes a deep breath, regaining her composure. "We need to keep searching. Every person who knows Megan, every place she frequents, we need to cover all possibilities." She gathers what she needs and steps outside with a group of uniformed officers.

The house feels empty, the silence deafening. It is just Everett and I standing in our home. The home that will never be the same. He and I will never heal from this, no matter the outcome. We're broken and there is no putting us back together.

Everett says something—what, I don't know. His voice is muffled, distant, like he's speaking through water. My ears are ringing, a high-pitched wail that drowns out everything else. I can feel my heart pounding in my throat, in my ears, in my temples, so hard it hurts.

I try to breathe. In, out. In, out. But the air won't come. It's stuck, lodged deep in my lungs. My head is spinning, my body trembling uncontrollably. I feel like I'm suffocating, like I'm drowning in open air.

Where is she? Where is Megan?

The panic claws at me, vicious and relentless. My hands shake, and I squeeze my eyes shut, trying to block it all out—the thoughts, the fear, the guilt. But it's useless. It's all still there, lurking in the darkness behind my eyelids, waiting to consume me.

I've lost two of them now. Two girls gone.

FORTY-FIVE
EDEN

The car is back. I can hear it laboring up the steep hill that leads to the cabin. The hill I've been dreaming of climbing down for days. The hunger pangs have stopped and I wonder if that's a bad thing. If I'm transitioning into some other euphoric phase before my body starts to shut down. I can't remember the stats of how long a person can really go without food before everything starts to quit. The stream behind the cabin is a good supply of water but it's the food I can't stop thinking about.

Some things have changed since the last time my mother was up here. She won't be slapping me again. The shift in my soul is tectonic. It sent parts of my mind crashing together and splintering upward. I'm leaving here today. One way or another, this is the end of it. And I won't be her punchbag anymore.

Instead of looking out the window when she pulls up, I ready myself, my back against the far wall. She won't be able to storm in and have her hands on me in the first second.

What throws me off is the way she says my name from outside. It's the fake voice. The one she uses when she wants people to think she's capable of love.

"Eden, darling. It's Mum."

I nearly lose my footing trying to figure out what might be going on. I clutch the wall behind me to stay upright.

"Eden?" I hear a tiny voice say as Megan pushes open the door and sticks her head in wearily. "Eden, are you here?"

"Megan?" I call back in shock. On instinct, I charge toward her and pull her inside. Away from my mother. I don't know what the play is here or why she's brought Megan, but I don't care. I feel instantly responsible for keeping her safe. "Mum, what's going on?"

"Things were getting quite bad down there and I felt like we needed to get Megan somewhere safe. I told her that we know something that would put her in a lot of danger and I needed to get her away."

"Eden, you're okay?" Megan wraps her arms around me and I hug her back. "What is going on?"

"She's old enough." My mother makes some odd expression as I hug Megan as if I'm supposed to know what to do next. When I don't talk, she continues. "We're not dealing with a little girl here. She's old enough to be told what is really going on."

"I am," Megan agrees as she looks around the small cabin with an expression of deep concern and confusion. "What is going on?"

"Eden had to come up here to stay safe. Just like you are doing. She found out something was going on in your house and she couldn't be safe there anymore. Now you're going to stay here too for a little while so everything can be sorted out." My mother oozes fake compassion.

"My dad?" Megan asks, looking to me for some kind of confirmation. I don't want to give it. I don't want to pull Megan into whatever twisted part of the plan my mother is trying to pull off now. She's gone too far. But I also know how vulnerable we are here at the moment. If I don't give my mother what she wants, Megan is in even more danger.

"It's a lot to explain." I bite at my lip as I look over at my mother. "But you're protected here and my mum will go and work out everything else. You'll be back home soon and it will all be okay."

"I'm going back there now to get it all sorted out," my mother promises. "You did an amazing job. I am sure it was scary being in the car boot. But I needed you to be calm until I could get you to Eden. I'll be back as soon as I can."

"Stay here," I tell Megan firmly, squeezing her shoulder before I follow my mum outside.

"What is this?" I demand quietly through tight lips when we are out of earshot. "Why did you bring her here?"

"You weren't enough." She looks pleased about this somehow. "This morning when Jo went to take a shower, I went to him. I told him what he needed to do to get all this to be over with and he didn't budge. So I had to take something he actually cared about."

"No." I'm incredulous. "There is no way you told him all he had to do was pay and I'd come home and this would be over. He'd pay. Of course he would."

"He doesn't care about you." She shrugs coolly. "But that little girl, he cares about her. I'll go and give him a second chance, and then everyone gets what they want."

"Megan can't stay here. It's not safe. There's no food."

She walks back to the car and grabs a bag. "Stop being a baby. I got you some food. Just stay put until I send you the message."

"And what do I tell her?" I wave back to the cabin that has been my prison.

"Anything you like. It doesn't matter. Daddy will pay up and she'll be back home and they'll tell her whatever lies they want. If I were you, I'd keep it vague and just sit tight."

"Mum." I curse myself for sounding so weak and childlike. "This isn't right. We can't."

"He deserves this," she hisses back. "They all do. Living like kings and queens while we starve. It will be good for that little girl to get a taste of the real world." She pushes the bag forcefully into my stomach and walks off. I want to scream. To run up behind her and hit her in the head until she falls to the ground. But I don't move. I think of Megan. My new mission. My mother is like an infectious disease. She's already got to me, but there is still time for Megan.

As I walk back inside, I see the worry etched on Megan's face. She looks around the small cabin, probably wondering why she listened to my mother and came here in the first place. I force a smile and hold up the bag of food my mother brought. "Look, we've got some supplies. We'll be okay. Don't be scared."

Megan's eyes meet mine, filled with uncertainty. "Eden, what is going on? Why did your mom bring me here? Is this where you've been the whole time?"

I try to keep my voice steady, reassuring. "It's complicated. But we won't be up here long. Everything will work out, I promise."

She bites her lip, glancing around nervously. "What about my parents? And Ashton? What if they're worried?"

"They know you're fine. My mum will sort everything out, and we'll be back home soon."

"But why didn't she just talk to them? Why did she bring me here?" Megan's questions are relentless, each one cutting deeper into the fragile web of lies my mother has spun.

I can't answer her. Not truthfully. Not without crossing a bridge I can never come back from. A bridge that would put me on the opposite side of a wild river from my mother. It's a switch of loyalties I'm not ready for. Not yet. But as I look at Megan, I see myself at her age. At a crossroads, afraid and unsure. And I see more than just that in common between us. We've both got his eyes. I don't know how no one noticed. But people only see what they want.

"Megan," I begin, my voice trembling with the weight of what I'm about to say. "There is something I need to tell you, and it's going to change everything."

FORTY-SIX

JO

Eden's room is calling me. I don't know why but I'm compelled to sit on the bed and stare out the window. I have no power anymore. My job was to stay at the house in case Megan comes back or calls. For some reason, this is where I choose to sit vigil. Eden's room.

I think about the vape I found. How sneaky we all are. People in general. I know the skeletons in my closet rattle loudly. The things I've been willing to do to keep my family from finding the truth about my own failures are plentiful. But the secrets are the key. It's what I have to look for.

Standing, I start glancing around the room. Just casually at first, waiting for something to leap out at me. Then I'm more systematic. I pull open the drawers and not only check every inch of them and all their contents, I also run my hand across the underside of each of them. I think of where I hid things when I was young and lying my face off about most everything in my life. I lift the mattress. Pull the sheets off the bed. I tear apart the closet. The suitcase. Every pocket. My arm is all the way down the front compartment when I feel it. A necklace. I pull it out and stare at it for a long moment.

Eden stole Megan's special necklace? The one that Everett bought her when she turned ten? He called it her double digits necklace. Real gold. Engraved. A large stone for her birthday. Except this is an opal stone, not a sapphire like Megan's. Did Eden steal it and change it?

I shake my head at the stupidity of my question. Of course she didn't do that. With the necklace in my hand I rush across the hall and dump Megan's jewelry box out onto the bed. I pick up her necklace and compare it to the one I found in Eden's bag. They are the same design with different stones. I turn them over to see the inscription. Identical.

A Daughter. A Blessing.

My brain can't compute. Why would they both have this necklace? A gift from Everett to his daughter on her tenth birthday. His daughter. Megan.

His daughter. Eden.

They both twirl their hair. I'd missed it. Both girls have a dimple only on the left side. I'd thought my daughter was morphing herself into a mini Eden because of some kind of hero worship. But now as I swipe through pictures of Eden from the last few weeks on my phone and hold them up to Megan's school picture that hangs on the landing, it becomes so obvious.

I'd thought it. It had crossed my mind about how lucky we were to get matched with Eden. She and Megan were similar in so many ways...

They could be sisters. They could be... and they are.

When I hear the front door open, I'm ready. Like a warrior ready for battle I stand at the top of the stairs positioned to charge down and confront whoever it is. Ivy or Everett. They both have to answer for this insanity. The necklaces are in my fist as I hear Everett's voice boom from the kitchen and I freeze.

"Bring my daughter back here, now." He slams something

down on the counter and I hear Ivy laugh. A crazy cackle I can't believe. I'm relieved suddenly neither of them has spotted me.

"That's a rich statement coming from you. It really blows my mind how resolute you've been on not telling the police. It shows your priorities. You'd rather face criminal charges than just admit you were wrong, or actually give away a little of your kingdom here. A rich man who won't pay up or speak up to get his daughter back. You knew the ball was in your court the whole time to make this go away. You just couldn't do it. Too much pride. You had to keep this death grip on the pretend life you have here."

I inch silently down the stairs toward them.

"I will not tell you again. Bring my daughter back here. Now."

"Or what?" Ivy laughs again. "It's not like you're going to have me arrested. You sure aren't going to tell your wife the truth. We've established you don't do that."

"You don't want to find out what will happen if you don't tell me where she is." I hear his feet move and Ivy jump back. "Tell me," he demands, and I hear a frightening yelp and muffled breaths. I can't stay here. I can't hide while he does something he cannot come back from.

"Everett, stop!" I come around the corner to see his hands around Ivy's neck. Her eyes bulge as she claws at his arms. In an instant he seems to snap out of the trance and let her go. She gasps and clutches her neck as she falls forward.

"Jo, you don't understand," Everett pleads. "This is not—"

"She wants money?" I walk toward Ivy as if I'm looking at a science experiment gone wrong. Some inhuman creature with no soul. "She took Megan and she wants money? Give it to her. Give her whatever she wants."

Everett too is catching his breath. "It won't stop there. She's insane. She'll never stop until she punishes us all."

I put the two necklaces on the counter and watch as his face drains of all its color. He knows that I know. And none of it matters until I have my child in my arms.

FORTY-SEVEN

"I'm so sorry, Jo," Everett whispers as he turns toward me and tears gather in his eyes. "I've tried so hard to not let this impact our family."

"Family." Ivy lets the word hang there.

I can't even pin down where to start. But the most confusing thing is how we all got to this place. How our house became ground zero. "Why is she here? You didn't even know Eden was coming. I planned all of this. It was my idea. How?"

"Oh, please." Ivy is circling around us so Everett has to look at her. "You were easier to play than a piano. The fancy school. The allergies. I'll admit there was a good amount of leg work to get everything in motion, but you fell for it all. It was easier than I thought to get her into your house. You see, Everett had been trying so hard for so long to make sure you never knew she existed. And I got you to invite her here. That's how good I am."

Ivy seems delighted to be able to explain. "Let's see, you guys have been together for nineteen years. Eden is seventeen. That math is a little suspicious. Could it be that while traveling for work, your dirty little husband decided it would be fun to hook up with the barmaid in some sleepy seaside town in the south of England?"

"We weren't married," Everett interjects weakly as though that is some kind of comfort. I count back the years of our life and think of what it was like for us then. Happy. The exciting first couple of years of our relationship, filled with promises and dreams. All the while he was out in the world breaking those promises and destroying those dreams.

"Right, when he did propose to you, that's when things got a little rough for me." Ivy folds her arms across her chest like a child pouting. "That's when he stopped coming around. Stopped calling. He tried to just cut us out completely."

"Us?" I whisper, realizing that while I was being proposed to at the country club his parents belong to, he had a daughter on the other side of the world that he was trying to cut off.

"Yes. He'd actually been a decent father that first year. He sent money. Any time he was in the country he found a way to get to us. There were gifts and sweet moments. That's where he went wrong. He should have just blown me off from the beginning. Been a deadbeat right at the start. But we got this little taste of what life could be like and then when he proposed to you, he tried to snatch it all away. Sure, he'd send little things like a necklace or a card, just to keep her thinking he cared. But I knew better."

"How could you keep that from me?" I try to bore holes in Everett with my stare. I want him to look up, but he doesn't.

"We were young." He runs his hand through his hair and shakes his head. "I knew the second I asked you to marry me I'd never screw up again. I just needed that fresh start."

Ivy reaches for a glass on the counter and throws it down at his feet where it smashes loudly. I scream and though the sound comes from me, it feels far off.

"Screw up? That's what your daughter is? Something you screwed up? She's a *child*. Your child, and you abandoned her.

You abandoned us like some mistake you wished didn't happen."

"Ivy, you know what you did." He kicks the shards of glass away angrily. "Don't pretend you hadn't planned exactly what happened and how it happened. That's what you do. You turn everyone into your little puppets. What we had wasn't... it was never going to be. You knew that. You got pregnant and you thought I was your ticket out of the life you didn't want."

"Do you know how he's kept me quiet all these years?" She's asking me now, and the way her eyes dance with excitement is unnerving. She's been dying to tell this story.

"I just want to know where Megan is. That's all I care about." I keep my voice unaffected. Direct.

"Right. Of course. You don't want to hear the messy details of how your husband shut me up and abandoned his daughter. Because you plan to just put this all behind you. You'll do anything for this life. To hold onto what you've got. It's so funny, I was never a woman Everett could love because I was just some trash. But you, you weren't much better. Just a few degrees above me in the world of the elite. You came from a poor family. You were barely scraping by. But apparently that was enough. Everett did want to slum it, but I was a bridge too far."

"Ivy, stop this." Everett is through with it. I can see his patience growing thin and as much as I want answers, I want my daughter more. If he has a way to get this from her, then I want it done. "You are insane. Tell us where Megan is now."

"He could have paid me." Ivy points her finger at me to get my attention back on her. "That's all I wanted. Eden went missing, I put the screws on him and all he had to do is pay. You could have gotten your whole life back, but he was too selfish."

I look at him and this time with the vilest expression. He knew. He knew this whole time that Eden was a pawn in this game and he could have stopped it. He could have saved his children so much pain, but he refused. It's unforgivable.

"There was always something else." He's finally looking up, imploring me to believe him. "That's how it's always been. I'd try to find some kind of compromise that would work and she'd find some other way to infiltrate my life and taunt me. Threaten and blackmail me. It went on for years until I finally cut everything off completely."

"When we moved?" I think back to the urgency with which we moved after Megan was born. Everett had insisted that we'd have better school choices and work opportunities if we moved out west. A fresh start. It was away from the friends we'd made and the places we knew, but he was ready to take a risk for his career and he wanted to know I had his back. Now I can see there was far more to it.

"I'd already given her plenty that she asked for." Everett looks frantic as he tries to explain and I can see this is what he's rehearsed in his head for years. What he tells himself late at night when the guilt must gnaw at him. "There was never enough."

"Never enough?" Ivy gestures around the house. "Because you were so strapped for cash? You had nothing to spare? Or was it just that you could only funnel so much away without your wife noticing?"

Everett continues his explanation. "She threatened to tell you for so long, and then I realized she wouldn't do it. The second she did, all her leverage would be gone. It was time for me to finally cut her out."

"You had a daughter." I want to strike him hard across the face. Maybe even with a frying pan. Even if Ivy was as cold or as cruel as he was saying, and she was certainly sounding it, it didn't justify abandoning his child. "Eden is your child. Did you know it was her when she came? Did you just act like she was a stranger?"

"He knew it was her." Ivy didn't give him a chance to lie and I'm glad for that. "And she knew it was him. Did he seem freaked out? I have to know. Was he totally spooked to see her here?"

"Not at all." I'm in awe of his ability to lie to me. He seemed perfectly at ease as he pretended to meet Eden on our front steps. I never would have guessed.

He shakes his head as he explains. "Jo, you sent me a picture from Eden's first day at school." He gulps back the guilt I hope he's feeling. "I'd been caught up in the shitstorm happening in my job and hadn't heard from Ivy for a couple of years. This wasn't on my radar at all. I didn't think Ivy would do something so psychotic. To orchestrate a way to send Eden into our home. I shouldn't have underestimated her. When you sent that picture of all of you together and I realized it was Julia."

"Eden's her middle name." Ivy's full of pride as her devious plans unfurl in front of us.

I can't get my head around what possessed Everett to keep the lie going. "You saw your other child in our home, here with us, and you still didn't tell me? How could you come home and act like nothing was going on?" It hits me like a lightning bolt. "That's what Megan picked up on. The way I saw Eden looking at you. The way she shot me those fleeting, nasty glances. You weren't sleeping together, you were... I don't know what that is. Pretending together?"

"Eden wasn't trying to hurt any of us." Everett steps onto the glass at his feet, his shoes crunching it down to even smaller pieces. "At first, she and I were obviously not on the same page, but very quickly I think she started to realize I'm not the monster her mother has painted me to be. I just tried to keep things normal. Eden was enjoying herself. She and I, for the first time, were having conversations that weren't poisoned with her mother's lies. I know I was playing with fire but I saw some hope. A possible path forward. Eden was never the problem. Ivy was."

I can't believe what he's told himself all these years. "You are the problem, Everett. It's you. You convinced yourself you deserved to just drop them and move and, in the process, you created this huge conflict that has carried over into our lives. You wouldn't face this like an adult and now every single person in your life has been damaged. The moment you knew that Eden was safe and alive you should have done whatever Ivy asked. You could have paid her and ended all of this. You should have told me what was going on and stopped this nightmare. You chose your own pride and secrets over our family. And now she has Megan?" I turn to Ivy and try to look sincere. "I'm so sorry this happened to you, and for any part I played in this. Please. Bring me to my daughter and we can figure out what comes next. Is she with Eden?"

"They're safe." Ivy looks slightly moved by my words but not completely ready to give up either. "I need to go talk to them first. I'll bring them back here."

"No." My voice is sharp and I accidentally give away just how little I trust her. "Please, let me go with you. I just want to know she's okay. I want to be with her right now."

"Tell your husband to give me what I want and I'll go get them."

"He'll give you whatever you're asking for. Anything." I don't bother looking at Everett. I'll make him comply. If it's the last thing I do as his wife, he'll do what I tell him to.

"She wants two hundred and fifty thousand dollars." Everett gives me the number as if I care. She can have it all. The house. The vehicles. Our whole bank account. I want my child.

"Give it to her. I don't care how you have to get it, just get it. I want my daughter. And you should want both your daughters safe."

"I'm going to get them," Ivy announces through a devilish

smile. "But I won't come back here until I know you have the money."

"Do we call you?" I feel like every inch closer to the door she moves I'm losing my chance at getting Megan back safely. It all feels like it's slipping away.

"I'm not taking my phone. You'll track it. I'll call you here in two hours. Have the money. I'll give you a place to meet."

"Wait." I hold up my hand to stop her. "I don't know where you have her but maybe it will be cold as the sun starts to set. Take her coat. Please. I just want to know she's warm enough."

Begrudgingly Ivy snatches the coat from my hands. "If you can't come up with the money—"

"We will." My voice is level now. "Just, please call in two hours. We'll give you anything you want."

"See?" Ivy stares at Everett. "That's what a parent is supposed to do."

Ivy steps out the door and I hold my stomach and brace myself against the counter. I hear her car start up and pull out of the driveway.

"We need to call the police." I start to hyperventilate as I think of Eden and Megan at this woman's mercy. Or lack thereof. "We need to tell them it's Ivy."

Everett doesn't budge. "We can't. You don't understand what she is like. You don't know what she's capable of. She's greedy and she hates me. Ivy knows the best way to hurt me will be to hurt Megan. You should have let me..." His eyes glaze over as he's clearly taken back to the moment his hands were around her neck.

"You're as crazy as she is." I edge as far away from him as possible. "Just give her what she wants and get my daughter back."

"I'm going to call the bank and our financial advisor. I'll pull the cash together. I can do it if they understand it's urgent. Just be here when she calls. Tell her I have it, even if you haven't heard back from me yet."

"For once in your life just be the damn father I need you to be. Get that money. I don't care where it comes from or how you get it."

"Jo, I know how terrible—"

"Don't. Don't make a case for our marriage or your actions. You are as much a stranger to me as Ivy is. You walked around this house for weeks pretending you didn't even know that girl. You had every opportunity to tell me the truth about everything and instead you lied. And that's not even the worst part. It's the fact that it looked so easy. Your secret child was in our home and you didn't even flinch. Didn't even break a sweat. You're a pro."

"It killed me to have her here and have to pretend. She's a good girl, but her mother is insane."

"You might want to look at the common denominator here. Are all the women in your life crazy, or are you breaking them to the point they go mad? You back us into a corner with no other choices. You take our wings and leave us with only claws and then get mad when we slash at you. Shut up and get that money." The disgust I feel for him must be written all over my face because he moves away from me and does as I say.

I need him gone.

I need him gone so I can do what needs to be done. There is nothing in life that has prepared me for this. But there is also nothing in the world that could stop me. I grab my car keys and take the biggest risk of my life.

FORTY-EIGHT
EDEN

I didn't know if the truth would set me free, but I did know it would hurt Megan too much to hear. Though I swore I was over doing so, I take my mother's advice. I leave Megan mostly in the dark about what is happening, and perhaps when this is over her parents can still convince her everything is fine. They'll be living a lie, but at least they'll be living. I can't see anything waiting for me after this.

My mother's vision of what will come next seems impossible now. And the small hope I'd been holding onto that maybe there was a place for me in my father's life is gone now, too. He'll never want me around after this. The child he actually loves is in danger and all he'll know is that I had a hand in it.

It was the first time he drove us to school that I started to imagine it. Jealousy and rage were all I felt when I originally stepped into their home. Megan was living the life that my mother had made clear was stolen from me. Her room in her huge house was perfectly decorated. Her closet full. I wanted that. All of it. And then in the car to school I imagined we could all have it together.

I sit on the floor behind Megan, gently parting her hair into sections and starting to plait it. I try to keep my voice steady as I speak, weaving a story about my friends back home and their silly antics in school.

"...and then Rachel tripped over her own shoelace, can you believe that? Like something out of a cartoon. We all laughed so much, even my teacher couldn't keep a straight face," I say with a soft chuckle, fingers moving deftly through Megan's hair.

Megan giggles, but then her face grows serious as she half turns to look at me. The whole point of doing her hair was so I could sit behind her and not have to see the fear in her eyes.

"Eden, what's going on?"

My heart skips a beat. "I'm not sure of everything that's going on. I've been here for a while." Deflecting has worked for a little while but I knew she'd push for more answers soon enough.

Megan looks down, fiddling with a loose thread on her jeans. "The news... they said there's something wrong with my mom. That she's crazy and dangerous. Is that why Ivy brought us up here? To be safe from her?"

My hands freeze for a moment before I continue plaiting. "That's not true, Megan. Your mum loves you very much. Things just got out of control, that's all. She would never hurt you."

"But I heard everyone talking about the journal they found in your gym locker," Megan says, her voice trembling. "It was all stuff about how crazy my mom is. They found it and took my mom to the police station. Why did you write all that if it's not true? It must be true and my mom must be crazy."

A lump forms in my throat. I take a deep breath, trying to find the right words. "Megan, sometimes people write things when they're scared or confused. I was trying to make sense of everything that was happening. But that doesn't mean what I wrote was true. Your mum isn't crazy. She's just going through a really hard time."

I was so distracted by the need to keep Megan calm that I missed the sound of my mother's car pulling up. She's pushing her way in with her hair wild and her eyes sparking like fireworks.

"I think you need to answer that question." My mother is spiraling. Something I've seen plenty of times before but I now feel less prepared than ever to manage it.

"Mum, you're back. Can we go?"

"Why did you leave that journal with all those awful things about Jo written in it? We didn't plan it like that. It makes no sense to try to pin your disappearance on her."

I stand abruptly and yank Megan to her feet. In a quick move I push her behind me. Just as quickly my mother lifts her arm and waves a kitchen knife in our direction. Swiped from the Hargrove knife block.

"Put that down. You're not thinking straight."

Megan yelps with fear and I pray she doesn't do it again. She needs to be small and silent. This is between my mother and I. I can't protect her if she's drawing attention to herself.

"It's something your father said that really made it all become clear. He said, you two were getting along so well without me around. He thought maybe... just maybe."

I'd hoped she wouldn't have made this connection but I can see now it's more than just a seed planted in her mind. It's bloomed into the full idea, and one that'll drive her mad.

"You must have been thinking the same thing. Coming here with an agenda to hurt him and take his money and then he does what he always does. Charms people. You fall under his spell. He's so funny. So brilliant. Then it gets a bit mixed up in your mind. You don't want to extort him; you want to keep him. You want to know him. But what's really stopping you? *Her*. You started to think it was Jo that was in the way. That was the only reason he wouldn't want you here. You can't really be that stupid."

"I was confused and lost focus for a while." The admission won't really help me, but I need time. Time to figure out how to get Megan out of here.

"I'd warned you. How many times did I tell you not to fall for his crap? Of course he was going to be nice to you. You had him by the balls. All this time he spent trying to cut us out and you infiltrated his home. His family. It was masterful. He wanted thousands of miles and an ocean between us and you were able to get to his whole family in the one place he felt safe."

I feel Megan's hand squeeze down on my arm but I shake her loose. We can't be holding onto each other right now. Not when I'm the one my mother wants to stab.

"It was incredible. Your plan was perfect. You should have seen his face." I try to feed the beast in her. The part of her that demands accolades and compliments for just how evil she can be. "He never saw it coming. The first time we were alone in the kitchen he even said as much. That it was masterful how you'd pulled this off. The fake allergies you gave me. The way we'd written the application. He couldn't believe you'd actually done it."

"Then what?" Her lips curl into a devilish smile. "You were supposed to demand money from him. You said you did, but he shot that down. That's very brave of him. What really happened?"

The truth is dangerous, but so is my mother when she detects a lie. "I waited. The timing didn't feel right to ask for the money. There were still weeks left before my time in the program would be up and I wanted to get all the benefits I could from being there. Plus we already knew at that point I'd be coming up here. Pretending to be missing so we could get more money."

"More. That's the operative word. You were supposed to squeeze him when you first got there, and then I'd get more when the pressure was on and you were in hiding. But you fell for it. You got sucked in to their perfect little life. And you thought Jo was standing in the way of your happily ever after."

"I thought she was the reason he cut us out." My cheeks blaze red and I feel terrible that Megan is hearing all of this, but I know it's what my mother is demanding of me. "They got engaged and then we were nothing. Then I could just see the hold she had on all of them. The way she watched everything they did and kept all these strict rules. I wrote it all down in the journal. Embellished it and thought, maybe if she was to blame for me being gone, she'd be out of their lives and—"

"And he'd suddenly want you? She wasn't the problem. You're the problem. That's the bit you don't get. There will never be room in his life for you because he sees us as trash. You can get the grades and try to be all interested in the kind of work he does, but it won't change how he sees you. This was our only way to make him pay and actually get the lives we deserve."

"I think things did change." I take two steps forward and push Megan back so that she's against the wall. "I went to work with him one day. I talked to him. Really talked to him, and he told me all the things you've done over the years trying to manipulate and extort him. He took responsibility for what he did wrong, but he couldn't see a way to be around me without having to deal with you. And dealing with you meant he'd lose his family."

"And you ate it up." She's got that look. The laser focus on my face that comes before a slap. But this time, with the knife in her hands, I'm not sure what to expect. I'm weak from being up here and barely eating. She's always been stronger than me and I know for sure I'll struggle to fight her off. The best I can think to do is wrestle with her long enough to tell Megan to run.

She pounces and I grab her wrist, trying to keep control of the knife as she pushes it toward me. Megan is screaming and I can hardly hear myself think as my knees buckle and I hit the ground. I can't fight her off. The knife is coming closer and closer to my face as she seethes with anger. "You're not going to look like him at all when I'm done."

I close my eyes and wait for the pain. "Run, Megan," I finally shout as I tighten my grip on my mother's wrist. This day was always coming. There was no way to keep her from turning on me. It was inevitable. I feel the point of the knife connect with my cheek and then I scream. I scream so that she knows she's losing the last person on this planet who cares about her.

The thud is like something out of a cartoon and I feel my mother's body go limp on top of me. Catching my breath, my eyes peel open slowly to see a figure standing over us with a tire iron in her hand.

"Jo?"

FORTY-NINE

JO

I watch as Ivy's body hits the ground with a thud, the jack handle slipping from my trembling hands. The coat I'd asked Ivy to bring to Megan had an AirTag tracker in it. Just one of my many insane ways of trying to keep tabs on my children without looking like an absolute crazy person. Though that term is taking on a new meaning by the second. I'm surely not the most insane one in this cabin.

I'm standing over an unconscious Ivy and a bleeding Eden. Megan is behind me, crying loudly, her wails piercing through the chaos. My heart races as I take in the scene, my mind struggling to catch up with what just happened.

"Eden," I gasp, dropping to my knees beside her. Blood trickles from a cut on her cheek, and her eyes are wide with fear and pain. I can feel my pulse pounding in my ears as I reach out, my hands shaking. "Eden, are you okay?"

She nods weakly, trying to sit up. "How did you find us?"

"A little bit of stalking technology I use on my kids. Your mother came to our house and told us she had taken you and Megan. I tracked and followed her."

"Megan... she needs you."

I glance back at Megan, who's sobbing uncontrollably against the wall. My heart aches seeing her like this. "Megan, it's okay. You're safe now," I say, trying to keep my voice steady.

Megan doesn't respond, just continues to cry. I turn back to Eden, my hands hovering over her as I try to figure out what to do. The cut on her cheek isn't deep, but it's still bleeding, and I can see the exhaustion in her eyes.

"We need to get out of here," I say, my voice firmer now. "Can you stand?"

Eden nods again, and with my help, she manages to get to her feet. I support her as we move toward Megan, who flinches when we get closer. "Megan, it's me. It's Mom," I say softly, reaching out to her.

She looks up at me, her eyes red and swollen. "Mom... what's happening?"

I pull her into a hug, holding her tight. "It's going to be okay, sweetheart. We're going to be okay."

"I'm so sorry." Eden is clinging to me. The blood is staining her shirt quickly and I wonder if I should try to find something clean to put pressure on it.

"Megan, go get the coat out of Ivy's car. We need to put something on that cut for Eden." Megan moves tentatively as if more danger might jump out of the nearest bush. My eyes are fixed on her but I can feel Eden sobbing up against me. "I can't believe I did this. I can't believe I let her convince me that..."

"You're going to be okay, Eden." I don't tell her that I forgive her because I don't forgive anyone who puts my child in danger. But I did hear her tell Megan to run to safety as I charged at the cabin. That means something.

As Megan reaches the car, I hear the clatter behind me. Ivy has scrambled to her feet, and as Eden clings to me we both turn back to face her. The knife is above her head and she charges at us. Dropping the tire iron now feels like the stupidest thing I'd ever done.

I can see the fear and determination in Eden's eyes as she steps in front of me, trying to shield me from Ivy. "Get Megan out of here," she pleads, her voice trembling but resolute.

But I know that's not how this works. Eden is a child. That's the part that's been missing in this whole situation. She's a child, manipulated and failed by her parents at every turn. Maybe she's never known that kind of love, but mothers are supposed to protect children. Even children that are not theirs.

"Eden, move!" I shout, my voice leaving no room for argument. I give her a hard shove, pushing her out the door of the cabin. "Get Megan."

I turn back to Ivy just as she lunges at me with the knife. The blade slashes across my hand, a sharp, searing pain radiating up my arm. I grit my teeth, refusing to let it stop me. With my uninjured hand, I grab Ivy's hair and yank her head down, her body following the motion.

She struggles, slashing at me wildly, and I feel the knife slice into my arm and side. The pain is excruciating, but I hold on, refusing to let her gain the upper hand. I manage to wrestle the knife from her grip, tossing it across the room.

Ivy is relentless, clawing and punching, but I get my hands on the tire iron again. With every ounce of strength I have left, I swing it, connecting with her ribs. She cries out in pain, stumbling back, and I swing again, landing a few more solid hits.

I have her on the ground, breathing heavily, and for a moment, I think it's over. But then Megan breaks free from Eden outside and runs in to be with me. She throws herself at my side, tears streaming down her face. Just enough time for Ivy to stand again, ready to lunge.

"Megan, no! Stay back!" I shout, trying to keep my focus on Ivy.

There's a brief moment where I see something flicker in Ivy's eyes, a hint of humanity, of recognition. There is a little girl here. An innocent child. But it vanishes as quickly as it appeared, replaced by a cold, vengeful glare. She lunges at us again, but before she can reach us, Eden comes from behind with a large rock, striking her mother hard on the head.

Ivy crumples to the ground, very still. I'm almost certain she's dead, but I can't take any chances. We're all breathing hard, the room spinning from the blood loss and adrenaline.

"Eden, get Megan to the car." I push Megan her way. She nods, tears mixing with the blood on her face, and I follow and manage to get into the back seat of the car. Eden applies pressure to the worst wound on my arm, her hands steady despite the chaos.

She hands Megan the keys. "Drive, Megan. We need to get off the mountain and call for help. It's one road. A straight shot. You can do it."

Megan looks at the keys, her hands shaking. "I can't drive. I'm only a little kid."

I reach out, placing a blood-streaked hand on her cheek. "Megan, you can do this. You are so very strong. I'm sorry I've spent so much time trying to convince you that you're not. That you're not ready for the world. You are. You can do this. I need you to."

"Dad let me practice a couple of times in a parking lot." The admission doesn't seem like such a big deal now that our entire world has been turned upside down. She swallows hard, nodding, and turns the key in the ignition. The car roars to life, and as we pull away from the cabin, I see spots. Things are going dark and I wonder if this is the last time I will see my child. I can't die here. Megan won't survive that pain.

FIFTY

EDEN

My mother is dead. The one person on the entire planet who was there. Not some dependable emotional support, but physically always there in my life. Now she's gone. And I'm the one who did it.

The tinfoil-looking blanket they wrapped me in is not very cozy but I can hardly feel my body anyway. I heard the news about my mother on the police radio as they worked to help the people in the ambulance get Jo loaded up. Megan is at my side shaking and clinging to her own foil blanket.

"Your mum's going to be okay," I whisper into her hair as I rest my chin on her head. "You did a great job getting us down here. And she's going to get all fixed up at the hospital."

We're leaning against the car she drove that's parked crooked in the middle of the street surrounded by police and an ambulance. They've used some glue to join the cut on my face temporarily, and the next ambulance is supposed to take Megan and I to the hospital to get checked. They assure us it's on the way and we lean on each other while we wait.

Before it can reach us, I see his car. Everett is driving quickly toward us and stopping abruptly as he practically falls out of the car. He tries to run in our direction but two officers grab him and start asking questions.

"That's my daughter." He points at Megan and I take a step to my left. "Where is my wife? Is she in the ambulance?"

"Dad," Megan calls, dropping her blanket and running as fast as she can toward her father. I can't blame her. If I had someone to run to, I'd be sprinting.

Everett makes no move to come to me. He embraces Megan tightly as the officers explain Jo's injuries and where she will be brought for care. Megan tugs Everett in my direction, but he doesn't budge.

"Come on, Dad, Eden needs us too," she pleads. "Her mom attacked her and—"

Everett looks at me, but only for a second. He shakes his head and turns back to Megan. "We need to get in the car and drive behind the ambulance to the hospital. We can't leave your mom alone."

"But Eden—" Megan protests, her voice breaking.

"Megan, we need to go. Now." He ushers her into the car as the ambulance begins to pull away.

I watch as they drive off, Megan's face pressed against the rear window, her eyes locked on me until they disappear around a corner. I'm left standing there, feeling more alone than ever.

A few moments later, a woman approaches me. Her face is unfamiliar, but there's a warmth in her eyes. "Eden, I've been looking for you. You've been hard to find."

I stare at her, the words feeling distant and disconnected from reality. "So hard to find I can't even find myself," I say.

The woman reaches out, gently taking my hand. "I'm Detective Stephanie Delray. Let's get you to the hospital. You need to get checked out. You've been without food and care for a while, haven't you?"

I nod, the questions stirring in me. "I think I'm in big trouble." My mother is gone. There is no one else here to blame for what has happened. Clearly Everett has no more interest in me than he ever has. As a matter of fact, he most likely hates me even more than he did before. I was always just a bargaining chip my mother played. I don't think he ever really saw me as a person. As his child. Now, I'm the partner in crime. Just as guilty as the woman he always hated.

"I'm still trying to piece it all together," Detective Delray admits. "This has been quite the case. But the good news is, you're alive. You're here to tell me your story. I've been involved in too many cases where the victim isn't around for that. You tell me what happened, and I'll be here to listen."

"My mother is dead." I just want to hear it out loud. To make it real when everything else feels like a nightmare.

"Do you want to wait for the ambulance, or ride to the hospital in my car?"

"I'm really fine. I can go ho—"

"Not sure where home is right now?" She looks empathetic as she asks the question. "That must be hard. I know it probably feels like nothing will ever go back to the way it was or be normal again, but I promise you, parts of your life will come back. Things do settle down. You need to get checked out at the hospital. I'll take you over there now and we'll figure out what comes next."

"You might arrest me." It feels foolish to dance around the idea. "I killed my mother."

"I know that. And you've got plenty of time to tell me why." She guides me to her car and opens the door for me to take a seat. I don't know how I'll tell her what happened without looking like an absolutely horrible person. And maybe that's the point. There is no way to spin all this so that I look innocent. So I won't spin it. I'll tell it all, even if it means I shoulder the blame. I have nothing to lose. Nothing to gain. I have nothing at all.

FIFTY-ONE

JO

The lights above me are too bright and I open my eyes for only a moment before snapping them shut again. Groaning, I begin to hear the voices in the room as they make their way to me. I feel groggy and disoriented, but the familiar voices pull me back to consciousness. Everett's low, comforting tone, Megan's soft whispers, and Ashton's childish, worried ramblings are like a balm to my frayed nerves. My eyes flutter open, and I squint against the harsh lights of the hospital room.

"Mom?" Megan's voice is tentative, and I turn my head to see her worried face. My heart swells with relief.

"Hey, sweetie," I manage to say, my voice raspy. "Are you okay?"

She nods, tears welling in her eyes. "Yeah, we're okay. We were so scared, Mom."

Everett steps closer. He looks apprehensive that I might kick him out. I offer back a weak smile for the sake of our children.

He takes this as an invitation to talk to me. "You need to rest, Jo. You're very lucky. None of the wounds required surgery, but you'll be in pain for a while. Save your energy."

I try to sit up, but a sharp sting shoots through my side, and I gasp. "Where's Eden? Is she okay?"

Everett's face hardens slightly at the mention of Eden. He exchanges a glance with Megan, who looks down at her shoes.

"Just rest, Jo. You've been through a lot."

"No, I need to know," I insist, looking directly at Megan. She seems unsettled, her eyes darting between me and her father.

"Please, Everett," I press, my voice trembling. "I need to see Eden."

Everett sighs, rubbing his temples. "She came in to get her injuries checked. She was treated for dehydration and malnutrition. They said the police were going to take her shortly."

Megan's face crumples, and she clings to my hand. "Mom, she's been through so much. She saved us."

I can feel the tension in the room, the unspoken emotions swirling around us. "Everett, she's just a kid. You can't let her go through this alone." I stop short of saying, *she's your kid*. That's a longer conversation with my children, and one they deserve to have thoughtfully delivered.

"She'll go through whatever the police deem appropriate. Maybe she was trying to make this work at some point but the moment they took Megan, everything changed for me. Eden was a willing participant. I can't even bring myself to think about what could have happened to Megan."

"Her mother was pulling all the strings. You can't blame her—"

"I can. This was no last-minute, thrown-together decision on her part. You understand how much calculation and manipulation went into her getting into our home. And at any point up in that cabin Eden could have left. All she had to do was walk out of there and get help. That would have saved us so much of the misery we went through. And you, you could have been killed. I'm not going to just pretend she didn't have a part in that."

I want to remind him how quickly he could have resolved all of this, too. How he was the one saying Eden was a good girl back when he was trying to cover up all his lies.

"Can you two go sit in the hall, please?" Megan doesn't wait for any kind of approval from Everett. She steps out into the hallway and Ashton follows close behind her. She knows I'm calling the shots right now.

"You are Eden's father and you've failed her again and again. You don't get to hide behind two of your children while you condemn the third. I don't care how you feel about her, and whether you think this is her fault or not. I'm not asking you to bring Eden in here so that we can all be one big happy family. I am telling you to get someone to bring her here, because we were in that cabin together. Because I saw what she did for my child. And how she saved my life. I don't need your permission, but since I'm not able to get out of this bed, I'm telling you to do it for me."

"I'm not going to let our children be—"

"Everett, you're not letting anyone do anything. You're going to remember exactly what you did to put us all in this situation and you're going to do what we tell you to do. Anything you and I ever had together is over. You destroyed our marriage – you forfeit the decision-making. We're done."

"Is this how it's going to be?" Everett looks defensive, which only makes me sure I'm doing the right thing. "You're going to use the kids to punish me?"

"I have no interest in punishing you. Everyone has been through enough. But you and I are not going to be doing this together. We'll get our children the help they need and do what we can to heal them. But it's not you and me anymore."

"Jo, I know I have a lot to make up for and a lot to work on but we both made mistakes over the years. We can't throw away our marriage. Not now. Not after the kids have been through so much."

"We never had a marriage. Everything we based it on is a lie. But three amazing children came out of those lies, and that's the only part we can control. I can't begin to understand what Ivy did over the years but she's gone. It's up to us to put the kids first. But we can do that separately. We'll be doing everything separately now."

Everett opens his mouth to make some argument I'm sure I don't want to hear but he stops short when all three kids come back in the room. Megan has done what I hoped she would and gone to get Eden. Detective Delray pokes her head in and then gestures that she'll be waiting outside.

"I'm going to step out too," Everett says, and I worry that he plans to tell Delray his twisted version of this story. I consider interjecting but instead fix my attention on Eden.

Eden stands there, looking fragile and scared. I reach out a hand to her, and she slowly steps forward, her eyes filled with uncertainty.

"Eden, come here," I say softly. She hesitates, then moves closer, allowing me to pull her into a gentle embrace.

"I'm so scared," she whispers, her voice trembling. "I think they're going to arrest me."

"Shh, it's okay," I whisper back, stroking her hair. "Just tell the truth. Whatever happens, you have my support. You did something incredibly brave up there. You saved us."

Megan moves closer, wrapping her arms around both of us.

I'd like to get out of this bed. To walk with Eden wherever she has to go. That might not be possible at the moment, but I can make sure she knows she's not in this alone.

FIFTY-TWO

We're sharing it all. Everything. That's what we promised to do when we made these plans. It was the only way I could see our moving forward. We're calling it a girls' retreat. Pretending it's just a regular kind of outing. But we all know it's more. Sitting in the woods by a camper and listening to the crickets chirp was the only setting I could think of for this. It needed to be somewhere peaceful and far off. Camping sounded like our best option.

We've never been a family that camps, but this is glamping really. I rented this fancy trailer and someone from the campsite already came and lit the fire for us out under the stars.

"We're going to burn things that need to be burned," I explain, gesturing to the bag we packed. "And we're going to say what we need to say to each other. Nothing is off-limits. It's about the truth. We've all been through hell. No, we're still in hell, and the only way to get out of it is to keep going until we get to the other side."

"Can we curse?" Megan asks as she reaches for the bag of candy I've brought.

"If you feel like you need to. Yes." In the firelight I can see the apprehension on Eden's face. I knew this would be a lot for her but the therapist thought it would be helpful. "Eden, you only say what you feel comfortable sharing. We leave it all in the fire. Nothing has to follow us home."

"Who goes first?" Megan asks, stuffing her face with chocolate and passing the bag over to Eden.

"I'm the mom, so I will." I reach over for a piece of chocolate and stare into the fire. "I have pretty severe anxiety. Working with the therapist has helped me come to terms with that. I was wrong to let my storm get you guys wet. Megan, I'm finding more ways to trust you and hopefully build our relationship back to where it used to be. Ashton needs the same. My fears over his allergies have to be held in check. I was very wrong, and I'm getting help."

Megan goes quiet and stops snacking. Her nostrils flare and I can tell she has something to say. "You were right." She nibbles her lip. "I wasn't sure how to tell you this, but I know Detective Delray will eventually find out and tell you."

I hold my breath for a second. "What is it? This is the time. It's what we're here for."

"It started over a year ago, when I got a friend request from a boy named Jayden on a messaging app. I know I wasn't supposed to have an account but I found a way to access it on my school computer. Jayden seemed to understand me in ways no one else did. We started chatting every day, and I found myself looking forward to our conversations more and more. He listened when I vented about your strict rules. He said I deserved to be treated better. Jayden said you were overprotective, unreasonable, and trying to control my life. I started to believe him. More than that, I fought back against every rule you tried to enforce. You became my enemy and Jayden was my ally."

I've been working on my poker face for moments like this. I

nod and keep my eyes focused on the crackling fire. "It's okay, Megan."

"I told him everything—where we lived, our routines, my frustrations. He was always there, feeding my anger, making me feel like I was justified in my hatred."

"Talking to strangers online is dangerous—"

Eden cuts in. "It wasn't a stranger, was it?"

"It was Ivy," Megan reports as her face crumples. I can tell she's been holding this in for far too long. "It was a couple weeks after Ivy's death that I finally figured it out. I looked at the time stamps. The location on the messages. They were coming from the town Eden was from. The messages stopped after Ivy died. The friend I shared every detail of my life with wasn't a friend at all. I'm the one who gave Ivy every detail of our lives. The road map for how to get in our home and try to destroy us. My angsty blabbering became the weapons she used against us. I'm so sorry."

"Did you know?" I ask Eden, not a hint of anger in my voice. I've moved past any feelings of blame. She's a child. A pawn.

"I didn't know. I just guessed when Megan started explaining. It sounded like something she would do. I'm really sorry that—"

"Don't apologize for her." I give her a sweet smile. "She was an adult and you were her child. And, Megan, what you shared with Ivy, she'd have found some other way to find it out if not from you. It's not your fault."

"I guess it's my turn." Eden nibbles nervously at her thumbnail. "I've told Detective Delray everything already. But there might be things you're wondering, too."

"Share whatever you feel comfortable with."

"I guess the first thing is what we were supposed to do. What the original plan was. My mother worked hard for two years to line up our application in a way that made your house the most obvious choice. You know now that I'm not really allergic to anything."

"Besides penicillin," I correct with a smile. I like that I know these real details about her.

"Right. I was interested in STEM but my mother got me fully obsessed with it. Study everything I could. I needed it to look as if Windsor Knoll was my dream come true. There were a lot of other parts to it too. But I was supposed to come to your house to make Everett feel claustrophobic. My mother wanted me to do crazy things to make him think I was just about to tell you the truth. But when I got here..."

"Was it different than you thought?" Megan offers Eden a chocolate and she takes it.

"Very different. My mother made it sound like you were the worst people in the world. As if you'd stolen everything that should have been ours. But when I met you, it was all just normal." She shrugs as she continues to try to search for the right words. "We were the ones who weren't normal. It's a level of madness that I can't even get my head round now, but then, it just felt like what people do."

"I have something else to say," Megan offers sheepishly. "I'm actually really glad to have a sister. I know the whole thing was batshit crazy." She pauses to see if I scold her but continues when I don't. "But the parts that weren't crazy, were actually pretty amazing. These last couple of weeks when it's just you, Mom, Ashton, and me, have been okay."

I know that "okay" is a ringing endorsement from a preteen. "I agree." I make sure to say this with my full chest and without missing a beat. "I really feel like the dust will settle and we'll find some way forward that makes sense."

We sit for another two hours, laughing, crying, and telling each other exactly how we feel. Or mostly how we feel. I can tell Eden is holding back. I knew this would be great for Megan and it was. We cleared the air on a lot of things and she had the opportunity to ask questions I knew were lingering in her mind after Everett moved out. She asked if I hated him, to which I replied no. She asked if I'd divorce him to which I replied, yes. To my surprise this made her smile.

When her eyes are heavy and her cheeks warmed by the crackling fire, Megan makes her way to our fancy camper for bed. At first, I'm panicked at the idea of her walking the thirty feet alone. About her going to bed without me in there. But I work through the steps the therapist suggests and the tools do work.

"It's never going to work," Eden says, spinning her long hair into a bun. She looks so much like Everett with her hair up that it's spooky now. I don't know how I didn't see it sooner.

"What won't work?" I ask the question though I already know the answer. I've seen the doubt in her eyes every day over the last few weeks.

"I really appreciate everything you've done for me but I'm a few months away from turning eighteen. Everett has offered to open a trust for me that will sustain me financially in England while I get settled. I can finish school and start a job. Whatever we're doing here, it won't work."

"Things have been pretty great over the last few weeks, though, don't you think? Therapy has been helping all of us, and all three of you kids seem to like the new school. We talked about you finishing the school year here and then—"

"Then what? You'll send me to university? I'll just be one of your kids? I'm not yours. I'm the person who's just imploded your whole life. At some point, you're going to remember how much danger I brought into your home. You'll resent me. And I don't blame you at all."

"Eden, I can sit here and promise you that won't happen, but you won't trust that. You're always going to be worried that what we're offering you will be yanked away. I might not be your mother, but you know what is great about that? I'm nothing like your mother either. I would die for my children. Kill for my children. I've got a lot of learning to do, but at my core, I am a fierce mother. And that extends to all the children I care about."

"Doesn't it scare you?" Her eyes are wide as she waits for my answer.

"No." I smile warmly across the fire at her. "I'm really not afraid at all."

"How is that possible? With everything that happened, how can you not be afraid of having me in your life?"

I tip my chin back as I explain. "I'm good at this. Really good at it. There are many things in my life that I'm terrible at, but I know how to love children. Am I still finding ways to manage my own emotions? Yes. But I know how to be a mother. I'm not afraid. I'm built for this."

She closes her eyes for a long beat as though she's conjuring up a memory. "I've never had that before. My mother..."

"You are my children's sister. Maybe it's messy, but it's true. And I know my words don't mean that much to you right now, but there is something else that might convince you."

She raises a brow and looks hopeful. "What is it?"

I reach into the pocket of my sweatshirt and pull out the folded envelope. "I get this letter nearly every month now. I race to the mailbox every day to make sure no one else in my family finds it first. To make sure no one else reads it. But I'm done hiding it. It's time you find out what I've done."

FIFTY-THREE

Eden stares at the letter in my hand much the same way I've looked at it over the years. As if it's far heavier than just a folded-up piece of paper.

"Eden, the reason I forgive you for everything that happened is because you and I are the same. And I've been waiting most of my life to pay for my wicked choices. I'm done hating myself, and I'm certainly not going to spend my time hating you. We're the same. And we both deserve forgiveness."

I lean over the fire that's burned down to just one log and embers. Handing her the envelope, I feel raw and unprotected. But I know the only way she'll believe she deserves to be in my home and have a good life is if she sees how broken and flawed I am, too.

"What is this?" She peels open the envelope and begins to read. Occasionally she looks up at me but I don't speak. Waiting for her to finish, I feel a prickly heat of embarrassment crawling across my scalp. I can recite it from memory.

Dear Angel of Death,

As the years continue to pass, I often find myself thinking about those days at Saint Mary's Hospital and, more specifically, about you. I've prayed for you for many years now, and I want you to know that you are never far from my thoughts. I write this letter with a genuine concern for your soul and the eternity it will spend burning in hell.

I know what you did. Honor thy Mother and Father. That's what you were called to do. What a failure you were in that way. What a crime you committed. A crime against God and nature.

Please, for the sake of your eternal soul, confess your sins. You can't keep running from this. You can't hide from the truth forever. How would your children look at you if they knew you were a sinner? A killer?

Do you sleep at night or are you haunted by his face, as I am haunted by yours?

I will write until you make this right. It will never go away. I will never go away.

When she finishes reading, I find the courage to explain.

"That is from a nurse that worked at the hospital where my father was at the end of his life. I don't remember her specifically but she certainly remembers me. It was a Catholic facility and, as you can tell from that note, she spends a lot of time worrying about my eternal soul. She wants me to repent. She prays for me. But there is something more than just fear for my soul."

"A threat?"

"That's how it always felt to me. Like if I didn't finally see the light and come to terms with what I'd done, she'd expose me. To who, I don't know. It was always just this big boogie man in my life. I've never told anyone. You'll be the first."

"You don't have to if you don't—"

"We're the same, Eden. That's really important. It answers

your question as to why I could ever love you and let you into my house. It's because we are the same."

"I lied to you. I put your children in danger. You had to have so many stitches because of me. Your marriage—"

"What I did was worse." I hang my head in shame. "Maybe once you know, you won't want to stay with me. But at least you and I will have a clear understanding of each other." I draw in a deep breath as I start. "My parents drank. I never really noticed it when I was young. It just seemed like a part of their lives. A normal part. But as I got older, I realized that it was making them sick. My mother was diagnosed with breast cancer and never went for treatment. She just drank until the cancer took her. I was fourteen. My father turned to the bottle even more after that. I was his caregiver. The person who tried to keep him from losing his mind. It was a lot for a teenager, and we didn't have much money. I spent all my time dreaming of the life I would have. It was more than a dream really. It was an obsession."

"I can understand that. It's the only escape you've got."

"I plotted. I dreamed. I schemed. My life was going to be good. I was going to be the mother I never had and my children would be my whole world. I'd make sure they were well educated and well-traveled. They wouldn't worry about their next meal or want for anything. As my father yelled and cried and vomited, I imagined myself ten years in the future with everything I ever wanted."

"And for a while you had it." Eden looks guilty, still feeling like the one who stole it all away from me.

"It's how I got it that's the problem. When I was your age." I laugh at the irony. "Your age exactly, actually. My father got very ill. He went into the hospital with liver failure. I was a few months away from graduating high school. I had great grades but no plan. I was working at the local fast-food place and picking up graveyard shifts at a truck-stop diner. I had it in my head that maybe I could scrape up enough money to go to the community college. It was so far off from the life I'd dreamed up for myself, but at least I wasn't standing still."

"I've had those same thoughts." She's fixated on me completely and I am desperately hoping the message resonates.

"I know." I sigh at the similarities between us that she never would have imagined. "My father was in end-stage liver failure. He needed a transplant. The problem was he wasn't committed to sobriety and couldn't be placed on the donor list. His only chance was if I was a match and willing to donate. I went through the process and found out I could save his life. I could donate part of my liver. The news actually came as a letter in the mail one afternoon showing my results." I look down in shame, staring at the fading embers of the fire. "I threw the letter out. I told my father I was not a match. I was his last hope, and I lied to him." The tears are streaking down my cheeks now and I feel like that young girl again. Seventeen years old, a road forking in front of me. "If I gave my father part of my liver, I'd have months of recovery. I couldn't work or go to school. I wouldn't be able to graduate with my class or put away enough money for community college. My father would need almost a year of care after the surgery. I'd never be able to leave him. We were already barely scraping by, but medical bills would sink us completely."

"Oh, Jo, I'm so sorry."

"If I made the choice to save my father's life, I'd be throwing away the pretend life I'd designed in my mind. All for a man who was unkind and selfish. I'd be trapped in that house with him for years, and the more ill he'd get the worse he'd treat me. There would be no Megan or Ashton. I'd die there. I was so sure of it then."

"Donating an organ is not an easy decision. You were young, and—"

"I'm not in a place in my life where I'm looking for excuses to give myself. I knew exactly what I was doing when I lied to my father. I knew he had life insurance. Enough to send me not to community college, but to a beautiful university with real opportunity. The chance to meet the kind of people I thought I deserved to be around. It would elevate me to a class of folks that were polished and sophisticated. I'd get the life I deserved." I put a hand to my forehead and sniffle. "And you know what I found? The people in this life are exactly as cruel as my father was, they just wear designer clothes. Everett wasn't my Prince Charming, ready to sweep in and save me from terrible circumstances. I got the life I deserved. It was full of infidelity, lack of fulfillment and endless insecurity. I made a deal with the devil and he came to collect."

"I don't think it's that simple. Look at what you have accomplished. You really are an amazing mother. I was overwhelmed by how you are with your kids because I'd never seen that kind of love before. I saw it firsthand. You had a chance to get away the day my mother was attacking us. There was a moment when you could have taken Megan and run. You put yourself between my mother and me. You saved my life when you had a chance to get away. That has to count for something."

"And you told Megan to run before I got in that cabin. You did the same for her that I was willing to do for you." I gesture to the letter. "I don't know how to forgive myself for letting my father die when I could have saved him. But for the first time in a long time, I'm not running from it anymore. I'm going to talk about it in therapy. I'm going to face it. Maybe I'll find that it was his choices that led him to that moment and cut his life short, not mine. Or maybe I'll have to come to terms with the fact that I traded his life for the idea of happiness I thought I could find. Either way, what I know for sure is that you and I are not that different. Our circumstances were messed up. What was being asked of us was too much. And when we hit that crossroads, we failed. Does that really mean we don't deserve love? We don't deserve joy and fulfillment? That can't be true."

"I think you need to burn this letter. Be done with it all and forgive yourself."

"And what about you?" I cock up a challenging brow, daring her to give herself the same grace she's offering to me.

"I wanted Everett to pay for abandoning me as much as I've wanted him to show up and love me. But now I think..."

"What?" I'm desperate to know what she wants.

"I think my mother couldn't love me because I was his. And my father couldn't love me because I was hers."

"Then come be ours," I say, with a wave of emotion washing over me. "Come be a part of our family and be loved for who you are. I'm not going to get everything right. I have a lot of healing left to do myself. But why should any of us do it alone?"

Eden stands and rounds the fire to fall into my arms, crying with her whole body. I remind myself that this is the part I'm good at. I'll screw up plenty but, in these moments, I can be what she needs and I'm determined to do so.

Eden talks into my shoulder through broken sobs. "You really think you'll be able to love me?"

"I already do."

A LETTER FROM DANIELLE

Dear reader,

I want to say a huge thank you for choosing to read *Three Little Lies*. If you enjoyed it and want to keep up to date with all my latest releases, just sign up at the following link. Your email address will never be shared and you can unsubscribe at any time.

www.bookouture.com/danielle-stewart

I hope you loved *Three Little Lies* and if you did I would be very grateful if you could write a review. I'd love to hear what you think, and it makes such a difference helping new readers to discover one of my books for the first time.

I love hearing from my readers – you can get in touch on my social media pages.

Thanks,

Danielle Stewart

www.authordaniellestewart.com

X   x.com/DJStewart198

ACKNOWLEDGMENTS

A special thanks to the amazing team at Bookouture who never fail to elevate a project and build a welcoming community.

PUBLISHING TEAM

Turning a manuscript into a book requires the efforts of many people. The publishing team at Bookouture would like to acknowledge everyone who contributed to this publication.

Audio
Alba Proko
Sinead O'Connor
Melissa Tran

Commercial
Lauren Morrissette
Hannah Richmond
Imogen Allport

Cover design
Lisa Horton

Data and analysis
Mark Alder
Mohamed Bussuri

Editorial
Nina Winters
Imogen Allport

Made in the USA
Columbia, SC
19 May 2025